A RELIC OF
MAGIC & GOLD

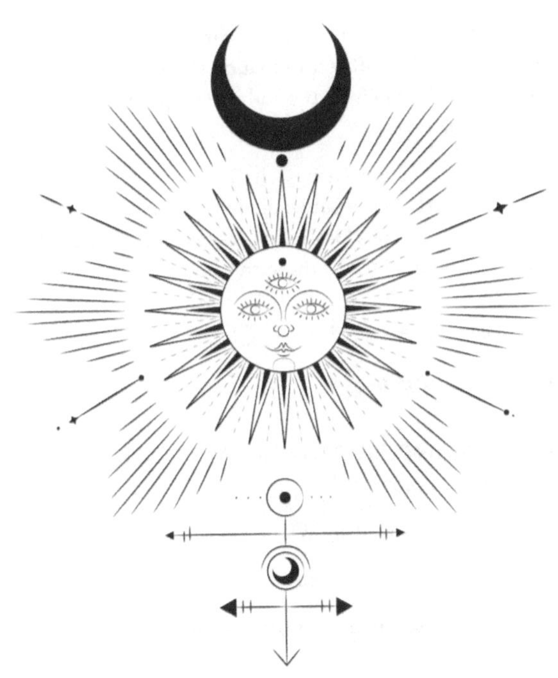

Ebook ISBN: 978-0-6454516-1-0

Print ISBN: 978-0-6454516-0-3

Edited by Sarah Proulx Calfee, Three Little Words Editing https://threelittlewordsediting.com

Proofread by Jo Speirs, Nurturing Words

https://www.nurturingwords.com.au

Front cover design by Amanda Pillar from Smoking Hot Covers

https://www.smokinghotcovers.com

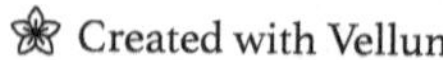 Created with Vellum

For two dads:

My father, Chris and my father-in-law, David.

Two wonderful people who ask the right questions and whose love and support my family and I treasure.

PROLOGUE

Rome, Italy

Some dreams are worth sacrificing everything for. Carrying her Watcher satchel in one hand, rubbing her amethyst pendant with the other, Eve ignored the annoying voice that whispered, *and some things aren't*, as her Templar escorts stopped at St. Anne's Gate. They weren't allowed past this point.

Butterflies rumbled in her belly, but she took a deep breath, and quelled their rioting wings. She had this.

Resisting the urge to check if her long dark hair was still smoothly tied back, Eve passed alone between the white columns topped with fierce stone eagle guardians and entered the Vatican City visitor's center.

From behind the security desk decorated with Christmas baubles and garlands, a priest in black pants and shirt approached. He was flanked by two Vatican City guards, resplendent and amusing—although she set her lips against the smile that threatened—in pantaloons and ruffled shirts. Their regalia hadn't changed in hundreds of years.

"I'm here for the ward," Eve said, keeping her chin high.

They all bowed low.

"This way, *strega*," the priest said with a heavy Italian accent. She nodded in acceptance of his calling her a witch. "We will take you beneath the Biblioteca Apostolica."

The click of Eve's boot heels echoed through the Vatican Museum's wide corridor as she followed the priest and the guards, her long strides easily keeping pace with them. Satisfaction filled her chest with every footstep. She'd done it! She was on her own as an active Watcher.

On either side of the tiled floor, centuries-old tapestries —threads as vibrant and rich as if they'd been woven that day—adorned the walls, depicting scenes of angels, cherubs and robed men. Scenes of the devil too, surrounded by lesser daemons brandishing double-ended hellblades.

They escorted her down a spiral staircase that descended deep into the belly of the building, coming to a narrow corridor. The way was lit by wall sconces and lanterns that looked like they'd been there for as long as Vatican guards had been wearing those pantaloons.

Several black timber doors, barely visible against the dank walls, came and went, and eventually, the guards stopped at a pair of thickly barred bronze gates. Only darkness was visible beyond.

Eve's heart wanted to pound, but she took a steadying breath. Calm. Focus.

The priest stepped ahead and withdrew a substantial set of keys from a chain around his neck and unlocked the padlock.

The guards each took one gate. Their expressions remained calm, but their bodies strained as they pushed.

Metal screeched and hinges creaked. Finally, when the gates were opened wide, both guards bowed to the vault, then to Eve, and took up a position on either side.

Well, this was it. The past ten years of training at the coven's castle in Cheshire were finally being put to use.

"*Strega?*" The priest's gaze darted to the darkened vault, then he took one of the lanterns from the wall and handed it to her. "Your light. Do you need anything else?"

"No, I have this under control. I take it you know the rule about not entering the vault once I commence the ritual?"

"*Si,*" he whispered.

"And the guards will stay on duty for the duration?"

"*Si.*"

"This will take several hours. Make sure they obey the rules, too."

She took a deep breath and blanked out the priest, the guards, the Vatican, and everything else apart from her task. Then she called the spell to pass the threshold. As Eve stepped forward, the existing ward made her calves tingle. But that was it. The old magic was decomposing. It should've caused a strong buzz, if not outright pain, even to someone with knowledge of the spell to pass.

The light of the lantern revealed a golden timber parquetry floor, with an ebony five-point star inlaid in the middle.

In the center of the room, a table held a small gold chest, no bigger than her hand, with little feet and ornate scroll-work covering the surface. The gold gleamed in the lantern light.

Eve's breath faltered. An actual relic—right here. But she forced herself to breathe evenly. Nothing else mattered but this task. And being awed by the past wasn't in her job description.

She opened her satchel, the snap of the clasps echoing through the silence of the vault. First, she took out her working crystals and precisely lined them up in a row across the table, clear quartz, malachite, turquoise, kyanite and black obsidian. Beneath the crystals, she laid her silver-hilted athame sideways, then her brass offering bowl and velvet pouch of salt below that. Finally, she withdrew three candles and placed one at each point of the triangle formed by her tools.

Eve made sure the candles were all at sixty-degree angles, then she rolled her shoulders and neck, checked her hair was tied back tightly and picked up her crystal pendant. The amethyst hummed against her palm as she got to work.

1

ON HER SECOND morning in Rome, Eve's screeching phone alarm made her jump upright in bed, legs tangling beneath the thick duvet. Ugh, was it time to get up already?

She fumbled a hand over the bedside table for her cell. Her fingertips grazed the warm stone of her pendant, and her knuckles bumped against her charging bowl, crystals clacking. Crap, where was her phone?

She sat up against the headboard, pulling the blankets with her to keep warm, and blearily surveyed the unfamiliar room in the dim light.

And there was the cell phone. On the shelf, right where she'd placed it last night to make sure she got out of bed. She peeled herself from under her warm blankets and shut the buzzing alarm off. At least her midnight plan had worked.

It was six o'clock, two hours before her workday started. The perfect time to go for a run and finally see the city.

She dressed in leggings and a long-sleeved running top, the shirt the same shade as the gray-upon-gray view of Rome that filled her apartment window.

Then the rising winter sun broke through the clouds, transforming the window into a kaleidoscope of colors reflecting the crystals from her bedside.

As Eve headed out, the near-winter solstice air—energized with the promise of the wonderful year to come—sent her blood pumping.

She kept her route to the few blocks closest to her apartment, and at the end, thank the goddess, found a place in a laneway near her building open for morning coffee.

With her coffee maker in a storage locker, along with most of her belongings back in Cheshire, finding a coffee shop had been a priority on her to-do list.

And the café was such a comfortable mix of solstice and Christmas decorations that if she didn't have to go to work, she'd have stayed and enjoyed her caffeine hit among the holly and the cinnamon.

Ah well, next time.

Eve took her hot beverage back up to her fourth-floor apartment and right into the shower. Hot coffee in a hot shower. Bliss. Plus, she saved time since she still had to prep her kit before the Templar escort arrived to take her to her next ward.

Although why, by the goddess, Watchers couldn't escort themselves—she grimaced at the old law—was beyond her. But she wasn't going to risk everything she'd strived for over the last decade by breaking the rules. No matter how much those directions chafed.

After her shower, Eve tied her hair back in a tight twist, secured her pendant around her neck and dressed in black ankle boots, jeans and a professional coat.

She'd just laid out all her craft implements on the dining table when a hard knock banged on her apartment door.

She checked her phone. Frowned. The Templars were

early. She'd have to adjust her preparation timings if this was going to be a regular occurrence.

"One moment," Eve called out, efficiently packing the tools away in their precise compartments. She left the salt till last and tied the pouch straps through the loop on her belt. It would be hidden from sight by her jacket, and who knew when she'd be called on to cast a circle?

She checked the knot of her dark hair was still tightly wound at the base of her neck, then took a deep, steady breath and centered her thoughts. Anticipation sang through her. Day two of Watcher duty, here she came.

After strapping her satchel across her shoulder, Eve opened the door. But instead of the Templars from yesterday, Caterina, her red-haired trainer from back in Cheshire, stood in the doorway. Two unfamiliar men in precisely cut suits stood at Caterina's back scanning the corridor.

"Caterina. Good morning. I didn't expect you to be here." Eve took a careful look down each side of the hallway. "Is something wrong?"

"Yes, Evangeline, something is wrong." Caterina's lips tightened before she stepped forward, crowding Eve back into the apartment. Caterina waved at the two men, and they followed her in.

"What's going on?" Eve cut the suits a look. "Who are they?"

"Templars. Field team."

"Caterina, what the hell ... What's going on? Why is a field team searching my cupboards?"

The suits opened every door and pawed through her crockery and saucepans. There was nothing to see in the pantry since she hadn't gone food shopping yet. Something she'd do after she'd wrapped up today's relics wards.

"Not sure what you're looking for." Eve crossed her arms.

"But maybe check the bedroom first. The wardrobe's bigger there."

The men stopped and looked at Caterina, who sighed and nodded before turning to stare back at Eve.

"Well?" Eve said. "I'm doing my best not to lose my temper here, Caterina. But you've got one minute to tell me what, by the goddess, is going on before I—"

"The relic you warded at the Vatican yesterday is missing. And since you were the last one with it, they need to search your apartment. And you need to come in."

Eve's stomach dropped.

"How could it be gone?" She turned her palms over, the buzz of yesterday's spell still fresh in her memory. She looked the other woman in the eye. In the bedroom, the sounds of the Templars searching her wardrobe ceased, but Eve kept her gaze on Caterina. "The relic was there when I left the vault."

"And that's why we're here. Where's your passport?"

"With me, of course." She tapped her satchel.

"Good. You're heading back to Cheshire to face the coven council."

"What? I'm not leaving—I just got here. I'm casting a protection spell today at the church of Santa Maria Maggiore."

"Oh, honey, I doubt they'll let you near a relic ever again. But hey, that's what they get for bringing in an *unfamiliar*."

"Fu—" Eve bit her tongue, as she had every other time over the past decade when someone had raised her lack of familial ties to the coven. "Caterina, I was there *yesterday*. The *relic* was there yesterday. I just need to get back and find out what's going on."

"You? Evangeline, even if you're somehow cleared of this issue"—Caterina's lips curled—"you ... we ... are *Watchers*.

Watchers ward, never engage. The Templars handle that aspect. I seriously have no idea why they selected you for this post."

Eve bit back a growl. She was the best spell caster the coven had. That's why. And the whole *Watchers never engage* thing ... What an archaic, limiting policy. How had the rest of humanity risen above such stupidity, but the coven hadn't? Her blood boiled, and instinctively, she reached for her pendant.

But something sharpened in Caterina's glittering gaze. Eve stopped, pretended to pat her chest as if she was catching her breath. Sure enough, Caterina frowned. Almost ... disappointed. *What by the goddess was going on here?*

Eve moistened suddenly dry lips. "Wait. If we go back to Cheshire, who will cast the protection spell today?"

"No, not we. *You* are going. I'll do the spell work."

"Caterina, this makes zero sense. Why remove me from my job? I never took the relic, so you're taking the last person who laid a spell around it. I can *help* you. And these relics need the strongest wards possible. You shouldn't cast a ward if it will be too weak to properly—"

"Stop." Caterina flicked a hand through the air, and the Templars were suddenly shoulder to shoulder with Eve. "You know the rules—obey your Senior. So listen very, very carefully."

Eve gnashed her teeth but did as she'd been trained.

"The council has recalled you, so you *will* return to Cheshire. But first, these Templars have questions for you. You're going to their base here in Rome now, and after they're done, they'll transport you to England. The coven will take over from there."

"What? Guilty without trial?" She cut both Templars a

look and then turned her gaze back to her trainer. "This is batshit. And you know it."

"Temper, temper, Evangeline. Watchers—"

"I'm not losing my temper. I'm losing all respect for you for thinking this is the way to handle this misunderstanding —or whatever is going on here."

"Ooh, disobeying orders too. Please, make that choice and let me see the oh-so-perfect Evangeline tossed out of the coven on her first post."

Eve opened her mouth to snarl a curse at Caterina but bit it back at the last second. Her trainer was awfully intent on Eve losing control. Why? And how by the goddess was Eve going to figure out what was going on?

She managed to feign a submissive dip of her head as her mind raced. "At least let me try a spell to locate the relic? Perhaps it's just misplaced—"

"You'll try anything, won't you? Well, enough is enough." Caterina spun on her heels. "Time to go."

The Templars started walking, their shoulders practically picking Eve up between them and forcing her forward.

As they walked down the corridor to the lift, Caterina's words played over and over in Eve's mind. The relic was missing—the relic Eve had placed her first Watcher spell on yesterday. Only a Watcher could get through that spell.

And Eve was an unfamiliar; of course they'd believe she'd taken it. Crap, there were those in the coven who'd relish having Eve responsible and Caterina leading the charge.

But Eve wasn't guilty. Hell, if needed, she'd open herself up to a truth spell and prove her innocence that way. But Caterina was so certain Eve had taken the relic that she was handing Eve over to the Templars for some sort of inquisition without any proof. And the red-haired trainer was a senior in the coven; she could easily convince the Council Eve was responsible, and no one would stop to question it.

Or ... what if Caterina had taken the relic? The relic held a potent power all of its own, which was why the Templars paid the Watchers to ward it in the first place.

A cold shiver trickled down Eve's back. She couldn't let the relic fall into the hands of *anyone* who wanted it for that reason.

No. If Eve was going to clear her name, *she* needed to be the one to find the relic. She'd make sure it was safely returned, and then the coven would have to hear Eve out. Not even Caterina could deny that evidence.

The first Templar pressed the button to call the elevator. A down arrow blinked in the little display. Crap. She had to act now.

"Wait. My apartment keys are in here." She tugged on her satchel. "Please let me lock up?"

"Fine." Caterina rolled her eyes. "But you're not going anywhere. Give them here."

Heart pounding, Eve opened the satchel and felt around for her storage locker keys. "Here you go."

"Don't move," Caterina ordered the Templars. She pivoted and headed back to the apartment. The Templars crowded even closer to Eve. Perfect. "And hold the lift when it gets here," Caterina called back over her shoulder.

Eve forced her expression to remain calm as she drew in a surreptitious deep breath, picked up her pendant, and rubbed her thumb over the crystal.

Please, *please* let this work.

"Set in stone that which moves," she whispered under her breath. "Hinder not what must be used." She turned her palm toward the Templar on her right, touching his thigh as lightly as possible. Then she sent the hastily called spell through him.

At the other end of the corridor, Caterina had reached Eve's apartment door. Time was up.

Keeping Caterina in sight, Eve cut the spell short and held her breath as she pressed harder into the Templar's leg. He didn't react. *Thank you, goddess*, the stun had worked. But the condensed spell would last minutes at best, so she had to move fast.

Down the corridor, Caterina inserted the key into the lock, took it out and tried again.

Eve whispered the stun spell again, as fast as she could, sending it into the second Templar.

The second Templar froze right as Caterina spun toward them. Realization dawned on her face, and she threw the keys on the ground. "No!" she screamed and ran up the corridor. She yelled her own stun spell and drew her arm back.

Eve's stomach dropped. Then adrenalin punched through her. The lift pinged at her back. She spun and lurched inside, flattened herself against the side and hit the button for the ground floor.

A stream of silvery magic hit the back of the lift.

"Crap!" Eve hit the close door button over and over. If Caterina caught her now—or if the Templars came out of their stun quickly enough—Eve had little magic left to call on. And no way could she cast two, let alone three, new stun spells. "Come on. Come on. Come on."

Another stream hit the back wall. The lift shook.

The doors closed.

And something loosened in her chest. But there was no time to relax. Plan. She had to plan what by the goddess to do next.

The lift doors opened on the ground floor, and Eve ran out through the lobby and turned hard right, then right again into the laneway with the coffee shop.

She was out of sight of the apartment building for now, but those Templars could be after her any second. Damn it, could the relic really be gone? Well, there was one spell she could cast to find out. She just needed to somewhere safe to conduct the incantation with what little energy she had left.

Eve brought up a map of the city on her cell phone. A largish shopping mall was only a few blocks from the other end of the laneway, in the opposite direction of her apartment. Perfect.

As soon as she reached the shopping mall, she went straight to the public restrooms and locked herself inside the end stall.

She opened her salt pouch and trickled the fine grains in a circle around where she stood, keeping her feet tight together to reduce the radius. The salt would hide her spell work from any witches tracking her magic.

With shaking hands Eve took out her cell again. Although even that was a liability now. The Templar's legendary tech capabilities could geolocate her any second. She zoomed in on the map of Rome until the Vatican compound filled the screen, with the Vatican Museum at one end and the Basilica di San Pietro in the middle.

Next she withdrew her pendant from beneath her shirt and held it above the map. Thank the goddess, years of practice and finetuning her amethyst meant the crystal also worked as a pendulum. *Please let this work now.*

But there was no time to waste. She concentrated on the little ornate golden box as she'd last seen it. The turned legs and carving deeply inlaid into every surface. The gleam of gold. The sense of ages passed.

Determination to find it—secure it—flowed through her.

"Swing hither, swing fro," she whispered, "sideways for yes, lengthways for no. Is the relic in the Biblioteca Apostolica?"

She held her breath ... and the pendant slowly swung up and down. Zero deviation from that trajectory.

A solid no.

Crap. Heart pounding, she zoomed out on the map until the entire Vatican City was visible.

"Is the relic inside Vatican City?"

The pendant swung up and down once more.

"No. No, no, no, no." Eve moistened suddenly dry lips. The relic had been there. She had laid the wards to stop anyone from entering the vault. Had she done the spell wrong? Goddess, maybe she should go to the coven and—

No. They still believed she had taken the relic. She had to prove herself innocent. Otherwise, she'd face a fate like her mother—at best. At worst, she'd get to experience the infamous Templar dungeons. And that was a *damn* no.

Not to mention, she'd worked too hard to accept any other outcome than working as a Watcher.

A hard knot lodged in Eve's throat. How had someone gotten through her ward? Goddess, she'd failed in her very first Watcher ward.

Swallowing the lump, Eve tapped rapidly on her phone to bring up a list of every flight out of Rome since eleven o'clock the night before. Her heart sank. So many flights! And to all over the world. Singapore, Beijing, London, Paris.

Shit, she had minutes—maybe—before the Templars found her. And her magic was growing sluggish, slow to respond to her call.

"Come on, come on," she whispered as she brought up

the flight that had left at midnight to London, surely the soonest someone could've taken the relic and gotten to the airport. She repeated the spell, finishing with, "Did the relic travel on this flight?"

The pendant swung up and down. Damn. She scrolled to the next flight. Brisbane, Australia. She whispered her question again, the hum of her almost-drained magic so quiet she could barely feel or hear it.

But the pendant swung from side to side.

Brisbane, Australia

In the lobby bar of the five-star Carlisle Hotel, Raph Smith shifted in the delicate chair and stretched his legs beneath the table. He held in a snort. What, fancy places didn't cater for anyone over six foot two?

Ah well, at least they had good caffeine. He took another sip of his coffee as he finished reviewing the papers for his hire.

"The contract looks good apart from one thing," he said to the little man sitting across from him. "The terms for the finder's fee and then full payment upon delivery, plus expenses, are all fine. But I don't commit to a completion date until I know I can deliver. If that's no good, then I'm sorry to have wasted your time. Although I see Parsons has already signed. He's not coming down?"

"I'll check with Mr. Parsons now." The assistant stood up

and withdrew a cell phone from his jacket. "Excuse me while I step away and call him."

While he waited, Raph looked around the fancy lobby filled with businesspeople and tourists. Large black-and-white photos of the art-deco-era hotel adorned the wall behind him, including shots of the gargoyles featuring at each corner of the building. The image nearest to him was an up-close study of a gargoyle with the face of Forneous, the devil's right-hand man.

Raph shoved a hand through his dark hair and grimaced. Normally he liked photography—it was a necessary part of his job after all—but he turned his back to the image, and moments later, the assistant returned and sat back down.

"Mr. Parsons has a last-minute meeting conflict, so, unfortunately, he can't join us," the assistant said as he withdrew a fancy pen from his briefcase and handed it over. "However, he has agreed to your term regarding no completion date. As discussed, he was simply thrilled to hear a private investigator of your reputation had taken the job."

"Your boss is paying well enough; he could have had anyone."

"Yes, but your reputation is you always get your person."

"Person being the operative word there. I did tell you I don't normally retrieve things." Raph restrained the urge to grimace even at the word. *Payday, Raph. Think of the payday.* "But it's his dime. I guess this trinket box means a lot to him?"

"It's a family piece. His relatives fell upon hard times years ago and sold it off." The assistant reached into his briefcase and withdrew one more piece of paper. "Now that you've agreed to the job, Mr. Parsons has had an image drawn of the keepsake, based on his early recollections, to assist you."

Raph eyed the pencil-drawn picture. It was of a small trinket box, about as long as a deck of cards and several times as high, with little turned legs at each corner. Symbolic carvings adorned the top and all panels.

"Can I keep this?"

"Of course."

Raph slipped the paper into the folder that held his contract. What the assistant had explained about the Parsons family financial woes matched up with Raph's research on his prospective client. But he still had one question.

"I'm curious why Parsons isn't looking for the trinket box himself?"

"When someone of Parsons' financial standing enquires about an object, the price goes up. Considerably. And that's if the rumors of its sale are true. Which is why he has engaged you."

"Well then, if the item's up for sale, I'll find it." Raph signed his name.

2

———

CLOSE TO THIRTY-SIX HOURS LATER, battling back the exhaustion that dragged at her eyelids and sapped her magic, Eve left the air-conditioned cool of the Brisbane International Airport and walked outside into a stifling, sticky heat and hauled in a breath of thick air.

She winced and glanced at the cheap watch she'd purchased after tossing her cell phone on the journey to Brisbane. Surely this heat wasn't right at eight o'clock in the morning?

Clutching the fold-out tourist map of Brisbane she'd used to narrow down her search, she shrugged out of her jacket and joined the queue at the taxi rank. Thank the goddess, a car arrived in less than a minute, and she dropped with a sigh into the backseat. And another thanks, the taxi had air-con.

She gave the driver the address her pendant had indicated after two hours of spell work—a street in a suburb known as West End. As soon as the driver said it would be a twenty-minute drive, Eve couldn't help but slump into the seat.

One step closer.

She sat low in the seat to hide from passers-by, and within moments, her heavy eyelids were almost impossible to lift. But no, she couldn't sleep. Not now.

Eve forced her eyes to open and mentally reviewed her assets.

Cash—thank the goddess she'd withdrawn the maximum available from her accounts at an ATM before leaving Rome. Because even if the Templars hadn't shut her accounts by now, they'd be tracking any use of her bank cards. Salt—she opened her leather pouch, and her stomach sank. There weren't a lot of the fine grains remaining after all Eve's spell work over the last two days. So, salt went on her to-buy list. She had her crystal pendant, of course—which at least was rechargeable under sunlight and moonlight. And last, and perhaps her strongest asset— her magic.

The faces of the Templar Knights when she'd stunned them flashed through her mind. Her stomach knotted. Oh goddess, she'd *stunned* two Templars. Plus, she'd disobeyed *and* run away from a coven leader. If either group caught her now, her next destination would be a Templar dungeon, no doubt about it. They'd never even let her try to explain herself.

But ... she'd also *done* it. She'd escaped a situation that had stank of the rottenest lies and setup she'd could think of. And she'd done it with her magic. Yes, the coven had a lot of witches. And yes, the Templars had their tech and more money than probably anyone else in this world. But she—Evangeline, an unfamiliar witch from outside the coven—had beaten them all and escaped.

Her breath whooshed out. She'd come this far, and they weren't getting her now. No damned way.

Eve had no problem keeping her eyes open for the rest of the drive until the taxi stopped out the front of an unremarkable red-brick building.

After a last gulp of the air-conditioned air, Eve paid the driver from her cash reserves and hopped out. Then she shrugged her jacket back on, because as awful as the heat was, her hands had to be free in case she met with any resistance.

Because *finally*, she was here. It had taken traveling to the other side of the world, but according to her pendant, the relic was in this building.

The street was a mix of residential and commercial structures. Her spell work had led her to the latter.

There was no name on the building, no signage to show its purpose. An alleyway led up one side, with a black sedan parked at the very end. And she was completely alone, no signs of anyone coming or going from the business or whatever it was.

But according to her pendant, the relic was inside, and she wasn't leaving without it.

Eve tried the front door. Locked. Crap. She'd call on her magic, but hours of tracking the relic had left her exhausted. Even her amethyst pendant, normally a reserve of energy, was tapped out.

Then two male voices echoed from the alleyway.

She peered around the corner. A side door to the building was open now near the car parked at the end. Two men came out carrying boxes of varying sizes and shapes that they piled into the rear seat of the car before heading back inside.

Who were they? They both wore long pants with shirts that had to be uncomfortable in this loco humidity and heat. They came out again a minute later, new boxes in their arms.

"Any more?" the younger of the two men asked.

"One from the vault. You keep an eye on the goods while I grab it."

Eve crouched low and made her way to the far side of the car and peeked through the window. Boxes covered the back seat, but they were all closed.

The other man returned, carrying a much smaller cardboard box ... the perfect size for her relic.

Heart pounding, she ducked down and pressed hard against the car. Goddess, please don't let them come around. Then the door on the other side opened. Something thumped on the seat.

"Wait here. I've got to lock up," the first guy said.

Eve risked another peek through the window. Sure enough, only one guy left. It was now or never. She eased open the door she'd been leaning against, but at the last moment, the handle clicked.

She glanced up—the young guy's eyes flew to hers.

"Hey!" he shouted and threw the car door open on his side. "Stop."

Crap. Eve snatched the cardboard box off the seat. The young guy dove for it and grabbed it too.

"No way," she snarled and yanked the box toward her, dragging the young guy across the back seat.

"Let go," the young guy yelled.

"You let go!" She planted her feet on the concrete and wrenched the cardboard box out of his grip. Momentum had her stumble back. But in her grip, the cardboard box had opened, revealing her relic nestled inside.

Her breath whooshed out. Yes! Adrenaline flooded her system. She shoved the cardboard box—and the precious relic inside it—into her satchel and took off down the alleyway.

Shouts and footsteps followed behind her, but she was fast. And she was determined. Eve reached the end of the alleyway and, without pause, raced down the street, pushing herself faster toward a crossroad with buildings on all sides. The chasing footsteps died off as she neared the blind corner.

"Stop!" someone else yelled from far behind her.

As if.

She poured every ounce of energy into her legs and rounded the building at the bottom of the street at speed.

A woman and child stepped out of a doorway in front of her. At the last moment, Eve sidestepped to avoid crashing into them, but her center of gravity shifted, pulling her off her feet. She tumbled to the concrete. Searing fire scraped over her palms and knees and hip.

"Shit." She scrambled to her feet.

"Are you okay?" the woman she'd avoided hitting asked, reaching out a hand as if to help. "Do you need—"

But the yelling was getting closer on the other side of the corner. No time to stop.

"I'm good." Eve adjusted the satchel's strap across her body and took a step. Thank the goddess, her legs didn't crumple. She shook her hands—beads of blood welled where she'd scraped her palms in the fall. "Wait, which way to the city?"

The woman pointed up the road.

"Thanks." Eve took off again up the sidewalk, dodging pedestrians going in both directions. But after several blocks, there were so many people around she had to slow down to a fast walk to avoid running into anyone.

She risked a glance over her shoulder. No sign of the two men who'd been chasing her.

On either side of the road, the buildings grew larger as she entered some sort of cultural precinct with signs for performing arts buildings and museums. Straight ahead, the sidewalk followed the road over a bridge with the city's skyline filling the sky in the distance.

Perfect. She'd well and truly lose anyone following her among the inner-city buildings.

Eve raced across the bridge; brown swirls of water rushing by. On the other side of the river, the bridge opened into a square filled with open-air market stalls and little tents.

She risked another look back, pretended to meld in with the other tourists checking out the view. None of the thieving assholes were following yet.

Then shouts echoed from the southern side of the river. Around her, people turned and looked in that direction. The hairs prickled along the back of her neck. Crap, the thieving bastards had spotted her.

Eve tightened her grip on her satchel and took off at a jog. They couldn't get the relic again. That was not an option.

But the adrenaline that had surged through her minutes earlier was waning, and the rest she'd had in the taxi seemed a million years ago.

At her back, the shouts grew closer.

She pushed her dragging legs faster, and ran into the market, where little tents protected the stallholders and their wares from the already burning sun.

Eve ducked between two stalls, hiding between the canvas walls. Hands on her hips, she bent over and sucked a desperate breath of much-needed air.

If she couldn't outrun the thieves ... She glanced at her bloody palms. There was one thing she could do that would protect the relic.

She peeked through a gap in the nearest tent. Jewelry covered a display table. She darted to the back of the next stall. Inside, three long tables formed a U, each covered in an odd assortment of antique items from fancy painted cups and saucers to colored glass vases.

An older man and woman were speaking near the front. A pretty vase stood on the table between them.

"Absolutely," the man said. "I can hold on to this while you do your shopping."

"Thank you, Mr. Stanley."

"Please, call me Arthur. Now, I'll box this up right away. I'll be taking the larger pieces back to the shop this afternoon, so you're welcome to stop by any time after four to collect the vase if you don't get back before then."

Eve's heart kicked. Yes! She kept Arthur Stanley in sight as he processed the sale of the vase. *Come on, Mr. Stanley. Where do you put your wares?* She couldn't risk not monitoring the market any longer.

Finally, he walked to the back and carefully placed the vase in a large crate.

More shouting echoed across the markets. Crap. The thieves could walk past any minute and see her. Goddess, please let her have enough energy to make this work.

She ducked back between the tents and took the cardboard box out of her satchel. Opening it up, she lifted the relic out.

Eve spat into her hand, wetting the dried beads of blood, then pressed her palm to the underside of the relic. The blood spell would be far easier to track than using the pendant.

She quickly scattered a fine line of salt—the pouch was almost out now—and, gathering her magic, whispered, "Mark me, hear me, heed my call." Heart pounding, she held her palm still. Waited, waited, waited ... Finally, the last spurt of her lethargic magic responded. The faintest buzz whispered through her skin as her blood connected her to the gold relic.

She tucked the relic back into the cardboard box and blew out a steadying breath. This was it.

Eve walked around the front of the tent and pretended to browse through the tables at the back. Then she slipped her cardboard box into the container heading back to Arthur Stanley's store.

"I'll be back for you," she whispered.

Tears burned at her eyes, but Eve didn't look back as she left the tent, merging into the rest of the market goers.

A yell sounded behind her. Crap. She staggered through a gap between stalls, then wound around the back of the tents, stepping over cables and around storage boxes. But she was out of sight, with a building on one side and the backs of the stalls on the other. She just had to get to the end and the street ahead.

"There!" someone yelled behind her.

Oh shit. She scrambled over the rest of the equipment behind the tents and raced for the street.

Several steps away, people walked past on the sidewalk. Cars and buses and motorbikes sped by on the street.

The older thief from earlier stepped around the end of the stalls. He had black hair and dark, beady eyes. He yanked her to his side and wrapped one arm around her throat. Then he spun them around. Only their backs would be visible to anyone walking past on the sidewalk.

Her heart slammed against her ribs.

"Charlie," the thief holding her called out. "Stand guard at the other end. Don't let anyone come up here. Got it?"

The younger thief nodded and disappeared from view.

"Now, hand it over," the older thief said into her ear. "And we'll let you go."

"It's—it's ..." Goddess, she had to get away before they figured out she'd hidden it in the market.

"Where?"

"Don't shake me," she spat. "You're scaring me, and I can't think."

"Maybe this will help." Something sharp jabbed through her shirt above her hip. Fire bit into her side. She gasped and tried to wrench away from the pain.

"Keep moving. It just makes it worse," the thief said, tightening his grip around her neck.

"You prick," she hissed.

"Get over it. It's just a nick. But if you don't hand over what I want, you'll sure as fuck feel the next one."

Oh goddess, she was almost out of magic. But she wasn't done. This was going to hurt, though.

She jammed her boot heel down on his foot and her elbow into his gut. He doubled over, but his arm jerked, and the pain dug deeper into her side.

She cried out, reflexively jumped back and grabbed at the wound.

"Get back here," the thief growled.

As if. Eve ran for the sidewalk.

People were everywhere, thank the goddess, and she darted in front of the nearest group.

They meandered past a hotel, and with one hand pressed to her side to hide any sign of the knife wound, Eve darted into the lobby, doing her best not to limp. A fast scan revealed the hotel's public restrooms, and she headed straight for them, locking herself in a stall.

Another damned toilet. But she was out of sight, that was what mattered.

And goddess, but her side hurt. She lowered her satchel to the floor and eased out of her jacket. Fire ripped through her again, and she had to grit her teeth against the urge to whimper.

Slowly, she withdrew her hand from her side. Blood stained her palm.

Crap, crap, crap.

Eve pulled up her shirt. An inch-long wound ran across her side. Blood sluggishly oozed from around the edges, and more dried blood smeared across her skin. But it wasn't bleeding profusely, so the asshole thief hadn't nicked any major organs or veins. Thank the goddess.

She waited until there were no other sounds in the restroom, then grabbed a handful of paper towels, wetting some and keeping the rest dry. She cleaned up using the wet towels and then wadded the rest under her shirt and pressed them into her side.

She gasped, gritting her teeth against the urge to whimper at the pain, but the makeshift bandage would have to do. She didn't have the energy or the time here to take on a healing spell.

But that's what she needed—which meant she had to find somewhere to hole up.

Damn. She fumbled through her satchel for the fold-out map of Brisbane. A border ran around the edge with ads for various local attractions and hotels ... and there was what she needed.

A three-star hotel near the airport, cheap enough she

could pay with her cash funds, and far enough away from the city that the thieves wouldn't look for her there.

Gritting her teeth against the pain again, she folded her jacket over her arm, tucking her elbow into her side and using the pressure to keep the wadded paper towels in place. Then she picked up her satchel, somehow feigned a calm expression and left the restrooms.

The urge to run to the nearest taxi rank surged through her, but she kept her head down and forced herself to stroll through the lobby. No sign of the thieves. But that didn't mean they weren't still around.

It was only when she gingerly slid into the back seat of a taxi and gave the driver the name of her hotel that she breathed easier.

3

———

AT NINE A.M. on Saturday morning, in the one hundred percent humidity, with the heat already like a giant oven scorching his bones, Raph Smith paused at the threshold to the antique store. Blissfully cool air drifted beneath the door, enticing him inside.

Raph balked at taking that step.

But hell, this was the job he'd accepted. He gripped the doorhandle for a second and took a moment to clear his mind. Then he channeled the image of the little gilt-covered trinket box. His gut tightened, and a low-level hum buzzed through him. Yep, this was the right place. He blinked and dropped the image straightaway—he was in the vicinity, so that was good enough.

Taking a deep breath, Raph entered the store. A doorbell chimed, and a croony Christmas tune played in the background. Even so, the presence of *things*—old, new, small, big, chipped, used, worn, owned, loved, coveted—bombarded him. He suppressed the shiver that wanted to creep up his neck. This was why he didn't do missing things. Missing persons, sure. Missing things, no bloody way.

Why did people want to have *things* anyway? But that wasn't his problem right now. He had a job to do and a paycheck to make. So, he was doing this and doing it quickly.

The soaring ceilings of the old building could have given the narrow space an airy feeling—except for the fact that shelf after shelf lined the long shop, and on every one of them, some*thing* was there.

A little Christmas tree sat on a counter in the corner, with several larger posters on the wall behind it advertising some fancy Christmas auction event.

"Good morning," a polite, crisp voice carried from the far side of the room. A white-haired man wearing a buttery-yellow shirt with a deeper yellow bow tie emerged from between the shelves and walked over to stand behind the timber counter. His wrinkled eyes surveyed Raph from behind rimless glasses for one heartbeat before a warm smile made the creases around his cheeks deepen. "I'm Arthur Stanley, owner and manager, and it's my privilege to welcome you to Past and Future Treasures."

"Morning, Mr. Stanley." Raph smiled back, hiding his discomfort. "I'm Raph. It's good to get out of the heat. Can't believe it's so hot so early in the day already."

"I have to say the air-conditioning makes a welcome addition to coming to work." Mr. Stanley adjusted his bow tie. "Is that what brings you inside? The cool air?"

"Well, it's a bonus. But no, I'm looking for a gift for my sister," Raph lied smoothly. First lesson of PI school was never to play your hand too early. "She loves old things." At least that was the truth, although why the hell she did was beyond him.

"Lovely, you have certainly come to the right place." Mr. Stanley's eyes sharpened. "I take it she already has a collection, then. If you'd like some help, I can guide you to something, but if not, please feel free to browse the shop. We have another section up the stairs at the back, too. The air-conditioning's not quite as good up that end, but you seem young enough to handle it."

"Thanks, but I think I'll have a look around first."

"Of course. And if something stands out, let me know and I'll pop over."

Some*thing* standing out? That was the least of his problems. Hiding a grimace, Raph nodded at Mr. Stanley and took off for the first aisle.

Shit, but this was going to be hard. These things screamed at him with their human history, their owners as present as if they were right in the room with him, a jumble of voices a cacophony in his ears. Their energy buzzed along his nerves like he'd been tasered a million times. Hell. He'd never find the memento box this way.

Raph jammed his hands in his pockets and clenched his fists. *Focus. Focus. Focus ...* He forced in a long deep breath, then just as slowly exhaled. Did it again. And again. And again. Four times it took to clear his mind and dislodge the fucked-up sensations of the things in the room. And then, finally, he unclenched his fists. The shop came back into focus.

"That is a lovely lamp," Mr. Stanley's voice echoed from behind him. Damn, the old guy had clearly read his staring at the bloody thing for interest rather than a stare into nothing until he could squeeze a breath back in again.

Whatever. He'd use it.

"Yes, it is," he replied smoothly. "Early twentieth century?"

"Nineteen ten, to be exact." Mr. Stanley's neatly groomed silver brows rose. "You know your antiques."

Raph contained a grimace. That was one way of putting it. "It's a lovely piece," he said. That's if you like a hundred plus years of human association. "But I think my sister's got one like it already. I'm thinking of something she doesn't have at all. She's got a lot of little trinkets and jewelry, you know? Do you have any jewelry boxes? Doesn't have to be the traditional type either. In fact, the more unusual, the better."

"Unusual? Of course," the man said with a smile. He swept a hand around the shop. "I can think of a few out here, and I also received some new items this week that might do as well, although their provenance is still to be known. Does your sister have a particular period she collects?"

"No particular period. She does love symbolism—especially carvings," he said smoothly, using the sparse details he had of the trinket box he was searching for to fill in the blanks.

"Hmm, I may have just the thing. There's something in the back section that has some interesting motifs. It's not unpacked yet, though."

Raph's gut tightened. *Bingo.* "Can I take a look?"

He let Mr. Stanley lead him to the back of the main shop and then up a small set of stairs to another narrow room. The ceilings here were lower than the rest of the shop and combined with more shelves and tables, with things packed and tucked into every available space; it was crammed and uncomfortable.

The job, Raph. Think of the job.

"Ah, there it is." Mr. Stanley stopped in front of a table filled with teacups and saucers. A cardboard box sat in the center, looking completely out of place.

A smaller trinket box was inside. It had a gold gilt lid

with surface engravings matching the drawing Parsons had supplied.

A surge of energy buzzed through Raph, and he stepped closer. Everything else in the store dropped away until that one box filled his vision—its voice was strong, stronger than anything he'd seen before, and it called to him—

The creak of the front door opening, followed by the chime of the doorbell echoed through the shop.

"How delightful, more customers," Mr. Stanley said. "If you'll excuse me, I'll just check on them. And please, feel free to have a look at the box."

The urge to touch the small gold gilt box surged through Raph again, and he had to clench his fists to keep from doing just that.

Then raised voices drifted up the stairs, followed by the sharp crack of glass shattering and a distressed cry.

Raph took off down the stairs, through the aisles and skidded to a halt.

The shopkeeper was backed up against the counter, two large men looming over him. They were dressed completely wrong for the hot day in long black coats and long pants. Shattered glass from the smashed display cabinets covered the floorboards like a gleaming carpet.

Shit. What the hell was going on?

"Hey, boys," Raph said, feigning calm and raising his hands to show he was unarmed. "Whatever beef you've got going on here, why don't you let the old guy be, huh? He's an old dude—look at him. And you might not know this, but there's a cop shop right around the corner, and you've probably already tripped all the alarms in the place, so why don't you head out now while you can?"

The shopkeeper cut wide eyes at him. His glasses were missing, and his bow tie was askew.

"And who the fuck are you?" the largest of the long coats asked, barging past the smaller guy.

Whoa. This guy was big. He had dark eyes and hair, with a face that only a mother could love.

Raph glanced at the narrow front door. He'd have to grab the old man and shove past the long coats to get out that way. But there had to be a back entrance to this place— no way the larger items came in through the front.

"I'm just looking for a gift for my sister. No one has to get hurt here." Raph kept his hands raised and stepped toward the old guy. "Seriously, why don't I—?"

"Why don't you shut the fuck up?" Long Coat One snarled as he glanced over Raph's buff chinos and white polo shirt, a sneer forming over his lips. "Just sit your pretty ass against that wall and don't move. Otherwise, you and the old guy will be getting hurt."

Long Coat One had written him off *and* ordered him to get behind Mr. Stanley. Clearly not the sharpest criminal mind.

"Sure, don't want any trouble here." Raph did as instructed and fake-stumbled to the wall behind the old man.

"So, Mr. Stanley," Long Coat One said, "our boss hears you've got something of his and won't give it back. And as I said before we were interrupted, the boss only asks once. Now we're here to take it. It's an old box that came into your possession at the markets two days ago, and it's got an engraved cross on the front."

Mr. Stanley gasped.

Fuck. Who were these guys? And why the hell did they want Raph's box? Or the box he was getting for his client, anyway?

"A-as I told your b-b-boss on the phone last night, the piece is for sale. You can just buy it—"

Oh, hell no. That box was for *his* client. And Raph wasn't losing his biggest paycheck ever, no matter who these dicks were.

"Uh-uh." Long Coat One sank to his knees. "Mr. Frinecki don't buy back his stuff. This is *his* property. He wants it back again. And you will return it. Now hand it over."

Raph stiffened. The Frinecki family wanted the box? What the hell for? And what did they mean they wanted it back *again*?

"Now see here," Mr. Stanley said from the floor. Raph had to admire the old guy's spunk. "If the goods are stolen property, of course, I would return them to their rightful owner. I just need to fill out a police report ..."

Long Coat One pulled back his jacket and revealed the dark handle of a gun tucked in the waist of his pants. The outfit made perfect sense now.

"But I—I—I'm sure that won't be necessary," Mr. Stanley continued. "And I know exactly where the box is."

Raph tensed.

"Fine, you go get it." Long Coat One grabbed Mr. Stanley by the arm and hoisted him to his feet. "Charlie here will escort you—he's a real gentleman like that. I'll stay here and keep an eye on the pretty boy over there and make sure no one else comes in. Don't want any other surprises now, do we?"

"Ah, excuse me," Raph said, still holding his hands up. "I looked at something that sounds a lot like that box up the back, and I moved it just before you ... arrived. Why don't I take Mr. Stanley and go get it? He doesn't know where I put it."

"This true?" Long Coat One tightened his grip on Mr. Stanley's arm, making him gasp.

"Easy," Raph muttered.

"Well, yes," Mr. Stanley stammered. "He, the gentleman, was looking at it, I don't know—"

"Fine." Long Coat One jerked his chin toward Raph. "You go. But keep your hands in the air. And if I see you make a single move ..." He patted his jacket again.

"Got it," Raph said. "Not a single move—other than walking to the box. I'll even help the old man."

"Oh no. I'm keeping him with me." Long Coat One pulled the old guy even closer. "Just to make sure you don't get no crazy ideas about doing a runner with our property."

Raph bit back a sigh. For a moment there, he'd been about to get Mr. Stanley, have only one long coat to deal with and get his hands on the box. And yeah, he could definitely take care of one lone long coat and their weapon, do a runner with Mr. Stanley out the back exit—wherever it was —with the box in hand and get Stanley to the police for safekeeping.

But if Raph left with the box now, Mr. Stanley wouldn't stand a chance. Shit a brick. This was why he didn't do bloody fucked-up *things*.

But he feigned acceptance and forced eagerness into his voice. "Sure, sure. Whatever you need. It's just up here."

Come on, Raph. Need a plan here ... Well, he could start with the box. At the very least, he could get it now and then focus on Mr. Stanley next.

"It's up the stairs in the back section," Raph called over his shoulder—hands still raised—as he carefully walked away.

Charlie didn't say a word, just followed, boots echoing on

the floorboards as they passed the lamp he'd been standing at earlier, past more things—brass and porcelain and glass and crystal. Upstairs in the back section, once again, the trinket box drew his attention. Its voice was louder and stronger than anything else there—anything else Raph had dealt with, ever.

"That's it there," he said. "On the round table with all the cups."

"Stand back," Charlie ordered. "And keep your hands where I can see them."

"Sure." Raph managed not to roll his eyes. These people were clueless about anything outside their mortal world if they thought raised hands would protect them from other-world abilities.

"Charlie? Charlie!" Long Coat One shouted from downstairs. "Where the fuck you at? We ain't got time for you to look at the pretty shit. We've got orders. And now this mess to clean up."

Raph's gut tightened. Clean up? That wasn't comforting. Charlie grabbed the box and motioned for Raph to precede him back to the front of the store.

Mr. Stanley was still pale, and Raph sent him a reassuring look. Time to get him and the box the hell out of—

The shop's front doorbell chimed, and a woman barreled through the door. She wore black cropped pants and a white T-shirt, and her hair was tied straight back from her arresting face.

She poured something white and powdery on the floor into a small circle around her feet.

What the hell?

"Beside me, before me, behind me, call to me!" the woman yelled, her hands shooting into the air, fingers flared wide.

A buzz of energy raced over Raph; the hairs zipped up along the back of his neck. *Magic.* She was a witch.

Charlie cried out.

"Who the fuck are you? What are you doing?" Long Coat One snarled, whirling around.

But the woman didn't answer. Her gaze cut to Charlie holding the box—and then to Raph.

"Hey, did you hear me?" Long Coat One shoved Mr. Stanley away from him.

Raph shot forward, caught Stanley before he hit the ground.

"Thank you," the old man whispered.

Raph nodded as he rose to his feet, holding in a sigh. Seriously, this job had gone ass up. Would he have to extricate this woman too? All he wanted was the goddamn trinket box.

"Did you fucking hear me?" Long Coat One snarled.

"Let's go with your second question," the witch all but purred to Long Coat One.

She cocked her head to one side, coolly surveying them all from a pair of dark, mysterious eyes. She was tall, maybe five nine, with deep brown hair tied in a severe knot at the base of her neck. Not a single strand out of place. Even though Long Coat One towered over her, she somehow looked down her patrician nose at him.

"I'm getting my property back," she said, and her midnight eyes flashed.

4

Adrenaline surging, Eve rapidly surveyed the scene, loosening her arms and widening her stance. She took in the multiple people in the shop. Then she forced herself to breathe evenly. In. Out. Calm. Steady. Her pulse evened out. Ready for anything.

But what by the goddess was going on now, and who were all these people? Was everyone after her relic? Well, they were in for a sorry surprise.

A male, easily six two, with wide shoulders and a lean frame, held the shopkeeper who she'd placed her relic with —Mr. Stanley—on the floor. The shopkeeper's hair was messed up and his clothes askew, but he didn't look injured.

A flash of guilt worked through Eve—if this was about the relic, then he was in this predicament because of her.

The male holding the shopkeeper had a tantalizing otherworldly scent that rubbed at her senses. She blinked— he *was* otherworldly. Nonhuman for sure—but what exactly? Something warm knotted in her belly. For a single moment, she stared at his broad shoulders, at the length of his body—

Oh no. Not the time for checking out—or reacting to—a male. Not even for the hottest male she'd ever seen.

Eve looked at the other two humans. One was unfamiliar, but the other ... he was the man who'd stuck her with the knife. Reflexively she rubbed her side. But through the help of her magic, the wound was healed, the pain gone—nothing more than the remembered insult of fiery shards—so she dropped her hand away.

And she was prepared this time. And while the spell's trace was faint, the blood magic on the relic still held, no doubt worn thin from both her weakened state when she'd cast it and the time that had passed while she'd holed up in her hotel room and healed from the knife wound.

But now her blood was literally tingling through her veins—rushing toward the thief holding the cardboard box —so her relic had to still be inside. As well as toward the otherworld male. Which made zero sense.

Eve concentrated on the thief with the box. Her heart punched hard against her ribs.

"I believe you have my property. If you give it back to me now, you can get out of here without anyone getting hurt." She raised her hands and whispered the words to a stun spell.

"You fucking crazy?" The thief who'd knifed her laughed and withdrew a gun from inside his jacket. He pointed the black barrel straight at her. "You've got three seconds to get over there with pretty boy. And, hey, I know you! You're the bitch who stole it in the first place."

Eve's side throbbed as if the wound being called out had made the pain fresh again, and the urge to grab at the spot surged through her. But she'd gotten through being stabbed once—could do it again if needed.

"That would be witch bitch to you," she said. "And you

can't steal your own property." She gathered her energy and whispered the spell, throwing her hand out in a hard jolt.

The buzz of witchcraft hummed through her arm, and a silvery stream of magic flew from her palm.

"Fu—" The thief holding the relic stiffened, his words dropping from suddenly still lips.

"Charlie? Charlie!" The guy with the gun spun and pointed the weapon at Eve. His eyes darted from her to the other thief. "W-what the fuck did you do?"

"Don't say I didn't warn you." Eve raised her chin, gathered her energy for the Spell of Shadows. It was risky—too much energy, and the shadows would get out of control. But she only needed enough to obscure herself and the relic, and the long, high walls of the shop should contain the shadows before they could escape her control. Theoretically.

"Rise and ruin, bind the dark. Hear my call and make my mark." She whispered the unfamiliar words as she poured her energy into her amethyst crystal—and then channeled it out. Electricity flooded her system, but she held tight to the pendant.

From the corners of the room, the gaps beneath the shelving units, the spaces behind the paintings, shadows darkened ... elongated. They prowled up the walls and over the windows, slithered across the ceiling and blocked all light coming into the room, obscuring everyone in it.

Thank the goddess, her blood called to the spell on the relic.

"Stop the shadows!" the otherworld male shouted. His voice sent a shiver over her, but she ignored it. And him.

More darkness spooled from the corners, shadow upon shadow poured into the room. More than she'd expected. Her heart began to hammer.

"Fuck," the thief with the gun snarled. "I don't know what the fuck is going on here, but I've had enough. The knife might not have hurt, but this will." A gunshot reverberated through the shop; glass and porcelain shattered and crashed. A sharp acrid tang hit the air.

The shopkeeper screamed. The otherworld male swore.

Eve tensed, but in the dark, the bad guy couldn't see her to hit her.

She let the tug in her blood lead her and darted forward, straight into the thief with the box. Yes! Still holding her pendant, she tried to grab the relic with her free hand—but something else tugged it in the opposite direction.

The shadows parted momentarily. A tall shape loomed over Eve, a serious face with a strong clenched jaw and a long, perfect nose. Dark hair. Narrowed eyes locked on hers. The otherworldly male.

Then his fingers grazed hers—another jolt of electricity zapped through her and she only just managed to keep her grip on the box.

"What—who—by the goddess are you?" she whispered.

"Let go" was all he replied through gritted teeth. "And shut the shadows off."

"No way." She poured more energy into her crystal. All she had. "This is *my* relic. *You* let go. And if you don't like the dark, get out of the room."

"What the fuck—are you a Templar?"

"What did you say?" Her gut tightened.

"The shadows. Stop them. Now."

"And I said, *let go*. And no, I'm not some high and mighty Templar."

"Then who are ... oh shit."

Suddenly the shadows roared into the room. Faster. Darker. Denser. Something oily gathered in her stomach.

"Turn it off!" the male yelled again as he pulled harder.

"Let go and I will!" she cried back, barely holding onto the relic.

Another shot rang out. More of that acrid tang stung her nose and made her eyes water. More shattering and clattering pealed through her ears.

But then a different cry—a high gasp of pain—echoed through the shop from the floor, followed by a whimper. The shopkeeper. Oh no. No, no, no.

"Damn it," the otherworld male snarled. "Where is he?"

Eve let go of the box and tried to drop the pendant—but she was stuck to the amethyst. The shadows were heaving now, so many and so fast her crystal vibrated.

"Kill the spell!" the male shouted again.

Damn. She was trying to. But she didn't bother glaring at him, just gathered every ounce of energy she had and wrenched her hand from the pendant ... Finally, her skin disconnected. The shadows in the room bulged larger—thicker—so dense they took up every available molecule of air to the point she couldn't breathe, then a crack echoed through the shop. The darkness dissipated.

Eve spun around and knelt beside the shopkeeper. "Goddess, are you shot? Where else do you hurt—"

"Not shot." Mr. Stanley raised. Shaking hand to his forehead. A gash ran across his temple, and bloody rivulets rolled down his temple, staining his cheek. "I think I got cut by flying glass."

Suddenly the otherworld male was there, dropping to his knees on the other side of the shopkeeper. The male's face was pulled tight, and anger glittered in his deep, jewel-like green eyes.

"Don't hurt him. I'll stun you right here and now," she bluffed. A cold weight filled her chest. After what had happened with the Spell of Shadows, she doubted she had enough energy to call on a spell to snuff out a candle right now. But still, she gathered what magic she could and raised her palm. If this male was going to hurt Mr. Stanley, she'd use the last of her energy to stop him—somehow—even if that meant letting the relic go again. The shopkeeper was in this because of her; she had to help him.

"Me?" the male hissed. "I'm not the one hurting him, am I? I'm checking him out. You keep an eye on Long Coat One."

"Who?"

"The guy with the gun—the only one not frozen. Stun him or something."

"*Something*?" She threw a look at the otherworld male. Was he serious?

Another crash sounded behind them. Eve spun on her knees. The baddie with the gun was tugging the box from the frozen bad guy's hands.

"Charlie, you in there? Charlie, let the goddamn thing go!" The bad guy wrapped one arm under the box and pulled it free.

Heart pounding, Eve rose to her feet.

"Now to clean up properly." The guy with the gun pointed it at her again.

Eve hauled in a desperate breath and gathered her energy for another spell, but as soon as she picked up her pendant, her thumb grazed a sharp edge running the length of the crystal.

Ice flew through her veins, and her breathing stopped. An internal fissure, splitting the edge on one side, ran from top to bottom.

That was bad. But how bad? Eve licked suddenly dry lips and poured her energy into the crystal—only the faintest ooze of energy sluggishly responded to her call. Shit. She was tapped out after the earlier spells, that was all. Surely. And absolutely nothing to do with the giant frigging fissure running through the amethyst. But it didn't matter. Either way, she had one option left.

Eve sprang at the thief with the gun, aiming for his arm as the gun went off with a booming crack. Her ears rang. Her vision swam, She wobbled on her feet. Was she shot? Didn't matter—because she couldn't stop. She lurched back to the gun-wielding thief, but her hands grasped at air as the room spun.

"Hey," the otherworld male's voice echoed in her ear. "Stop moving. Are you hurt?"

Something in that gravelly tone made her want to curl up close to his heat, have that voice fill her ears, while other things filled all kinds of other places ... As the room came back into focus, the warmth of his grasp on her arms bloomed through her. She glanced at the deeply tanned fingers wrapped around her bicep. Goddess, he was practically holding her up.

"I'm fine." Eve jerked backward. She didn't need any help. And the relic! She spun around. The thief was gone.

"So, you're not shot then?"

"No." But the relic was gone. Again. Dear goddess, no. She doubled over at the waist.

The male grabbed her shoulders again. "Hey, take a breath already."

She somehow inhaled, the airflow shuddering into her lungs.

"Let go. Now. I'm fine." Eve shrugged him off. No searing pain stabbed or cut through her with the motion, so she must have avoided being shot.

"Sure." The male dropped his hands. "But if you keel over and hit your head, don't blame me."

"The room's stopped spinning now." At least it had slowed. Eve clenched her jaw and planted her feet solidly on the ground. In the distance, police sirens echoed. By Hades, this entire thing had gone from bad to worse.

"How is he?" She turned back to the shopkeeper—his eyes were open now, and the blood at his temple wasn't running anymore.

"Gash on his forehead that will need glue or stitches, but apart from a few other scrapes, he's okay."

"No bullet wound?"

"No, the cut's the worst of it."

"Thank the goddess." Eve's knees threatened to buckle, but she locked them even harder in place. No weakness.

The otherworld male cut her a look. "What about you? You were bloody close to the gun when it went off."

Damn. Damn, damn, damn. *Damn.* And now the police were on the way, of course.

"Listen." The otherworld male moved like he was going to grab her arm but stopped at the last moment. An even deeper scowl furrowed his face. "Who are—?"

"I have to check out the guy I stunned."

"What? No, you need to get checked out. You can barely stand."

"I'm fine." Eve held out a steady hand. "See? No wobbles." She stepped over to the frozen bad guy. He couldn't talk, but he could have items on him that could help her work out her next steps. Whoever they worked for might have the relic for now, but she'd get it back. No question.

"Charlie, right?" she muttered.

Charlie's eyes were frozen, but he'd be able to hear her through the stun.

"I'm going to search your pockets."

"Pretty sure he won't mind. But don't go getting any ideas, Charlie," the male at her back called out.

"A bit juvenile, don't you think?" she said over her shoulder.

"You're the one apologizing to a thief."

"Manners never go astray." She cut him a withering look —which he completely missed since he was tending to the shopkeeper.

Which was at least a decent thing to do. And which she *would* have done if no one else had been there and able to help —and if she didn't have a critical emergency to deal with first.

She turned back to Charlie and quickly searched him. One billfold, one cell phone, and zero personally identifying documents. Eve used Charlie's jacket to wipe her fingerprints off the phone case and tucked it and the billfold back inside his pockets.

Two police cars pulled to a screeching halt outside the shop.

She whirled to the otherworld male, now staring at her, eyes narrowed. She almost took a step back from the heat in his glare. But no, she didn't back away from anyone.

"Stay with him." Eve nodded toward the shopkeeper while she tracked the police getting out of their cars.

They were speaking into radios attached to their vests. Would they already have the rear entry covered? Hopefully not.

"Of course I'll stay with him—he's injured." The man shot her a look. "And I think your stun is wearing off ol' Charlie here."

"But not before the police get here. You'll be fine. Now, which way did the other guy go—left or right?"

"The gunman?" The male's face tightened, and for a moment, his eyes flashed like molten emeralds. "Left. Down the hill. But, hey—"

"Down. Got it."

"Wait. Who the hell are you?"

"None of your business. And stay away from my relic," she called out.

5

____

After almost four hours spent with the police, Raph headed up to the hospital to check on Mr. Stanley. Raph had answered questions and made a statement, procedures he was familiar enough with after years on the force and as a private investigator.

In the hospital room, Raph found Mr. Stanley lying on a bed surrounded by family. Thankfully, Mr. Stanley's injuries weren't severe, and the doctors had glued the edges of the larger gash together on his forehead. The family welcomed Raph like he was some kind of hero—making his stomach turn. But he stayed until Mr. Stanley was discharged.

Then Raph got out of there as quickly as his feet would take him. He hopped straight into a taxi and headed home.

Fifteen minutes later, Raph was back at his apartment building, a renovated complex housed in what used to be the dockside woolsheds when the Brisbane River had been home to a bustling business of wool shipping. The old brown-and-red-brick buildings had fallen into disrepair until a couple of decades earlier when some savvy developers had seen the raw beauty in the old structures and the luxury of the prime waterfront.

Raph closed his apartment door, turned the air-con on and toed off his shoes, kicking them into the corner before heading to the fridge.

One ice-cold beer in hand, he grabbed his laptop, turned the television onto the all-news channel and dropped into a seat at his dining table.

Bloody hell, what a day. Still shaking his head at the absolutely fucked-up turn of events the supposedly simple job had taken, he slung back a sip of the crisp ale and let out a long, long sigh.

But Raph's mind didn't stop like he wanted it to. The witch had called the box a relic. Twice.

As soon as her vibrant voice with its British accent replayed through his mind, a punch of heat surged through his gut. Ah hell, she was like some fantasy woven from a fierce warrior queen, crossed with a serious schoolteacher with her severe hairstyle.

And now Raph seemed to have a thing for fierce, serious schoolteachers. Except that wasn't his type. He was usually drawn to lovers rather than fighters. And that witch ... she'd been all fight from the moment she'd blown like a tempest into the shop.

The contradiction made his hands itch to unravel her mystery. And why had the world gone quiet? A moment of peace he'd never experienced around so many things; in fact, the only time he had experienced internal quiet like that was up on the farm. Whatever had caused it had arrived —and left—with the mystery woman. Mystery upon mystery ... The skin itched on the back of his neck.

Damn, but he wanted to know more—except, he already had one mystery he sure as shit had to unravel right now.

What the hell was this relic? And once he knew that answer, did he stick with this job? Or turn down the kind of payday that could keep his family safe and hidden for another full year?

Raph sat the beer down beside his laptop and entered the characteristics of the trinket box into an internet search and added the word relic. It quickly returned multiple options, starting with a Vatican site. But all the relics were inside the boxes—was that the deal? Was something inside the box that made it so precious? He hadn't opened the lid and looked inside, so maybe that was it.

Finally, one reference to a tiny ancient gold chest came up, purportedly given to …

What. The. Hell.

He stared at the image on the screen. The scrolling around the edges, the simple turned legs, the carvings … and cast over two thousand years ago from gold out of the ancient mines at Hamdah.

But the precious metal wasn't the real value here.

A shiver worked down his back—completely unrelated to the air-con now blasting into the room. He quickly swallowed the lump that lodged in his throat and, unable to take his eyes off the image on the screen, grabbed his cell phone. There was one person he knew who *might* be able to help here—as much as Raph hated to call him.

"Raph," a smooth voice answered after a long moment of silence—the standard international call delay. "Long time no hear."

"Hi, Gray. Well, Hell hasn't quite closed over, and they haven't managed to kill me off yet."

"More like take you home, don't you mean?"

"Yeah, that too. And hey, sorry for the early call."

"All good," Gray said, voice way too bright for the time of day it had to be in Boston. "So, what's up?"

"Let's just say I'm curious about any rumors of something special ... going missing lately?" Eyes still glued to the screen, Raph took another sip of his beer. Waited. And waited. "Gray ... Grayson? You there?"

"Yeah, I'm here. Just getting my brain to work given it's 1:00 fucking a.m. here and thinking about all the *special* things there are."

"You're sounding pretty damned awake for 1:00 fucking a.m. So come on, out with it."

"You know what I do, Raph. So for you to be asking this ... I need to ask you something first. Why?"

Raph scrubbed a hand over his face. Hell. He did know Gray. And Gray knew him. He wasn't about to lie to the only ... friend ... he had any more than absolutely necessary.

"I've got a job." That was the truth. "And the item I'm looking for looks remarkably like something bloody *special*. Like something up your alley." Another truth.

"Why you?"

"The client thinks it's local to me. And wants anonymity to keep the price low." Another truth, or at least he'd thought that was the case. But now ... "If this is what I think it is, the payday is never going to be good enough to get mixed up with it."

"You really think it's something up my alley?"

"Don't know for sure. Which is why I'm calling you at 1:00 fucking a.m. to find out. So come on, I've answered your question. Now you answer mine. Anything really, really, *really* fucking special missing from where it should be?"

Gray's sigh echoed all the way down the phone line, as loud and emotive as if the other man was sitting beside him instead of a thousand miles away.

"Yeah, we've got something missing. And it's big."

Hell. Raph's heart sank.

Half an hour later, he hung up from Gray and spun his phone across the table.

And then the bloody thing started to ring. The name Parsons flashed onto the screen. His client. Double hell. He lunged across the table and grabbed the call. No use in putting this off any longer.

"Hello, Mr. Smith," Parsons said. "My team tells me there's news on my trinket box."

Raph rolled his eyes. *His* trinket box? But the guy was still a client. "Well, I definitely have news, Mr. Parsons. I'm afraid your ... item was stolen and is now the subject of a police investigation. Given that—I can't get involved from here on in. So I'm very sorry to say I have to cancel our contract. Of course that means I'll repay your retainer so far, and I won't be charging you any fees for the work done to date."

Raph waited. The only sound was Parsons' breathing on the other end of the line.

"That's disappointing to hear," Parsons finally said.

"Believe me, I'm disappointed, too. Best thing you can do now is lodge a claim with the police and go from there."

"I really thought you were the man for the job, Raphael. You've got quite the reputation for always finding your man."

"*Man* being the operative word there. I told you I don't normally work with objects."

"But given your ... background, I thought you were eminently more qualified for objects."

Raph stilled. What did that mean?

"Ah, I have your attention now," Parsons continued. "Well, how about this? If you open your email, you should see a communication from one of my team. It contains an attachment."

Ice slithered down Raph's neck and he wordlessly opened his inbox. One new email waited, and he clicked on it.

"This is our agreement," Raph said carefully. Looked like Parsons wasn't letting go of this one easily.

"Check closer, Mr. Smith. Look at our signatures. Do you recall the pen you used to sign the contract?"

"The one your man gave to me, you mean?"

"Yes," Parsons said brightly. "That pen. As I really do want this trinket box, I decided to use one of my permanent pens, if you get my drift. So I'm calling this contract due."

Oh hell. Raph shoved back from the table, checked his legs, his arms ... a tingling tightened around his left bicep. He yanked the sleeve up. Fucking hell. A tattoo was etching into his skin—a triangle with a circle entwined.

"You cast a binding contract," he whispered.

"And you signed it in my permanent ink. I have to say, I'm rather pleased I had the foresight to use that option."

The fucker. The absolute fucking bastard. Raph rapidly reread the contract—the only thing they hadn't stipulated in writing was an end date. Raph never committed to a timeline unless he was certain he could make the delivery, so no wonder Parsons' rep had tried to insist they add the due date. Thank the stars Raph had been more insistent. He at least had time to figure out how to get out of this mess.

"I need this trinket box, Mr. Smith," Parsons continued. "And as my man was unable to secure a binding due date, another email is coming through shortly."

What the hell? What else did Parsons have up his sleeve? Dread coiled in Raph's gut as he opened the next email. It contained an image of a woman standing amid a menagerie of animals.

"You're the best person to find my trinket box, Mr. Smith. But just in case you're thinking of taking your time on delivery, I understand you have a sister with the same hereditary ... gift as you. Perhaps I'll go to her instead if your delivery is taking too long. Only, my means of convincing her to take the job won't be so gentle."

What. The. Fuck?

"Did you hear me, Mr. Smith?"

"Are you threatening my family?" Raph gritted out.

"No, no. Persuading. You do your job and no further action is required. That's all."

"And how long is too long?"

"Well, surely an experienced investigator with your gifts won't need too long. Let's say seven days."

Raph gripped his phone so hard that his knuckles went white.

"No? I take your silence to mean that's not enough time? Then eight days is my final offer, Mr. Smith. By next Sunday, I have my trinket box, you get your payday, and all will be well."

Raph's throat was so tight all he could manage was a growl. And then the phone went dead.

Bloody hell! A fucking binding contract. And how did Parsons know things about Raph and his family that very, very few people in this world knew? Just who the hell was Parsons?

Raph rubbed the binding tattoo. The magic had settled into his skin, but his arm still tingled. He *had* to give the relic to Parsons. There was no choice. And given what Parsons had accomplished so far, Raph had to take his threat to Isa seriously.

He clenched the phone so hard he almost snapped it. Tension kept his hands stiff as he placed the cell phone on the table very carefully instead of giving into the urge to hurling it across the room. No time to waste time on being angry.

He had a relic to find. But where was the bloody thing?

Fact one—Frinecki's people had it now. Fact two—at least one other person was after it, and she may have been involved in its theft from the beginning, given what Gray had told him earlier. Which led him to fact three—based on what had happened today, she was as determined as him to find the relic, and she had mad skills that Raph didn't.

So that was the play. Find the witch. Find the relic.

Returning to her hotel room, Eve sighed as she closed the door and rolled her neck and shoulders. Every part of her body dragged, and all she wanted was to topple onto the bed and sleep for twenty-four hours.

But sleep was out of the question. She had to find the relic.

She'd tried to follow the thief from the antique shop and had called the blood spell for over two hours all over the city. But the magic must have worn away because she hadn't picked up a single trace of the original incantation. She'd finally run out of salt so had exchanged the last of her euros for Australian dollars and found a local grocery shop.

At least the euro had a decent conversion rate. Her cash funds should last a few more nights at the hotel, which was critical.

But she'd found the relic before. She could find it again. She just needed salt, time and her pendant.

An oily slick washed through Eve's stomach, and she reflexively rubbed her thumb over the fracture in her crystal. Gods, she'd never lost control of an incantation before. Was it because she was tired? Was it the Spell of Shadows? No one in the coven had ever said shadows were hard to control.

And what effect would the fracture have on her spell craft?

Eve withdrew a small pack of salt and scissors from the shopping bag. Please let this store-bought version work—it was the first time she'd used anything other than coven-procured salt for as long as she'd been casting circles.

But she had no other choice than to use it. The Templars could already know she was in Brisbane, and if they did, the coven wouldn't be far off locating her too—in fact, they could already have located Eve given their magic would beat the Templar's tech any day.

But Watchers only watched, so the coven would tell the Templars, who'd then send another field team to bring Eve in.

All she needed was for the salt to hide her spell work and buy her enough time to find the relic.

Eve took the salt into the bathroom and poured a circle of the fine grains around her. With one steadying breath, she took hold of the crystal, thumb once more running back and forth, back and forth over the fracture. *Focus, Eve ... focus.*

She lowered the pendant over the map of the city and, closing her eyes, tried to bring an image of the relic to mind. But the beat of her pulse thundered in her ears, and all she could see were a pair of green eyes. Shit. She dropped her head back to stare at the ceiling. *Come on, Eve. Get it together.*

She regripped the crystal, staring so hard at the map her eyes stung. She snapped them shut and shoved the dark, otherworldly gaze out of her mind—forced the relic instead to fill her thoughts. The ancient simple carvings. The turned legs. The hum of power.

She whispered her spell and waited ... waited ... Finally, the pendant began to swing up and down.

Her breath left her in a whoosh. Thank the goddess— the crystal still worked. But then the pendant made the slightest deviation from top to ... right. Then to the left. Then back to the top.

Eve's stomach dropped. Blood roared through her ears as she stared at her amethyst. It had failed. *She* had failed.

She'd lost the relic. Again. And then a pair of otherworld eyes flew through her mind. Why was he after her relic?

Her heart picked up pace. Maybe she had one avenue after all. She just had to find him.

6

At half past eight on Sunday morning, Raph stood out the front of the antique shop. The front door had a 'Sorry, We Are Closed' sign facing outward, but with seven days to hand the relic over, Raph wasn't waiting until Monday.

Luckily, through the glass, Mr. Stanley was visible beyond the intact display cases. His bow tie was back on, all neat and tidy, this time a pale blue matching his pinstripe shirt. A dressing covered his forehead, and several small scratches marred his cheek. The old guy was a tough nut to be back already.

Raph took a steadying breath. Back into the fire. Though this time, the payday wasn't the motivation.

He tapped the timber doorframe. Mr. Stanley glanced up; his eyes widened, and a smile covered his face as he bustled through the shop—between piles of damaged goods —and opened the door.

"Good morning, Mr. Smith," Mr. Stanley said. "I didn't expect to see you, but I'm so glad you're here. And please, come in. At least the air-conditioning is still working."

"Hi, Mr. Stanley." Raph plastered a smile over his face

and forced the voices of the things in the room away as he took in the shop. "You've already started to clear up."

"Please, call me Arthur. And yes, my family and employees cleared up as much as they could after the police left last night. I've had to leave all the damaged pieces in the corner until the insurance people can get here, sometime this morning, apparently. But that means I'm not able to open yet, unfortunately. But oh dear, are you still after a piece for your sister? I would be more than happy to help when I reopen."

"No, please don't worry. I'll come back when you're ready. And it's Raph." He automatically blanked his mind as they shook hands. Physical contact enhanced his curse, and he'd spent most of his adulthood perfecting a method to stop the barrage of a person's past flowing through him. "Thought I'd stop by to see if you needed some help clearing up." And he did intend on helping—he just didn't mention the other reason for the visit.

"Well, you're a lovely man to be so helpful, Raph. Though as you can see, at this stage I can't do much more. But *I* want to thank *you*. Yesterday was ... well, it was the most unusual day I've ever had."

"Yeah, about that ..." Something tingled on the back of Raph's neck, and he reflexively rubbed the spot.

Then the bell above the shop's front door chimed—and the voices of the things in the room dwindled to silence. A silence he recognized. And then Arthur's eyes widened again as he stared over Raph's shoulder.

Yes. His hunch had paid off far faster than he'd expected.

"Good morning," a smooth voice poured over him. Goosebumps prickled over his skin in the wake of that liquid-silk British-accented voice.

Turning around, he stared—no doubt, just like Arthur—

at the witch in the doorway. Satisfaction flared through him. Not because she made his blood fire, and brought some weird as all hell sense of ... quiet, but because his gut shouted that she could take him to the relic.

And that was the only important thing right now.

The witch wore the same calf-length pants she'd been wearing on Saturday, but this time with a plain white fitted T-shirt that made her skin glow. Her dark hair was pulled back again in a severe ponytail, highlighting sharp cheekbones and those liquid-chocolate eyes. Her gaze locked on him, and her mouth tightened.

"You," she said. Then she glanced at Arthur, and her expression unstiffened. "Sir, good morning. How are you?"

Did the witch ever smile? But that didn't matter. His blood quickened. She was here. Just like he'd hoped— although way faster than he'd expected.

"And good morning to you, too, my dear. And apart from this"—Arthur waved at the bandage on his head—"I'm fine."

"That's good to hear." Her eyebrows gathered, and her mouth turned down. Was that remorse in her eyes? But then whatever was in that gaze was whisked away, replaced by pure steel. "But should you be on your feet?"

"Why, of course! I've had worse head knocks over my seventy years."

"Well, I'm very sorry about what happened because of my relic. I had no idea they would track it to you."

"Your relic?" Raph cut in.

"Yes." She flicked a look in his direction. Something in him cheered to have all that liquid silk focused on him. "My relic."

"Well, shame you didn't stick around yesterday. You could've filed a report with the police." Raph regarded her carefully. Had her eyes tightened? "So you just came back to check on Arthur here?"

"That," she murmured, her gaze moving around the shop before settling squarely on him. "And for you."

"Wow. I'm flattered, princess."

"Don't be." Her expression turned glacial, which shouldn't have turned him on as much as it did. "I need information—and you clearly know about ..." She swiveled to Arthur. "I'm so sorry for our rudeness, sir. Please, let me introduce myself. And ignore Mr. Rude over there. I'm Evangeline—but call me Eve. Is your name really Arthur?"

Evangeline. Raph played the name over in his mind. It sounded fierce, sexy with a dangerous edge. He wanted to whisper her name to feel it on his lips. Would it be as decadent to say as it sounded? Suddenly an image of her name rolling past his lips as he kissed her flowed through his mind. Right, well, that was clearly not gonna happen. The warrior princess was too uptight to ever go there—and she was totally not his type anyway. Plus, he needed something else from the mysterious Evangeline.

"Arthur Stanley at your service, my dear."

"It's lovely to formally meet you, Mr. Stanley. And perhaps you can help me as well. I need to find the man who took the ... box. Do you know who he is?"

"They were not very nice men, I'm afraid. I think you should do as Mr. Smith here suggests and speak with the police."

"Mr. Smith?" Evangeline flicked him a glance.

"Raph to my friends." Raph rocked back on his heels, forcing a calm expression. "And Arthur's right; the police are a much safer option."

"That's an alternative, of course," Evangeline said. "But I

would very much like to know who I'm dealing with before that. So, those men are ...?"

"Yes, well, you see—" Arthur toyed with his bow tie, and the wrinkles around his eyes and forehead deepened—"if I give you their name, and you were to ..." He turned to Raph, clearly looking for help.

Raph bit back a sigh. He couldn't turn his back on Arthur's unspoken plea.

"Listen, princess—"

"Eve."

"You're dealing with some pretty dangerous people. Why don't I fill you in—but away from Arthur. Avoid any more harm for him, hey?"

Eve turned her captivating eyes back on him. His body tightened, and his blood heated. But Raph hid how much he wanted—shit, *needed*—to talk to her and didn't say anything else. The most important thing here to figure out was if she'd be a help or a hindrance while he searched for the relic.

The stunning witch clearly wasn't giving up her search, so sticking close would both stop her from finding it on her own—an unacceptable outcome—and put him in a better position to take the relic himself. But if she ever knew the truth about his intentions with the relic, she wouldn't want anything to do with him. In any capacity.

Regret pinged in his chest, which was absurd. He barely knew the warrior-queen-esk witch. He resisted the urge to scrub a fist over his sternum and shoved that soft emotion deep, deep down. There was no time for any emotional bullshit.

Let her think he just saw her as an attractive woman— and hell, that wasn't anywhere near a lie.

"Fine." She dipped her head once like some kind of

queen—maybe he wasn't so far off with his princess call after all. "Arthur, would you like to have a seat, and we'll clean up? We should be the ones doing the heavy lifting here."

We? What, like he'd brought this on the shopkeeper? But Raph just rolled his eyes. He'd already been prepared to help Arthur out, but he quickly filled Eve in on Arthur having to wait for the insurance people.

"Thank you, though, my dear. And please feel free to come back. Perhaps I can even tempt you with something lovely once I reopen."

Raph hid a grin. What a guy. "We'll come back and check in with you soon, Arthur. And yes, we'll both be more than happy to support your store by finding some of your beautiful things to buy."

Raph took a few more minutes to double-check Arthur really was okay, then he and Eve said their goodbyes.

Eve swept past Raph, a warm, beguiling scent following her through the door. Raph's blood thickened. Followed by another body part. *Down, boy.* He had work to do.

At the corner of the block, Eve strode into a street-side café behind the otherworldly Mr. Smith. His firm, muscled backside filled out his navy three-quarter-length pants perfectly —but she dragged her gaze away. Lush tushes weren't on her agenda. And the sweat building on her skin was purely to do with the unholy, thick heat of this city—not the tantalizing view.

She purposely looked around the interior and gratefully

sucked in a breath of cool air. A counter ran the length of the little space with two baristas behind it busily making coffees. Eve's mouth watered at the rich aroma.

"What would you like? My shout." Mr. Smith stopped in front of the coffee machine and turned to her. "Grab us a seat while I order, if you like."

"Coffee. Black. No sugar." Even as the words fell from her lips, the aroma of roasted beans fortified her flagging energy. Thank the goddess for coffee. And for someone else buying her one. Except—how could anyone drink a hot drink here? "Actually, I need something cold."

"Iced black coffee, then? Got it." Mr. Smith turned away from her and left her staring at his back.

Was iced black coffee even a thing? Well, apparently, she was about to find out.

As Eve wove between the mostly empty tables toward the back of the room, Mr. Smith repeated her order and then added his own, a caramel latte with sugar. That was a lot of sweetness. She hid a shudder and sat at the farthest table, back to the wall, and surveyed the other customers—and Mr. Smith, her information source.

His charming smile was back, casual, flirtatious ... but there was a tension about his shoulders at odds with the rest of his demeanor. Behind the counter, an attractive woman continued to chat to him well after he'd ordered. Were all baristas this friendly in Australia? Mr. Smith was chatting back, although she couldn't make out any words from their conversation. But his eyes cut to Eve continuously.

Beneath Eve's fractured pendant, her skin tingled.

She rubbed the spot before she could stop herself. That had never happened before. Eve picked up the crystal, her thumb finding the tiny fault in the amethyst, and ran over the seam back and forth.

At the counter, Mr. Smith stilled, and his gaze cut back to her. But this time, it stayed. And even from across the room, that look caught her. His lips tightened, and his eyes narrowed. In her belly, something began to warm and coil in answer.

No. Oh no. She was *not* adding sex to the mix with everything else here. She dropped the pendant.

The woman making the coffees spoke again to Mr. Smith, and he blinked, jerked back to her as she handed him two takeaway coffee cups.

Eve blew out a low breath. Who was he? And could she trust him enough to use what he said?

"Here you go," his smooth voice rolled over her as he easily maneuvered between the tables.

"Thanks," she muttered. At least the coffee gave her something else to focus on. And much-needed caffeine.

"So," Mr. Smith said as he sat down opposite her. His knees grazed hers. Tingles shimmied through her legs. Crapola.

Shifting away, she took a sip of her drink. It was … refreshing. Rich and icy. Bitter to taste. And it focused her.

"All right, Mr. Smith."

"Raph."

"Mr. Smith." She cut him a look. "What can you tell me about the man who took the relic?"

"According to my research, he's Michael Frinecki, nephew to the one and only Giovanni Francisco Frinecki, Frankie to his friends, and the head of the family who deals in all manner of business, the most well-known on the street to be illegal. Also, he's kind of Australian crime-family royalty."

"What?" Eve's gut dropped. "Do you mean they're like a mob family?"

"That's exactly what I mean."

What by the goddess did a crime family want with her relic? Would they have had enough ties to Rome to get into the Vatican vault?

"And that's why you should seriously reconsider going after the Frineckis," Mr. Smith continued. "They're very well protected—otherwise, they'd have been removed by this point. Just trying to get to the relic straightway will be near impossible. And now I've got a question; why are you after the relic?"

"Oh no. I've got a question for you. What do you want with my relic? Is it because you're otherworld?"

Mr. Smith stilled, and his lips tightened for the barest moment—or had she imagined that? His disarming smile was straight back again.

"Princess—"

"If I have to call you Raph, you have to call me Eve."

He cut her a look. "Here's the truth, I'm a private investigator—Raphael Smith, check me out—missing person specialist. I was in Arthur's shop yesterday looking for a birthday gift for my sister, just ask Arthur. He'd steered me toward what we thought was a family trinket box just before the Frinecki goons arrived."

Family trinket box? Eve snorted. That was one name for it.

"I thought you were trying to steal it, too," he continued. "And I couldn't just stand by and not help out Arthur."

"So you're not after my relic?" She regarded him over her coffee.

"I had no idea it was even a relic until you said the word yesterday. Promise. But now I have a proposal for you. You've already figured out I'm otherworld, so you might as well know my heritage means I can find things. You should hire me to help you find the relic."

"Hire *you* to get my relic? Why? You've told me who's got it. This Frankie Frinecki."

"Yeah, Frinecki's man took it—but we don't know where it's gone now, and Frinecki has a lot of properties, so the relic could be at any of them."

Damn. This was getting harder and harder.

"Listen, you need to find something. I'm a PI who needs a payday. I can provide references if it makes you more comfortable, and as I don't normally take on jobs to locate objects—you'll see that on my website—I'll even do this at a lowered rate. Hell, I'd practically help out for free if it gets the guys who messed up Arthur's shop."

"If you normally find missing persons, how can you help me with a missing thing?"

"Okay." Raph glanced around the café and then leaned forward. "This is just for your information, but I have a contact who works closely with the Frinecki organization. That's why I'm your best bet at getting your property back."

"Why should I trust you?"

"I had no idea what the box even was—remember? You're a witch. Don't you have some way to know if I'm telling the truth?"

Eve's gut tightened. Crap. She could find out if he was telling the truth through a spell, but she didn't want to cast one outside of a circle.

Although ... just how much did he know about magic? Could she bluff him?

Eve resisted biting her lip—forced an even expression, while inside, her heart was racing. She had to get this right. The relic couldn't fall into the wrong hands—and she needed to be the one to find it.

"Fine," she said, leaning in over the table. "I'm going to whisper a spell right now, and then you tell me you didn't know the ... trinket box was a relic until Saturday. Plus, tell me you're not after the relic for yourself. This relic is the most important thing to me. And I will find it—but if I can find it faster with your help, then I'll take you on. As long as I know you're being honest."

7

____

"I HAD no idea the trinket box was a relic until Saturday," Raph said truthfully. "And I'm not after the relic for myself."

He held his breath. Technically the second statement was true too—Raph wasn't keeping the relic for himself. And given her claim about how important the relic was to her and how certain she was of finding it no matter what, he was bloody well making sure he kept close to her.

That determination was straight-up sexy. So sexy, an image of all that purpose channeled somewhere else ... like wrapped around him ... flashed through his mind.

But Raph shut that thought down. She'd want fuck all to do with him when she found out what he was really after. Plus, according to Gray, Eve could very well be a thief. He told himself that over and over as Eve hunched over the table and closed her eyes, her dark lashes feathering over the tops of her cheeks.

Focus, Raph. This had to work.

Eve held the crystal on the end of her necklace that she had channeled the shadows from yesterday—he shuddered at how close that had been to an even more fucked-up situation—and whispered something over and over. Her eyes were closed, so at least she wouldn't see him holding his breath.

Bloody hell, please let his carefully worded statements pass her truth spell. He'd never heard one before, but she was clearly good at this, given what she'd done yesterday between the stun and the shadows.

And how in the hell had she even done that? A shiver prickled up his neck. Thankfully her eyes were still closed, and she missed his reaction. Her face was an interesting mix of angles—from her sharp chin to the long nose and those high cheekbones.

Eve's lush lips, with their fuller lower curve, drew him closer still. Were they as silky as they looked? What would they taste—?

"Okay, Mr. Smith—Raph, you're hired. At your lowest possible rate," she murmured as she opened her eyes. Then they narrowed on him. "What?"

"You, ah—I was going to—" Raph cleared his throat, sitting back with the thud. Had he been about to kiss her? Where the hell was his focus? "So, I'm hired, then? And my lowest fee. Of course. Let's discuss that in the car?"

"Car?"

"I have to head up to see my sister today." He bit back the urge to grind his teeth. He had six days to find this relic. And his sister might be the one advantage he had to make that happen. But he had to see her in person to make that work. Plus, he needed to check on her security.

"You have a sister?"

"Yeah. What's so odd about that?"

"You don't seem like a ... family type of person. Not that it matters." A frown covered her face. "But you want to see your sister instead of working on my job? I don't think you understand the urgency of my situation—"

"Yes. Yes, I do." She had no idea. "It'll be faster if we talk in the car. I *have* to see my sister, and I don't want to waste time and let the trail go cold. We can discuss my rates, and you can fill me in on the job on the way."

"Wait—on the way where?"

"Maleny. It's about an hour-and-a-half drive northwest of the city, so if we leave now, we can be back later this afternoon, and I'll drop you back off at your ..." He cut her a look. "Hotel?"

Eve's eyes stayed narrowed as she regarded him—man, she was short on trust, wasn't she? That made her a smart cookie. But he needed to get around her distrust. And quickly.

"Okay, I'm still sensing trust issues, even though you did your spell so you know I'm telling the truth. Here, look at my PI license. And my driver's license. See, names match and all."

Eve looked carefully at his documents. "Raphael? That's for real?"

"Yeah." His lips twisted. "Mom was into the classics. So, now you know I'm legit. Come on, I want to check in on Arthur one more time."

"Good. I want to check out your story."

"Scratch issues. You've got trust demons; you know that, right?" Raph's chest went tight. Fuck. Why had he said that?

"Only with untrustworthy people." Eve shot him a look before standing up, her chin raised, and leading the way out of the café. Thankfully not picking up on his reaction.

Roughly half an hour later, as Eve slid into the passenger seat of his car, Raph took an easy breath for the first time that morning.

Finally. Now he could get up to Isadora and Dad. He'd called Isa last night about taking precautions, but based on the photo from his other client, Parsons, she hadn't been taking any. Shit, his other-*other* client. He'd actually gone and gotten himself three clients for the one job. A major breach of integrity. And something he abhorred.

But he'd picked his course. Which meant one client was going to be happy. The others ... well, he'd deal with that when he had to. Raph slid into the car and strapped himself in.

"So, Raph, fee or job first?"

"Job. As I said, I'd take this for free to help Arthur." And the longer he could avoid signing his name to another contract, the better his conscience would be.

"He seems like a sweetheart." Eve turned to look out the window. "I'm glad you were there to help him," she said softly.

Raph glanced at her. He couldn't see her expression, but she seemed ... somber.

"Yep, he's a sweetie," he said as he turned the car on. He cut another glance at Eve. "Is that a smile?"

"No." She turned to him, her face close to expressionless until one of those arched brows rose. "You don't need any more encouragement."

"I feel so seen." Raph forced a chuckle. Not that she wasn't amusing—she was entertaining for all her seriousness. Or maybe it was her seriousness that got to him—she was holding on so rigidly to her detachment he was surprised she'd agreed to even hop in the same car as him.

But he didn't want her to know how serious he was, so he kept up the amused, laid-back persona.

"Okay, we'll talk job first, fees later," Raph said. Time to put that persona to work and see how much she was open to revealing. "First up, what's so special about this relic?"

"It's ... difficult to explain. And there are some things I'm not at liberty to tell you."

"At liberty? I'm a PI remember? You can tell me anything."

"No. No, I can't. But I can tell you that the relic is solid gold, with a long history. I'm in charge of it, and it went ... missing ... on my watch." Eve's breath hitched.

Her voice had a ring of truth to it. But if she was telling the truth, why hide the relic from the Templars? Maybe she was a really good actress.

He glanced at her for a second before turning his attention back to the road as he exited the multistory parking garage and turned onto the street that would take them out of the city.

"You know, eventually you'll see you can trust me," Raph lied smoothly. "Then maybe you'll tell me the full story. But fine, so we've got a gold box-type relic. So what's the evaluation on it?"

"It's priceless."

"Yeah, I get you think that. But what is it actually worth? It's got an evaluation for insurance, surely?"

"Well, to some, it is truly priceless. But I suppose the intrinsic value in the gold—it weighs over two pounds—would have it at about fifty-five thousand euros. The relic was taken from me while I was in Europe. Rome, to be precise. So that's why I'm thinking of its value in euros."

"Wow." Raph let out a long whistle. "That's close to one hundred-thousand US dollars. That's a lot of reasons to steal it."

"But it's worth more than the money. As I was saying before you interrupted, it has an intrinsic value based on its weight. It's highly unlikely anyone who knows what it really is would take it for that reason."

"What, mysterious people who know the truth … the truth that you won't tell me?"

"Yes. Them."

"Okay, so I'm tracking a solid gold … trinket box, weight approximately two pounds"—hot damn—"with a greater value than the obvious dollars to some people, who you can't tell me about, for a reason I can't know. But we do know that the Frinecki family have it. And based on what I've pieced together, you must have had the relic until … recently? Otherwise, how are you responsible for it ending up in Arthur's shop?"

"Well, yes, I did have it."

"Come on, Eve. You've hired me." Verbally anyway. "This is the time to give me every single detail so I can find the relic."

Raph merged into the road heading north. Waited. Waited. Fuck, she really wasn't going to say any—

"Two days ago, I arrived in this country and located the relic. I took it back, but in the act of …"

"Retrieval?"

"That will do. One of the thieves stabbed me—a little— in the side."

"What the fuck?" Raph's hands clenched on the steering wheel. He threw a look over her. No obvious injuries. Clothing and hair perfect, again. "How can you be stabbed a little? It's like being pregnant, you either are, or you aren't."

"A little as in no vital organs were hit."

"And how are you …?" He waved one hand in her direction.

"How am I healed?" Eve asked.

"Yeah. Except, wait—someone actually fucking stabbed you?"

"Not *someone*. It was the thief who got away with the relic. And to be fair, he didn't know he was stabbing me. Just someone that had taken back their property."

"Like that's any better."

"It was a gouge more than anything, so I was lucky there. I used magic to heal the wound."

Raph couldn't help but cut Eve a look. She said that so casually, but magic like that ... he mentally let out a long whistle. "Wow. That's some spell you must have to heal a stab wound. But okay, then what?"

After Eve had filled him in on the details of her escape and the subsequent time holed up healing in her hotel room, he bit back a curse.

"You could've been killed; you know that, right?" Raph said. "Since the relic's so goddamn important, why don't you get help?"

"I don't need that kind of assistance."

He couldn't stop himself from shaking his head. Whatever motivated her to pursue the relic on her own, she was taking a huge risk. Maybe she was up to her delicious eyebrows in something nefarious after all. He was going to have to keep a very close eye on her, and now he was taking her to his family. Shit.

"You might have a beef with the Templars, but there's always the police," he said, testing her one last time.

"Enough. No police. No Templars. No one else."

"You're bristlier than an echidna, princess."

"Eve. And what by the goddess is an e—e—what did you say?"

"E-kid-na. It's an Australian marsupial covered in quills."

"Like a hedgehog?'

"No, not really. But that'll do. Back to getting the right help—"

"Mr. Smith, are you going to work on my job or spend the next hour and a half trying to convince me to go to the officials? If so, pull over, and I'll get out right now. I'll find my relic on my own."

"No, no. I'm on the job. My common sense was just getting in the way. No more talk of officials—promise. Okay, so let me get this straight. Frinecki stole the relic from you. You stole it back. You then stashed the relic with Arthur. Frinecki found it again and now has it."

"Well, I can't say Frinecki is the one who stole it from me. All I can say is that Frinecki's men are the ones who had it when I arrived in Australia."

"Right, and how long was it out of your sight before two days ago?"

"I last saw it three days earlier than that."

"Rome, right? Where exactly?" he asked casually. Would she be honest here?

"I can't tell you."

Well, at least that wasn't an outright lie.

"And that's the way it has to be." Eve's lips set, and her jaw locked. She might as well have had a 'Do Not Go There' sign flashing above her head.

"Fine." Except no fucking way was it fine. He had to determine what drove Eve's involvement in this missing relic and just how much of a risk she posed to his goal. "Okay, let's shelve that for now. We can focus on establishing if it *was* Frinecki who took the relic from you in the first place. Three days is more than enough time for an item like your relic to pass through a number of hands."

"Why worry about when it was stolen? We need to find who has it now."

"Princess, we need to establish players and motive, then we can work forward to where it'll be next. You have a relic that's been missing for what—five days in total?—and for forty percent of the time it's been missing, you don't know where it was or who it was with."

Eve crossed her arms, her lips set, and stared out the window.

"Man, you're stubborn."

That pointed chin rose higher. Raph took a deep breath and quelled the urge to shout that he was the PI here. Yelling at your quasi client wasn't a good option.

"Okay," he said when the urge to curse had passed. "Let's put the missing days on the back burner—for now—and focus on Frinecki."

"Finally. And you're speeding, by the way."

"What?" He glanced at the dashboard. "I'm only slightly over."

"We just passed a sign posting the limit. And you're over."

"Are you serious? We're on our way to find your relic; you've been casting spells all over town, stunning people, calling out Hell shadows—please don't do that again—and you won't go to the police or the Templars, but you're worried about breaking the speed limit?"

"I didn't—don't—have a choice about those other things. But speeding is dangerous for others too, not just you and I."

"Fine, fine." Raph eased back on the accelerator until he was on the limit. She eyed the speedometer and nodded. Seriously? "Okay, give me a few minutes to think about our options."

So how to find the bloody relic? He had his contact inside the Frinecki organization, but he'd have to be careful he didn't put them in any danger either ...

There was one other option, of course. And Raph could grab one of the daemons coming and going from the seventh gate that could pass a message through if he asked. But no. He and Isa had chosen to steer clear of that world.

The sign for the turnoff to Maleny came into view.

"Only an hour to go," he said to Eve. But her cheek was turned into the headrest, her eyes closed.

She was sound asleep.

Eve's cheeks were pale—he hadn't noticed before; somehow, her energy and focus had hidden that. But now, she seemed delicate. Fragile even.

Fragile? He snorted. No. No way. She might look like that, but her inner core of steel had been evident from every word she'd said and every move she'd made. Hell, she'd been stabbed and still managed to escape Frinecki's men. Even if Eve was in on the theft, reluctant admiration welled inside him.

It was a shame she was going to hate him at the end of this.

The side-to-side swaying motion cut into Eve's consciousness, and she opened her eyes to a sea of deep green foliage and a drop-off she couldn't see the end of as the car rounded curve after curve, driving up the steep road.

Oh goddess, had she fallen asleep? She jolted up—and a pain twinged at the base of her skull.

"Hey, princess. How's the neck?" Raph's smooth voice had her turn to him. "Your head was at an odd angle for a while there."

"Eve." She rotated her neck—winced as a knot cricked. "How long was I out?"

"About forty-five minutes."

What? She sat up straighter. How could she have slept when the relic was who knew where?

"We're almost at the top of the range now," he continued.

"Did you say 'range'?"

"We're driving up the hinterland mountain range; subtropical rainforest climbs all the way to the top," Raph said like some tour guide, oblivious to her horror. "Once we reach the summit, you'll be able to see all the way to the ocean. And we've only got another fifteen minutes to go, so good time to wake up."

"I shouldn't have slept at all," Eve said.

"Not sure how magic works, but I'm guessing it took a lot of energy to do all the spell work. And you've been running nonstop for the last three days—plus getting over being stabbed. Makes sense you needed to sleep. Your mind recognized you were safe, and so you slept. Pretty simple."

"That's not the point." She held in the urge to gnash her teeth. The only thing that mattered was recovering her relic. Falling asleep was the last way she was going to do that. But her PI ... no, that sounded too much like he was *hers*, which he wasn't. And quite frankly, with his laid-back, ladies'-man, too-smooth approach, he'd be the last person she'd ever want to have as hers anyway.

No, Raph was in her employ—she nibbled her lip. Technically, she didn't have any money at the moment to pay him, but she would as soon as she had access to her funds again. So yes, he was in her employ. That was the right approach with an otherworlder like Raphael Smith.

Something made the hairs on her arms prickle, and she rubbed them.

"Is the air-con too cold?" Raph asked. He fiddled with something on the steering wheel. "Here, I'll warm it up."

"No, not at all. Thank the goddess you've got air-con." She cut him a look. "You're very observant."

"PI, remember? Comes with the territory."

"I'm fine." She dropped her hands away from her arms. "Have you given any thought to how to find my relic?"

His grip tightened on the steering wheel. And another current of something prickled over her again. Eve shifted in her seat. Was that coming from him? Just who was he?

Well, he was straight-up sex-on-a-stick hot. That was an inescapable fact. From those long fingers—what else could they wrap around?—to the strong, tanned forearms ...

Crap. Eve whipped around and stared out of the window.

"Everything okay?" his voice rolled over her.

"Yes, yes, of course. Just thinking."

"The relic?"

"Of course. There's nothing else I'd be thinking about right now." She snapped her mouth shut.

"Well, don't worry. I'm going to find it."

She stiffened. "Well, I *am* worried, Mr. Smith. And nothing you can say will stop me from being concerned until that relic is back where it should be." And her name was cleared.

"Right. Well, I get this is important and all, but in this exact moment, the best thing we can do is not stress. Anxiety leads to reduced mental acuity, and we need to be at the top of our game to work out the best approach. So, while you were napping"—Eve rolled her eyes—"I made a list of all my contacts in the antiquities and rare objects world. I'll get started with them to work out why Frinecki wants the trinket box and what might be his next move."

"You've been working." She swiveled back to look at him. "Good. Tell me who is on this list?"

Raph glanced at her once before shaking his head.

"What?" she snapped.

"You're a bossy thing, aren't you?"

"I have no idea what would possess you to think anything else." She folded her arms. "Are you going to answer?"

"Of course. But listen, we're almost there. Look out your window now."

Annoyance flashed through her.

"Seriously. Look. You'll regret it if you don't."

"Fine." She turned to the window. "But you'd better ..." Oh. Wow. All the way to the horizon, the land fell away in a patchwork of greens and yellows until the land met a distant blue, the color shimmering beneath the midday sun. Three rocky outcroppings jutted out of the ground like craggy teeth. "It's like we're at the top of the world. And what are those things, rising out of the ground?"

"They're called the Glasshouse Mountains. Not like the mountains that you're used to, I guess. But they're pretty special here. Those rock faces are what's left after millions of years of sun and rain and wind wear away all the topsoil, all the growth. All the nonessential detritus until only the exposed, raw rock is left."

As the deep roll of his voice ended, Eve blinked and turned back to Raph. His gaze was on the road, but that gravity in his voice and the stillness of his body spoke of a serious regard for those mountains.

"That was well said." She surveyed him carefully. Where had this serious, eloquent man come from?

"What?" He cut her a look. Instantly his lips turned up at the ends, all seriousness replaced with relaxed humor.

"Huh, probably read it in a guide somewhere. So, the farm is only a few minutes away. If you keep traveling along the ridgeline, you come to the actual town of Maleny—it's more like a village than a town, but it can get touristy, especially on the weekends."

Eve let Raph chat away, noting the long, windy roads, the rural farmlands, but all the while, her mind was racing. Who was the real Raph Smith? The relaxed, casual man from the antique store, or the serious, poetic man who loved the mountains?

"So, this is it," Raph said. "Now, the farmhouse is pretty plain. But we won't be here for long."

"Are you sure your family won't mind me arriving unannounced?"

"Nah, why would they?"

Eve glared at him. The man was unbelievable.

"This will be a bit bumpy," Raph said. He turned the car onto a winding gravel driveway bordered on both sides by a timber and wire fence.

Eve shot him a look as they did indeed bump their way past green pastures that spread out in every direction, with trees and cows and horses, even the occasional building, in the far distance.

Finally, they rounded a line of trees, and a farmhouse, a few smaller outbuildings, and a huge barn came into view.

The front door of the house opened before they'd pulled to a stop, and a stunning young woman appeared. At her side, a giant red-haired dog rushed out the door—evaded her hands as she tried to catch it—and bounded toward the car.

"That's Isa—my sister. We're pretty much the spitting image of each other even though she's ten years younger. The dog is Leilu. We haven't seen each other in a while so she's going to be excited." Eagerness coated Raph's voice as he turned the car off and unbuckled his seatbelt. "Come on inside and meet Isa and Dad—he'll be here somewhere—then I'll grab you a coffee and we can get down to the business of our relic."

Raph practically jumped out of the car, but before he'd closed the door, the big red dog was on him. He dropped to his knees and ruffled her hair, laughing and dodging Leilu's licks.

As Eve unbuckled her seatbelt, a smile spread over Raph's face before his sister threw herself at him, kind of like the dog had, and wrapped Raph in a hug.

He squeezed her back, their bond evident.

Something pinged in Eve's chest. She rubbed the spot—her fingers brushing the pendant. Who was this man?

8

Raph gave his sister one more squish. Isa's shoulders were a little sturdier than when he'd last been up—and what, that had to be over six months ago now?—and he took a deep breath, almost sent a thanks to the gods, but didn't go quite that far.

"You plan on leaving your guest to die of heat exhaustion in the car?" a gruff voice called from inside the house. Then the front screen door swung open, and Dad came out to stand in the doorway.

"Dad." Raph met Isa's gaze and shared a smile before he turned to his father. "You letting all the cold air out?"

"Cold air? Only sissies need air-con."

"Dad, I got you that unit so you, Isa and Leilu would be comfortable. And no, of course I'm not leaving my guest in the car. But sure as shit, she'll want that air-con when she walks inside the old tin can you call a house." Raph smiled and covered the ground in several steps, wrapping his dad up in a hug. "Good to see you, old man."

"You too, son. Been too long between visits."

"Yeah, well—" He glanced over his shoulder. Shit. They

had to be careful what they said around Eve. She'd left the car and was busy smoothing down the hairs of her bun, which had come undone while she'd been asleep. Her movements were efficient. Not meant to be sexy at all. But for some reason, his gaze got fucking caught on the curve of her breasts as she reached back—

"Staring much?" she said in that warrior-queen voice.

He yanked his gaze up to her face. *Busted.*

"What? Just making sure you get all those pesky little flyaways. Don't want messy hair now."

Her lip curled before she turned from him and nodded at Isa and his dad. "Hello, I'm Eve. Mr. Smith here—"

"Raph."

She didn't acknowledge his eye roll but kept going. "—is investigating a matter for me, and we were meant to use the drive here to discuss that business. My apologies for arriving unannounced at your home."

"Can't see any reason to apologize for a beautiful young woman landing on my doorstep," Dad said.

"See, princess—"

"Eve."

"I told you, no worries at all." Raph clapped his dad on the back and grinned when Eve eyed him again. "Now, let me introduce you properly. Dad and Isa, this is the princess. This is Dad and Isa."

If Eve's lips pinched any tighter, she'd be lipless.

"*Raphael.*" Isa gave him a withering look fit to match Eve's pinched lips as she joined them on the porch. She held out a slim hand to Eve. "Hi, I'm Isadora. Call me Isa, though."

"And I'm Donald," Dad added. "Call me Don."

"Thank you, it's lovely to meet someone civil. My name is Evangeline—or Eve. Not princess." Raph managed not to roll his eyes at Eve's dig. But at least she was believing him in the part he'd chosen to play.

"Eve it is," Dad responded. "So what does a nice woman need help from my son for? Is it about—?"

Hell. Raph grabbed his dad's arm. "Now, now. We can't talk about a client's job, Dad. You know that. But I'm here to have a chat with you and Isa too. How about Eve heads inside, and the three of us can stay out here to talk?"

"Actually, I'd prefer to stretch my legs after the drive," Eve said. "At least the heat here is a bit more bearable. I take it I can have a wander around the yard while you have your chat. And then we can get to business?"

Raph traded a look with Isa. Her slight nod indicated the yard was fine. "Sure," he said to Eve. "I won't be long. Just steer clear of any machinery or the barns, and you'll be fine. And if you head out the back, you get a great view down the other side of the range."

Raph waited until Eve had started to walk off before he pulled both Isa and his dad inside. As soon as the door closed behind Isa, he held a finger up to his mouth and gestured for them to come closer.

"What's going on?" Isa whispered.

"Okay, here's the thing. Eve's a witch."

"I knew something was—" Isa said.

"Not now. That's not the big thing. But she's got some potent magic, and I don't know the extent of her powers. But there's something more important here."

"What is it then?" Dad asked.

"Isa's been spotted by someone who knows what we can do. I got this photo." Raph opened the email from Parsons on his phone and turned the screen for them to see.

"What the hell?" Isa's cheeks paled. "Why?"

"Here, sit down." Raph led her to a seat and filled them in as succinctly as possible.

"The contract is binding?" Isa said. "And they're using me to threaten you? Raph, no. I can—"

"No. No way. These guys are not to be messed with. I did all my usual due diligence before I took the job on, and everything looked above board. Faking that level of background takes a lot of tech capability and money. And the fact is, he knows about our curses, *and* he's got a picture of you. That means he's got reach."

"Gift, Raph," Dad said. "Not a curse."

"So you say. But these *gifts* haven't exactly helped us out, have they?" Raph just shook his head. This was one argument Isa and Raph never agreed on—and it wasn't going to change now either. "And as much as I hate to ask, I've got seven days to fix this. Can you try to see the relic? Our curses—"

"Gifts."

"—are always stronger when we're together."

"Of course, I'll try. But you know how bad my control is."

"Thank you. I'll figure out how to convince Eve to stay here for a few hours. Hopefully that will be long enough. And Isa, you need to be on your guard from now on. Any strangers approach you—anyone at all—you get out of there and run. Actually, that might be the perfect way to stall for the afternoon. I'll ask Eve to cast a protection spell around the farm. I'll exchange the spell for payment for the job."

"The job to find Eve's relic, you mean?" Dad said. "The job you're lying to her about?"

"Sh, keep your voice down. I don't have a choice. And for Isa's sake, we all need to do this, okay?"

Isa's eyes narrowed, and Dad cursed, but they both nodded.

Eve rolled her shoulders and stretched her arms as she followed the driveway around the farmhouse. A huge barn and several smaller structures sat off to the side of the house. Around the back, the gravel gave way to grass and flower beds. A timber and wire fence in the distance separated the yard from unending paddocks dotted with cattle and trees.

It was pretty. But too open. Too nice. Too not the busy, crowded city where her relic was. Although Eve could go for a good run around here. Her legs were practically begging her to get out and hit the pavement.

But right now, Eve was on the hunt for her relic. Where was it? How to get it back? Her thoughts spun as she kept walking until she reached the fence. How much should she tell Raph? He was an investigator, so clearly, he was going to want to know everything, but there was so much she couldn't tell him. Like the truth about what the relic could do if it fell into the wrong hands. And why *she* had to be the one to return it.

"Sorry about that," Raph's smooth voice floated across the yard.

Eve turned and waited as he joined her. His warm skin glowed under the sun, and he looked ... rougher than he had in the city. Dangerous. Brutal.

And all that intensity dropped away, replaced by a

casual, relaxed smile. The hairs on the back of her neck prickled again. Who was this man?

"Thanks for giving me a moment with my family," Raph said. "Do you want to head inside to discuss the relic?"

"No, this is good. No one can hear us."

"It's only my family here at the moment. But sure."

"It's best for them to know as little about this as possible."

"Right. And that's why we need to talk about the relic. So, is there anything else you want to tell me?"

Eve pursed her lips and considered him. His eyes narrowed, and she could tell he was annoyed she wasn't giving him what he wanted. But she couldn't. "No, not yet. But you can tell me about Frinecki."

"Well, I've sent a message to my contact inside the Frinecki organization. She'll get back to me when she's clear to send a message."

"Who is she? How is she involved with Frinecki? Does she know we're after a relic? Can we trust her?"

"Whoa, slow down. No, she has no idea what it is. Yes, we can trust her. I found a missing person for her. But I'm not telling you her name—she's *my* contact."

"Mr. Smith." Eve crossed her arms. "I'm your employer. You're meant to be far more accommodating here."

"Well, princess, maybe if you told me what's really going on—"

"Eve." She gritted her jaw. "My name is Eve."

"Then maybe I'd be a bit more open to giving you all my secrets."

"Secrets? Your contact is a secret?"

Raph tunneled his fingers through his thick hair. Really, what man had hair like that?

"Okay, let's cool things off here," Raph said between

clenched, perfectly even, white teeth. "Listen, I need to stretch my legs too. Since you want privacy for this talk, how about we walk up to that tree on the hill and back?"

"What? Walk in the paddock with those things?" She nodded at the animals in the distance.

"After everything you've done in the last three days, you're not scared of a little cow, surely?

"That was with people," Eve said. "I know people. I don't know cattle at all—and they're not small."

"Trust me, we'll be fine. Come on, we need to get back on track."

"You think?" She shot him a look but followed him through the gate. She eyed the cows closest to them carefully. "Listen, I'm only walking through this paddock to discuss—"

"Just watch out for the cow pats," Raph drawled.

"Cow pats?"

"Yeah, those." Raph nodded at a crusted, dark mass on the ground. "Cow manure."

"Oh goddess. They're giant."

"We're in a cow paddock. Did you think there'd be some fancy cow loo somewhere?"

"What? No. Of course not. Just—never mind. Back to the relic, please."

"The main thing here," Raph said, "is that I have a contact who I'm waiting on for information. I've also started looking at known Frankie Frinecki contacts in the antiquities market. He has an import-export business that deals with rare items—my police contacts seem to think the business is likely a front for his more illegal dealings. So possibly Frinecki's using the relic for that and has no idea about our world."

"Finally, you're sounding like an investigator." Raph cut Eve a look, and she met his gaze. "What?"

"Anyway ... as I was saying, Frinecki might be treating the relic like a highly valuable item. The man is all about money. He's not known for having a particular interest in collecting antiques, which makes me think he could be looking at the relic purely for financial reasons. After all, it's a shit ton of gold. He could melt it down and have a good profit right there."

"No!" Eve's stomach dropped. Oh goddess, no. Was this all her fault? What if she was responsible for the relic of gold being *melted*?

"I'm not saying he will." Raph grabbed her arm. "Hey, watch out for the cow pats, remember?"

Tingles of heat bloomed where he touched her skin. Eve hauled in a breath and turned to him. Why did he have this effect on—?

"Calm down," Raph said.

"Excuse me? Calm down?" Adrenaline surged through her, and she shrugged his hand away. "Don't tell me to be calm. I am calm. I'm also rapidly reassessing the urgency of finding the relic. As in now. I can't—we can't—let the relic be smelted."

"Of course not. And it's very unlikely—even if he doesn't know exactly what he's got. Frinecki would know the relic is worth more in its current form than if he scraps it. So let's plan our next steps—"

"No. No planning next steps. We need to act now."

"Yeah, that didn't work too well last time. But sure, tell me how you're going to find it."

Crap. That was the problem. She needed Raph Smith's help to find it.

"Okay, so like I said earlier," Raph continued, "we need

to find out where the relic is and where it's going to be. That's what I'm working on now. But yes, if you have any spells that can help, then please do."

Damn it. That was the problem. Eve wanted to—she just needed salt to hide her activity. She could also try to find a new pendant, but her amethyst had been with her since she'd started training as a Watcher. How long would it take to find the right gem, and then train the energies within the crystal to work with her?

Eve took a deep breath and forced down the urge to run back to the car and return to the city where her relic had to be.

"And while we're talking magic," Raph said, "I have a proposition."

"What?" She frowned up at him. His glittering gaze was locked on her mouth. Warmth instantly pooled low in her belly, and she reflexively moistened her lips. Her heart began to pound. "Proposition ...?"

"Proposition ..." Raph's sculpted lips caressed the word.

How would they feel caressing something else? Then his eyes met hers; their depths darkened close to black.

"Ah, yeah." Raph cleared his throat. "I was going to suggest that we could come to an arrangement."

He wanted an *arrangement*? Eve licked her lips again, unable to look away from his face. Was this how he did business? And yes, he was hot. No, hot wasn't even right. He was a walking smorgasbord of deliciousness. And she'd been aware of him on a hyper level since the moment she ran into the antique store. That traitorous warmth in her belly grew, and her nipples pebbled.

"Witches use magic in business, right? Well, I'm after an alarm spell for the house. To help keep my family safe. You need to find the relic. So why don't we agree to rub each other's backs and save dollars?"

Rub each other's ...? Hold on. What?

Heat washed over her cheeks, and she backed away. Crapola. *Mind out of the gutter, Eve!*

"Well, yes," Eve said, "of course that's an option."

And damn, usually it would be. Ward spells were her specialty. Except she was in the least prepared state for her craft than she'd ever been. Although, she wouldn't have to worry about having zero funds to pay for this job. Eve took another step back.

"Excellent. So an entire house isn't too big?"

"The entire house?" Now *that* would be a challenge. Exactly how far her could her wards extend? The coven never let the Watchers test their spells on anything larger than the cells and vaults where the relics were stored.

"Yeah, the whole farmhouse. Is that possible? Hey!" Raph lunged at her. "Look out!"

She grabbed her pendant and whirled, her foot landing in something squishy and wet. And then her foot slipped forward, and she fell backward into something warm and oozy.

A putrid odor assaulted her nose. Made her eyes water.

Oh goddess.

9

<hr>

INSIDE THE FARMHOUSE, Raph held the bathroom door open for Eve.

"Towels are in that corner cupboard," he said as she shuffled by him, holding her arms away from her body. He took a step back. Well back. "While you have a shower, I'm going to drive into town and pick some stuff up for Dad. It's not far."

Eve stopped in the middle of the room and faced the mirror. Her stunned expression shifted to ... horror?

"You'll be fine," he soothed. "A shower—a long, *long* shower—and you'll get all of that ... uh, stuff, washed away. And we'll do your clothes. So don't worry about that."

She pivoted to him, the horror giving way to murder and mayhem.

He automatically stepped back. "Salt," he blurted. "I'll get you salt, too. And anything else you need. Just say what and how much, and I'll take care of it while you ... take care of that."

"You think salt will make this right?" She turned back to the mirror. A little whimper escaped her.

"Yes?" he said hopefully.

Eve closed her eyes and took a deep breath. Was that a good or bad sign? He was still learning to read his newest ... client.

"I'll need a lot of it," she finally said.

"Right. Okay, absolutely. How much?"

"How many yards to walk the exterior of your house?"

"Ah, I don't know. But I can work that out."

"I need half a cup for every yard."

Raph whistled. "That's a lot of salt."

"Before you go, do the walk yourself, and make sure you get it right."

"Yeah, yeah. Man, you're ..."

"I'm what?"

"Nothing. What else do you need?"

"Does your dad or Isa have candles?"

"Yeah, I guess."

"Guessing's not good enough. I'll need at least three. Check if they do, and if they don't, get them. Then I need crystals."

"Crystals?"

"Yes, crystals. Please don't keep repeating everything I say."

"Of course not. Totally, no more repeating." Somehow, he managed not to laugh. She was so bossy—even covered in stinking manure. And that bossy got to him because even now, his cock was stiff. He shoved his hands in his pockets to hide the tent in his pants as she listed the crystals she wanted by preference.

One of those fierce brows rose, and she walked over. Slammed the door in his face. "You didn't take notes," she said through the door. "Repeat what I need."

He rolled his eyes but did as Eve had instructed. "Is that all, princess?"

The rustle and slide of clothes dropping to the floor echoed through the door. Eve was naked.

"For now," she called out. "But if you make a mistake in what I need …" The creak of old pipes as water rushed through them, followed by the patter of water hitting tiles, filled the silence. She was in the shower. "It's your ward spell that won't go right."

Her crisp voice and bossy attitude, along with the mental image of her in the shower … Oh man. He needed a shower too. A cold one. Raph cleared his throat.

And then a string of mumbled words echoed through the door.

"Are you muttering curses in there?" he called out, unable to stop himself from baiting the uptight witch. Why the hell did he like taunting her so much?

"Count yourself lucky I'm not! Otherwise, you'd be something small and slimy right now."

Huh. Was that even possible? Eve had some powerful magic under her control, so maybe? "Not sure how many times I can say sorry. But I did warn you—"

"Not helping!"

Raph couldn't stop a grin.

"I can tell you're laughing at me."

"What? Your magic lets you see through doors?"

"No need. Your voice is dripping with glee."

"Never," Raph said. "Although I am sorry, it means delaying the return trip to the city. But, ah, we couldn't exactly drive back with you covered in …"

"Enough. Now, Mr. Smith, I've had enough of this … this farm time. No more talking. I need to clean up. You need to get going."

And bossy Eve was back. But he was okay with that. Eve in the shower ... Eve naked under all that steam ... He held in a groan. "Be back soon."

The wood-paneled bathroom with its shower over a clawfoot tub had a certain old-fashioned charm, which Eve only took in when she was finally free of the stench of manure. She turned the shower off and stepped over the edge of the tub, then wrapped one towel around her hair and another around herself.

Raph knocking on the other side of the door had her tightening the towel at her torso. Shit. He couldn't see her like this. Except ... that kernel of attraction was saying—

"Eve, it's Isa. I've got a dress here."

And that was *not* disappointment pinging in her gut. She took the summer dress Isa passed through the door and held it against her body.

"Thank you," Eve called out. She eyed the dress. Isa was at least a size smaller than Eve and a good foot shorter. But this dress would be better even if too short and tight than clothes covered in stinking manure.

"No worries," Isa called out. "Just sorry you had to get such a close-up look at the farm! Are you sure you don't want me to put your clothes in the wash?"

"No! I mean, no, thank you." She pulled her undies back on; thankfully, they'd survived unscathed. "I'll do it myself —if you'll let me borrow your machine. It was my own fault for not watching where I was going." And Raph's. Definitely Raph's fault too.

A few minutes later, squeezed into the dress that probably floated ethereally around Isa, Eve followed the smaller woman into the laundry.

The rest of the farmhouse was similar to the bathroom, with high ceilings and timber walls painted a fresh white with blue trim. Isa had explained the building was about a hundred years old, but it had had a couple of smaller extensions, plus a rumpus room and deck at the back. There were modernizations to the kitchen and bathroom, too, that made it comfortable for both her father and her.

"Raphael tells us you're going to do a ward to protect the house?" Isa said from the doorway once Eve had finished rinsing the worst of the mess off her clothes in the laundry sink.

"That's right," Eve replied as she placed the garments into the washing machine. "Although he hasn't said what you need protecting from?"

"Oh." Isa's gaze dipped away, and her shoulders stiffened. Eve kept her expression blank, but Isa's reaction was telling enough. The Smiths had a secret of their own. But it was none of her business—unless it impacted on finding the relic.

"Never mind," Eve said. The last thing she needed was Isa and her father on their guard, too, since she was going to use this enforced downtime to find out about her investigator. "So, how long has Raph been a PI?"

"How long? Some time now. Hey, how about some lunch while this is washing? Dad's working on something outside but will be in in about an hour. And Raphael should be back by then too."

"Sure." Eve hid her growing interest—and concern. Two for two Isa had dodged giving a real answer to Eve's questions.

Eve helped Isa make up half a dozen sandwiches—four went into the fridge for Raph and their dad—and then she and Isa took theirs to the small timber dining table.

"So, how long have you and your dad lived here?" Eve asked as they sat down.

"We moved up about three years ago."

"Up?"

"Um, yeah. We're not locals."

"And your father runs the farm still? He looks ..." Eve bit her lip. Mr. Smith Sr. looked at least seventy. Maybe farmers never stopped farming?

"Not how you think. We moved here as a retirement plan for Dad."

"You run a cattle farm for retirement?"

"No," Isa said with a chuckle. "That's our land, but we lease it to a local farmer so he can run his cattle on it. Helps keep the grass down. And brings in some money. I'm an artist—I'll work anywhere—so was happy to come up here. I've got a studio in one of the smaller barns out the back. This move was meant for his retirement, but Dad still does odd work around the place." Isa smiled and shrugged. "Apparently, once a farmer, always a farmer."

Eve smiled back, surprisingly comfortable around Isa. "You and Raph are close?"

"Yep, we might be ten years apart, but we share a lot of ..." Isa's cheeks paled, and she went still in her chair. Something icy prickled down Eve's neck, and she checked over her shoulder, half expecting someone to be there. But it was only the empty kitchen.

She turned around as Isa stumbled to her feet, eyes glassy. "Ah, excuse me. I have to go."

"Are you okay?" Eve jumped up and grabbed Isa's arm, steadying her when she wobbled. "What's wrong?"

"Nothing, just—please excuse me. I'll be back in a minute. A few minutes."

Eve stared at Isa as the other woman practically ran down the short corridor and disappeared into a room, the door slamming shut behind her.

Okay ... what, by the goddess, was that about?

Eve stared at the hallway for a moment longer before she dropped into a chair at the table. Right, well, clearly, there was a lot more going on here than she'd realized. But that couldn't matter—all that mattered was the relic. The gift of gold.

Goddess, what if it came into the hands of someone who truly knew what it was capable of? Because if someone held her relic along with its siblings, the gifts of frankincense and myrrh, together ... the power that came with that union was beyond anything else.

A shiver trickled down Eve's spine.

She would never let that happen. And at least the other two relics were still safe under wards.

But to get to her relic, she had to take care of the ward spell here first. And that meant she needed an enormous amount of energy,

Eve eyed the sandwich. Even though her stomach was in knots, food meant energy, so she forced herself to finish her lunch.

She was putting the dirty plates away when the door at the end of the hallway opened, and Isa reappeared, cheeks pale but steady on her feet.

"Sorry about that," Isa said with a weak smile.

"You look like you need a coffee. Here, have a seat. Don't want you falling on your backside."

"Thanks," Isa murmured. "Only, I don't do coffee. Could you make it a chamomile tea instead? And I'm so sorry about this—first you go and fall into a giant cow pat, then I flake out on you, and now you're making *me* a tea."

"Well, you lent me your dress. That's something, right? Now, where do you keep the tea?"

"And you look stunning in it. Tea's in the cupboard above the kettle."

"It's a bit tight."

"No—it shows off how toned you are."

"I'm a runner, but I also box when I get to the gym."

"Wow. No wonder you're so fit. The biggest workout I do is walking from the house to the barn. That's more than enough for me."

Eve laughed. "I'm the opposite. Running and boxing energizes me—plus, if I don't exercise, I tend to get cranky. Not that I've been able to run for the past few days. All my focus has been on ... finding the item that your brother is helping me with."

"Ah, I take it then that we can't discuss this thing?"

"Correct. Although your brother assures me he doesn't discuss business with you."

"Well, Raphael is very serious when it comes to his business."

"Really? He seems so ... casual. Like he doesn't take anything seriously."

Isa muttered something under her breath.

"What was that?" Eve asked.

She quirked one eyebrow when Isa regarded her silently. Isa's vivid green eyes were narrowed. Assessing. Wary. Which made sense. Raph was otherworld—so Isa was too. And if Eve was going to get any information here, she needed Isa on her side.

"It's okay," Eve lied. "You don't have to say anything about Raph. Actually, I think we should clear the air. I'm a witch." She didn't say exactly which witchcraft she practiced. "And I can tell you and Raph are otherworldly, though not your father. But I'm not looking for any details about your heritage if that's what you're worried about."

"Thank you for being honest about yourself. And what you've recognized in us."

Crapola. Isa's expression was completely open. The other woman believed Eve totally. And that was not guilt tightening in her gut. She had a job to do—the relic. This was all about the relic.

"No worries at all," Eve said. "I think we should know each other given I'm sitting here at your table and wearing your clothes. Plus, I'll be around your brother for as long as it takes me to retrieve a ... piece of property that was taken."

"Raphael can be complicated. And yes, there are things ... some things anyway ... that he takes very seriously. Too seriously at times. But he's an amazing big brother."

Eve forced her expression to remain calm. Serious? *Too* serious? That was the opposite of the man she'd known for the last two days. And okay, clearly, that was part of the issue —two days was a fraction of a blink in the eye of the universe.

"But I shouldn't talk about him without his knowledge," Isa continued. "I'm happy to tell you about me, though."

Yes. Eve had to stop herself from shifting forward in the seat. "Only if you want."

"Actually, I do. You know how I disappeared into my room before? Well, I was having a vision, you see. I have the ability to know—or more accurately, to experience the future."

"Holy shit," Eve breathed out. "You're a Seer?" She couldn't help but stare at Isa. While Eve had been at the coven base training to be a Watcher, she'd read and heard stories of Seers. But she'd rarely left the ground of the coven's base, and even if there was a Seer close by, Eve had never met one.

Isa's lips twisted. "Kind of. But I can't control it."

"Witches can use spells and the craft to divine the future, but a true Seer ... you don't need any magic at all, do you?"

"No, the future comes to me no matter what."

"You don't sound too happy about that."

"It has its moments. As you saw before, it can be challenging to be around others. When I said we moved to this farm for my dad, well, it was also for me. To get away from others."

"So you don't trade from your power?"

"Trade?"

"As in use your gifts to trade on," Eve said. "They're a skill like any other. Some people are gifted with numbers—they become accountants. Some people are gifted with animals—they become vets. I'm gifted with magic, so I became a Wat—witch. You're gifted with the Sight. You could be working for major corporations as an in-house adviser. Or working as a subcontractor at your own pace."

"I tried working for someone once. But my boss became ... reliant on me. So much so that I had some problems in our last hometown."

"Oh. I see. So that's why Raph wants me to ward the house? To keep anyone out you don't want in?"

"I guess so," Isa said.

"Well, if it works, you could get someone to ward your house anywhere—then you could live wherever you want. Do whatever you want."

"True. But I'm happy here, and I love my artwork. I'm happier this way."

"Well, as long as you're happy." Eve sat back in her chair. Something pinged in her chest, and she reflexively toyed with her pendant, thumb unerringly tracing the fracture. If Isa could see the future, what could Raph do? And where did such gifts come from?

"That's pretty."

"This?" She dropped the crystal. "It's been with me since my witchcraft emerged as a strength. It's a ... comfort, I suppose."

At their feet, Leilu raised her head, and her ears pricked before she gave out a yip.

"And that'll be my brother. Leilu's our first indicator that someone's coming."

"Great alarm system."

"Yes, she is," Isa said. "And we're so far away from anyone up here we don't get visitors without a reason."

Moments later, the rumble of a car engine echoed through the house.

"I'll hold Leilu if you want to make sure that's Raph?" Isa said.

By the time Eve had reached the screen door, Raph was pulling the car around to the top of the driveway. From the kitchen, Leilu gave another loud yip. Isa cussed. Moments later, the red dog barreled into Eve.

"Crap." Eve grabbed the dog's collar, arm jolting with the force of Leilu's lunge to get outside. "Whoa. Hold on, girl."

Fortunately, Raph stopped the car quickly, and as soon as the engine turned off, Eve pushed the door open and let Leilu go.

The red dog bounded to Raph.

Laughing and rolling her shoulder at the same time, Eve strode down the porch steps, her heart picking up. Which was totally due to the fact she was about to get her hands on salt—and maybe some crystal—and do some spell work. Absolutely nothing to do with the man himself.

Eve reached Raph as he unfolded his tall frame from the car.

"Hey, girl," Raph said as he dropped to his knees, rubbing Leilu's sides and laughing as she covered him with doggy kisses.

Eve's mouth went dry. And something in her chest tightened.

"Hi," Raph said between Leilu's licks. He stood up and wiped his cheeks, then leaned back into the car, the material of his cargo pants pulling tight across his tush, and pulled out a bag. "Got you candles, an assortment of crystals—basically one of everything they had since they didn't have a large range, and three large sacks of salt. I'll put those on the porch."

Eve jerked her gaze up to his just as he swiveled and held out a small shopping bag. "Thank you."

"Whoa." He straightened to his full height.

"What?"

"Uh, nothing. Just didn't expect you to be so ... relaxed." Raph's eyes dipped to her dress, then to her hair. "You know, I haven't seen it loose before. Didn't realize you have so much hair. You always keep it tied up in that bun thing."

Eve swiped a hand over her thick curls. "I washed it. And my hair tie was covered in ... Anyway, I need to put it back up." She twisted it in a knot, but it wouldn't stay that way for long. She never left her hair out—it'd be a rat's nest in no time.

"It looks good." Raph's voice dropped. Something warm glinted in his gaze. "You look good."

Butterflies rollicked in her belly, warmth spreading from

their beating wings to her core, to her breasts. Even her nipples tingled.

But Eve smashed the sensation down. She needed to focus on her craft—nothing else. She had salt, candles and crystals. It was spell time. Finally.

She pulled her gaze away from his. "Right, well, let me open this and see what crystals you found, then I can work out the best way to tackle the spell."

"Sure. I'll ... uh, just grab the salt and leave it on the porch. The three sacks will cover the distance—I measured the perimeter exactly as ordered."

10

A_s_ R_aph_ grabbed the salt, Eve opened the bag with the crystals and pretended to stare at the contents—but all she could see was Raph's glittering eyes. Goddess, the man was hot.

And she was attuned to him on a whole new level.

Even now, she didn't need to hear his steps to know where he was—the freaking hairs on the backs of her arms prickled in his direction. Like he was an electric current and her body was a lightning rod for him.

"Let me know if you need anything," he called out from the porch.

"Give me a few minutes to work out the spell, and then I'll join you inside."

The front door to the farmhouse shut with a bang, and she let out a long breath. Finally, the air cleared enough for her to inhale and not take in a lungful of Raph-scented oxygen. Wow, if anyone ever wanted to make a scent and sell it for a fortune, they just had to bottle up whatever elixir had made that man.

Come on, Eve. You have salt. You have crystals. You can get this ward done and spell for the relic.

She sat on one of the porch seats shielded from the afternoon sun. It was still hot, and she'd take whatever shade she could find. She laid everything out.

Five crystals—clear quartz, amethyst, tigereye, rose quartz and selenite. She picked up the clear quartz. A gentle tingle warmed her palm. Okay, there was energy there. She tried the rest—and the same reaction. Nowhere near the power of her pendant. She could use them to complete the spell, but she'd tap them all out in no time.

She picked her pendant up in one hand and held the store-bought crystals in the other.

Nope—even with all five together, they didn't have the same power as her one crystal, fracture and all.

Crapola. But at least they should get the spell for the house. Although which ward? And could she really spell the entire house?

Eve put the crystals aside and checked out the salt. Not that she didn't trust Raph, but she did a careful walk around the exterior of the house, using her paces to work out the distance. Sixty-five paces.

Raph appeared at the front door as she opened the first sack.

"I saw you walking around the house; was that for the ward?'

"Yes. Just checking your calculations."

"What was I saying about trust earlier?"

"It's called diligence."

"So?"

"It'll be tight. Also, what type of ward spell are you after?"

"What are the options?"

"Small would be triggering an alarm of some kind, medium level spells can cause a physiological reaction in the intruder, and the top end can be a barrier only those who are cleared can get through." Her gut clenched. *Only those who are cleared ...*

The relic—oh goddess. What if she hadn't messed up? Because what was more likely—she'd messed up her first ever live-in-the-field spell after years of training and let a thief through? Or someone who knew how to get past the wards had cleared a path?

"Hey, are you okay?" Raph asked.

"Yes. Yes, of course."

"Well, you've gone kinda pale. Is it the heat? You don't have to be superwoman all the time, you know. Here, come inside where the air-con's on."

"No." Eve pulled her arm out of his grasp. "No, thank you, Mr. Smith."

"Back there again, are we?"

"I get like that when people tell me what to do."

"Okay, I'll keep that in mind. So let me rephrase—would you like to come inside into the cool air-conditioning?"

"It's not the heat. I ... I just had a thought about my relic."

"Care to share?" His eyes narrowed.

"I'm thinking about it." Surprise of all surprises—she actually was thinking of telling him the truth. Everything. Eve shook her head at herself. How, by the goddess, could she trust someone she'd only just met? Except she did. It was pure and simple.

"You know we'll find the relic faster if you tell me the entire story."

"I said I'm thinking about it." She straightened her shoulders. "Don't push me."

Raph held his hands up. "No pushing."

"I think perhaps a colleague of mine may have taken the relic," she blurted. "That I might be her scapegoat."

"Whoa. That's ... intense. Do you have any evidence?"

"Not really." And that was a problem. Eve was as junior a Watcher as they came. Who would believe Eve over anyone more senior without solid, irrefutable evidence? But if she got the relic, she might have a way to bargain with the coven to get them to do a truth spell—on the person who had taken it.

"What are you thinking?" Raph asked softly.

"I'm thinking I need my relic back. Come on, let's get this spell done and then get back to Brisbane." She glanced at Raph. A funny look crossed his face. "What is it?"

"Just thinking you need a PI to do more than find the relic. But okay, focusing on this spell here and now. I just need to select the type of ward we want, is that right?"

"Yes, but the thing is, I don't have my normal tools, and although these crystals are good, they're not going to be strong enough—probably not even for a small true-barrier spell—and certainly not for a whole house."

"Okay, then what can they do?"

"Maybe an alarm—we could set it to trigger off in an object that you or Isa or even your father can wear. Or maybe I can try for some kind of reaction in the intruder."

"You can do that?"

"Hypothetically." Eve shrugged. "As I've said, I've never attempted to spell an entire house. We could try the shock option. Leilu is already a good alarm system, right? She'd alert you to anyone coming up, and then the shock will be strong enough to slow the intruder down, letting you decide how to deal with them."

"You go around shocking and stunning people a lot, don't you?"

"Of course. That's my jo—"

"Job?"

Eve stared at him and then gave him her back as she opened the first sack of salt. "So, the shock spell? And twenty-four seven, or just day, or just night? And that's not like a clock thing; the shock spell is purely tied to sunrise and moonrise. Once you decide, I need a piece of hair from everyone—humans that is—who you don't want to be shocked on entry."

"Whoa. So everyone else—everyone else who's not here right now—will be shocked?"

"Yes. That's what you want, right? A ward spell for the house?"

"Okay, okay." Raph rocked back on his feet. "What if we have someone else in the future who we want to let in?"

"Well, first of all, you should know that since I'm casting the ward, I have the knowledge to come and go without any impact. Second, the ward will only last six months at best. You'll need someone who knows my spell to repeat it. That's how they work." A hollow feeling echoed in her chest. If everything went right, she'd be back in Rome—or the UK at the least. She resolutely ignored the sensation and lifted her chin. "Second, I can make a potion that you can add a hair to for future visitors, but that's going to take time *and* ingredients I don't have. But"—she held up a hand—"after you find my relic and return it to me, I'll make that potion."

"Shit. Okay, I have to talk to Dad and Isa about this. Give me a few minutes."

"Fine, but don't take all day. We need to get to my relic. And once I start the spell, I need you all to stay where you are so I don't get distracted."

"Can I watch? I'd like to see you ... *it,* I mean."

Something warm uncurled inside her. He wanted to watch her? Watchers were never watched outside of training —and even then, that was only in their early days. But the idea wasn't ... unpleasant.

"Okay. But you'll need to be quiet and still unless I tell you otherwise."

"Done. I'll be back in a minute."

"When you come back, I need a large glass of water and a sharp knife."

Eve started with a cleansing rite for the crystals to remove the residual energy of others who'd handled them in the past.

Several minutes later, Raph joined her again, holding a large glass of water.

"Here you go." He handed her the glass. "Isa's got Leilu in her bedroom and won't let her out until you give the all clear. For the spell, we've agreed on nighttime only. And just the three of us for now. But we really want that potion, so how about we treat that like a job? We'll pay you the going rate."

"Of course, you'll pay me. But this isn't just about money. I'll need to find a practitioner who sells quality goods—and I have no contacts here. Plus, the potion takes at least one full twenty-four-hour cycle to prove. I can't just click my fingers and make it work."

"Fine. You tell me what you need, and I'll get the ingredients. And we'll double your normal fee."

"A spell like that would go for at least five hundred dollars."

"No problem. We really want that potion."

"And I really want my relic." Eve crossed her arms. "I'm not doing one more thing that delays that."

"Okay. *If* we have any moments where there's absolutely nothing more we can do in our relic hunting, you make the potion."

"Why do you need a ward if you're just going to let people through it anyway?"

"We don't want to hurt people intentionally," Raph said, "and who knows who'll come to visit unexpectedly."

"Fine. You said double, so that'll be a thousand dollars. And that's without the ingredients. They'll be on top. Now, are we ready to go?"

Raph muttered under his breath.

"Did you just call me a hustler? I'll have you know I come from a long line of professional witches. And you never mess with a business witch. So, are you holding the hairs?"

He slowly uncurled his fist, and there were a few hairs, one silver—had to be his father's—and two others midnight black.

"Okay, let's go," Eve said. A familiar surge of energy pulsed through her. Not the crystals. Not the pendant. But her. She was about to do the thing she was born to do. Make magic.

With the afternoon sun baking the gravel driveway, Raph stayed under the shade of the porch as Eve took another large drink of the water.

"Do you want more?" he asked.

"No, that was enough. I'm going to be out in the sun for a few hours. Now, I need to move this salt."

Eve picked up one sack of salt, arm muscles bunching with the weight. Raph reflexively stepped forward to help, but her dark eyes flashed a warning at him.

"Got it," he mouthed and stopped still. She dropped the salt on the ground at the bottom of the steps and did the same with the other two sacks.

Damn. Raph's hands twitched with the urge to help, and he folded his arms to stop himself. Just because he was lying to her didn't mean he wanted to watch Eve freaking pull a muscle. And if he'd known she was going to move them, he'd have done it himself.

Eve lifted one of the salt bags to her hip like she was holding a child, then took the knife from her pocket and shoved the blade into the bottom of the sack. Absolute concentration pulled at her features as she repocketed the knife and cupped one hand over the hole.

Then she walked around the outside of the house, a fine stream of the granules slipping through her fingers and falling to the ground in her wake. She rounded the porch and disappeared out of sight.

Shit. Did he move? Go watch her? He almost took a step —but then her words came back to him. Fine. He wouldn't move.

Not long later, she came back around the other side of the house, salt sack crumpled in her hands, and threw it onto the porch. She eyed him again—her chin rose, and her eyes flashed once more.

Don't move. Don't speak.

Okay, okay, the silent message was clear. He nodded and shrugged.

Her lips twitched, and she rolled her eyes—did she know he'd been so close to moving?—before she took the next sack and stabbed it.

Ouch. And then she was off again. Eve repeated the cycle with the third bag of salt until the granules made a full circle.

Finally, she returned to the porch, skin gleaming beneath sun and sweat. She held up one finger—okay, so clearly, he still wasn't to speak—and grabbed the glass of water and drank the rest.

"Right," she said. "I needed that. So, next steps."

"I can speak now?"

"Yes, now you can speak." Her lips twitched. "And I'm surprised—I didn't think you'd last a second after the circle was finished."

"So what, you shushed me just then for no reason?"

"I was hot." Eve shrugged. "And I needed water. Didn't want to have to even think about anything else until I had the water. And I could see those questions whirring in your brain."

"Fine." Raph bit back a laugh. She sure was funny for an uptight witch. "So, what happens next?"

"The next step is the spell itself. I need the hairs."

Raph opened his hand and let her pick the strands from his palm. Her scent tickled his senses. Her fingertip grazed his skin, and heat shot to his groin.

"Can I watch?" he murmured.

What would Eve look like? Her gorgeous skin gilded by the sun, that mane of hair that he suddenly had an urge to grab a fistful so he could bring her lips to his—

"Still?" She twisted her hair into a knot at the base of her neck.

He jolted back to reality, the fantasy image dropping away. "Uh, yeah. Professional purposes, you know." *Sure, Raph. Professional only ...*

Eve twisted the pendant chain around her fingers. Huh.

Why did that look like a nervous reaction? His senses heightened, and he waited while she looked at him carefully.

"I suppose. But seriously, this will take some time."

"Then I'll sit too."

"And you have to be still. And you can't make one single sound or step off the porch. I can't lose my concentration even once. If I drop the spell, I can't recast it until my energy restores, which could take twenty-four hours, or I get more crystals—probably both. And no way am I staying here for another day while my relic gets farther from us. And you can't pass over the circle. No matter what. Promise?"

"Got it. Silent and still. Swear."

Eve cut him a look, then removed her shoes and walked barefoot to the side of the house.

He followed to the edge of the porch, then she held up a hand and sank to her knees.

Raph sank to the porch steps. If she'd told him to move, he doubted he could've made his feet shuffle, let alone walk anywhere. Damn, but he wished he could see her face full-on.

Eve laid out the candles and crystals; then, she picked up the crystal pendant around her neck where it nestled between her breasts. Her warm skin glowed as if she was lit from within, then she began to chant her spell.

She was totally, utterly, captivating. And he needed to see all her face. Surely, one step closer wouldn't hurt.

He placed a foot on the ground. Eve's eyes flew open— her midnight irises now like crystal quartz—even as she intoned the spell over and over.

He opened his mouth to ask what was wrong—but the words jammed in his throat. She stared right at him, but it was as if she was looking *through* him. *Into* him. Connected *to* him.

Heat flared through his chest, his dick, through every single part of him as the world condensed until only Eve filled it. Her glowing skin. Her eyes. Her perfume that filled his senses and tugged him to her. He followed her lure, stepped closer—

And then her eyes shut.

Around Raph, the world came back into view.

Fuck! He jumped back on the porch. What. The. Hell? He hauled in a shuddering breath—but the remnant of that fire filled his lungs as if whatever had passed between Eve and him still lingered.

Whatever was going on, it needed to stop now. This was not the time—and sure as shit, not the place—for a romantic anything. The urge to get as far away from Eve as possible slammed through him, except he had had to force himself to sit still.

He couldn't risk moving and interrupting the spell.

So he fought back whatever that stupid-ass sensation was that had lodged in his chest and focused on getting the relic. Because only the relic mattered.

11

———

Five hours later, after eating dinner with Raph and his family, Eve let the farmhouse door shut behind her and, with a glass of chilled vino in hand, walked over to the porch steps. The true dark of a country sky, stars so bright she could practically reach out and touch them, greeted her. The vista should've been a welcome balm to the furor inside her, but nothing could blanket the competing turmoil roiling in her belly.

The need to get to the relic. And Raph.

Damn it, she should've insisted the sexy otherworlder stay inside during the ward spell. Because something must have gone wrong. What else could explain how her body reacted every time he looked at her—or she looked at him?

The way heat boiled low in her belly, coiling and deepening in her core, and the way her nipples pebbled.

Eve plonked down onto the top step of the porch, planted her feet on the bottom tread and took a sip of her wine.

Damn it. She shouldn't be thinking of Raph. Not when her relic was still in someone else's hands. At least she'd been able to sneak in one little spell to scry for the relic earlier on. The spell hadn't been enough for an exact location—without her pendant to use a pendulum that was going to be difficult to pin down—but the strong signal meant the relic was still relatively close. At least it hadn't left the region.

The tang of freshly cut grass and hay mingled in her nose. Thankfully the air wasn't as heavy during the daytime. She took a deep breath and forced her tense muscles to relax. She had to stay calm. Calm and focused.

"Starry night. It's stunning, isn't it?" Raph's cocoa voice rolled over her from the dusky shadows, and Eve shivered.

Then he appeared from the around the corner of the house. She held in a sigh. Of course he'd appeared like a dark god from the night.

"Would you like something else to drink?" he asked, coming to stand closer to her.

"No, this is lovely. Back home I'd be drinking mulled wine about now, but I'm enjoying this."

"Mulled wine? I've had that a few times, don't mind it either." He slipped his hands into his pockets. "Thanks for staying for dinner."

"Couldn't very well say no when your father explained it has been so long since you've been up here."

"Yeah, Dad can be pretty persuasive."

"I didn't expect you to be so ..."

"So?"

"So ... close. As a family. All of you really care for each other. Your bond is clear to see."

"Of course we do. We're family. Aren't you close to yours?"

Eve finished the last sip of her wine and carefully placed the glass on the porch. Close? She loved her mother. But she hadn't seen her in over a decade. Not since the coven had come calling. And her father was a nameless one-night stand that her mother had never seen again. So no. She wasn't close like Raph and his family. For the first time ever, a hollow feeling pinged in her chest.

"Hey, you don't have to answer that," Raph said. He turned his face up to the sky. The urge to drink in his beauty swelled through her, pushing away the uncomfortable sensation in her chest. "I usually end up out here if I come up for the night," he continued. "I swear those stars are so bright I could pluck one from the night. Like I said, stunning."

She couldn't help herself and stared up at him. Stunning. Oh yeah. She blew out a slow breath even as her pulse kicked.

And then he turned around. The night obscured the green of his eyes, and shadows carved the planes of his jaw. He was back to looking sinister. Hard. And achingly sexy.

What, by the goddess, had she gotten herself into now? Where had the too-casual, easy-to-dismiss Raph Smith gone? And who was this Raphael who'd taken his place?

Eve searched his face. His eyes. Was this the real man?

"Find what you're looking for?" His eyes narrowed.

She moistened her lips. "I'm not sure."

Raph took a step closer, and another, until he was at the bottom of the steps. His body filled her view, and his face was completely obscured by night; only the glitter in his eyes was visible. "And now?"

A warm wind carried his heady scent. Eve's lips tingled as if a wing had brushed over them—except nothing had.

Was this starry sky some kind of magical enchantment?

Her blood thickened; her heart pounded; her body thrummed. The skin beneath her crystal warmed.

Goddess, she wanted to kiss him. But that had to be the most loco thought of all.

"Now?" Eve slowly stood, her body so, so close to brushing every inch of Raph's until they were almost eye to eye. She was a tall woman—but even standing on the step, he was taller. Wider. Hotter. Heat rushed to her core.

In the dark, shadows played over his face, but his jaw clenched. His lips firmed. Lips she wanted to taste. "Now," she said, "I have no idea what I'm looking for, but I know what I've found." She darted a look at his lips, then back to his glittering eyes. "May I?"

Raph inhaled sharply. Eve's words and scent spiraled through him, and every part of him went taut. He wanted to run his palms up her silky skin, tangle his fingers in her hair and hold her still while he plundered her mouth. He clenched his hands in his pockets against the urge to do exactly that.

But she was right there. Those lips he'd been watching caress her words were right. Bloody. There.

Raph stared into her eyes. *May she?* Blood pooled to his dick. His head swam.

"Yes," he rasped. "Yes, you may."

And then those lush lips were on his. Wine. Heat. Temptation. Eve sharply inhaled. Her breasts rubbed his chest.

A growl tore through him and he couldn't keep his hands in his pockets any longer. He cupped her cheeks, molded her mouth to his, tangling their tongues and breaths. Raph ran his lips along that carved jaw to her neck.

Eve's scent infused his senses, and she tipped her head back—

"Hey, Eve," Isa's voice echoed through the night. "I need to tell you ..."

Raph jumped back even as Eve stiffened against him. Oh hell, what had he just gone and done? Kissing a client? Except she wasn't really a client. He was double-crossing her. So she was a fake client who didn't know it. He held in a groan. That made it even worse.

"Sorry," Isa called out; she didn't sound repentant. "Don't mean to, um, interrupt."

"No, all good," Raph managed to get out. Double hell. He couldn't even turn around right now—otherwise, even in the dark, the state of his body would be clear. And Eve knew it because her gaze dipped down and then jerked back to his.

She pursed her lips—as if to say that wasn't happening again—and stepped around him.

A cool shiver shook through him. Had to be because of the loss of body heat.

"No need to apologize," Eve said smoothly, her voice as cool as silk. As if she'd never even kissed him. Had their kiss affected her at all? "How can I help?"

"I just had another ... vision," Isa said.

Raph stiffened. Holy fuck—his sister had told Eve about her ability? Dread shoved its way along his spine, dousing the fire from Eve's kiss. What else had Isa said?

He spun around.

Isa stood in the doorway, holding the frame for support. Bugger the bloody visions. They always left her weak. He darted up the stairs.

"Here, lean on me," Raph said. "Do you need to sit down?"

"No, no, I'm fine," Isa replied. "But I need to tell Eve what I saw."

Raph couldn't contain his scowl. Why the hell was Eve in Isa's vision?

"What was it?" Eve said as she joined them, expression tight.

"You—with lots of makeup and your hair all out. Some kind of fancy party was going on in the background. You were staring down at something in your hand. A gold-trimmed card, like an invitation. The card said: gala event, rare items auction."

"Bloody hell," Raph muttered. Isa's visions were never wrong. He cut Eve a look. Her body stiffened, and her eyes narrowed.

"What else was on the card?" Eve said. "Did you see anyone else you recognized?"

"The angle of the invitation hid the actual date, but I saw a day—Saturday." Isa's eyes darted to Raph. "And, Raph, you were there."

By the time Eve and Raph finally returned to Brisbane, it was close to eleven p.m. Eve blew out a pent-up breath as Raph parked in the visitor area of her hotel car park.

She got out of the car as soon as it came to a stop—*not* staring at Raph's sinful mouth for the millionth time. Goddess, why was he so hot? And why, by the goddess, had she kissed him?

Because he was *so frigging hot.* Ugh. This hyper-attraction crap was ... was ... well, crap. Enough. She had to get a grip on her hormones. Or maybe that was the problem. It had been way too long since she'd last scratched this itch with anyone other than herself.

Could she bring Raph back to her room and pick up that kiss? He'd seemed keen enough earlier—would he be up for more than just lip-locking?

Raph got out of the car and stretched his arms and neck.

"So, princess, what time should I pick you up in the morning?"

And that was a giant no. She wouldn't be taking Mr. Smith back up to her room. Because she wasn't a princess. She was the farthest thing under the moon from a princess. Plus, he was her employee. You don't jump in the sack with an employee.

"You don't have to get out," she snapped over the car. Anger boiled in her gut. Damn him for being an ass. She'd been so close to getting that itch scratched ... Well, now she *had* to go for a run in the morning. Otherwise, she'd be a cranky bitch of a witch until the solstice.

"Just stretching my legs," Raph said all too calmly.

"And yawning. You should've let me drive, and you could've slept. I can drive, you know. Or do you have some Neanderthalic asshole issue with women driving?"

"What? No. It's just the road down the mountain is pretty tough to navigate, especially at night. You're inexperienced on the roads here, so I was safer at the wheel."

She recoiled. Was he for real?

"What?"

"You've been yawning your head off for the last hour, and you're saying *I* would have been a dangerous driver?"

He rubbed the back of his neck. "Yeah, well, you didn't want to stay at the farm overnight. So we came back."

"Don't blame me for making you drive. I offered. You

said no." Eve refused to feel bad for his tired ass. Slinging her bag over her shoulder, she took off toward the darkened entry to the hotel. "And no, I wasn't staying up at the farm. As nice as your father and Isadora are, I am. After. My. *Relic*. And now we know it's still in Brisbane. I just have to get to it before the auction. So we should get your Frinecki contact to ask around about it."

"Eve, we know where it's going to be in six days, yes. But we don't know where it is right now. And my contact *can't* outright ask about the relic. That would be way too big a risk."

"No, waiting any longer than I already have is the risk." She stalked ahead of him. The hotel glass entry was closed, but a night-light shone from the check-in desk, so someone had to be around.

"I'll keep working the case." Raph joined her at the doors and peered through too. "Where is everyone? Is there a night bell or something?"

"I don't see anything ..." Eve raised her hand to knock on the glass, then stopped. The crystal around her neck was warming up ... hotter ... hotter ... She reflexively grabbed the pendant. "Shit," she hissed and dropped it. She backed away from the entry, and the heat in the crystal steadied—it was still fricking hot. But it wasn't getting hotter.

"What is it?" Raph asked.

"Stop. Don't move a step closer." She gingerly picked up her amethyst pendant. The paler pockets at the outer edges had clouded over. "There's magic here. Hidden magic. And a lot of it."

Inside the building, lift doors at the far end opened, warm light spilling from inside the elevator. A man and woman emerged, talking to each other. As soon as the pair stepped out of the lift, two streams of silvery magic flew through the lobby and slammed into their chests.

The man and woman froze midconversation.

"No!" Eve cried. "They're stunning them."

"Shit!" Raph hissed. "Stay still."

Through the darkened corner beside the lift, two men appeared, gazes locked on the man and woman. Then they turned to the glass entry, mouths dropping when they saw Eve and Raph. They shouted something over their shoulders, and behind them, a woman emerged. Eve caught a flash of red hair before the woman moved into the shadows.

Both men launched into a run.

"Oh fuck," Raph said. "Eve, can you take them?"

"I'm still recovering after the ward spell." Her heart rammed in her chest, and she grabbed her crystal. "I can slow them—but not likely I can stop them. And whoever that is inside, I don't know."

"Get to the car, now. I'll hold them off."

"No. You get to the car and get it started. I'll hold them off."

"Eve—"

"Not the time for ego," Eve snarled. "I've got the magic. Start the car!"

"Shit." Raph met her gaze but then spun and ran. "No shadows!"

The two men crashed through the hotel doors, glass shattering and smashing to the ground. Goddess, how strong were they?

"Eve!" Raph shouted. "Get your butt in now!"

She ran for the car as the engine came to life, revving. She wrenched the door open, grabbed the crystal around her neck and shouted her stun spell.

The magic flew into the night.

Two steps away, the men hit her spell. Their expressions froze; their bodies stilled ... for a moment. And then their momentum returned, but goddess—she'd made them slo-mo. A hysterical laugh escaped her. That was a first.

"Eve! Get in!"

She jumped at Raph's words. Crapola, look at what she'd done. She threw herself into the car and slammed the door shut.

Raph reversed and took off, tires squealing.

12

———

BACK AT HIS APARTMENT, Raph slammed the front door shut behind Eve. "Okay, Eve or Evangeline, or whoever the hell you are, you need to tell me everything. What happened to all those people tonight? What the hell were those fucking balls of magic?"

But Eve didn't answer. She was looking around.

"Listen," he tried again. "What just happened wasn't right—"

"No, it wasn't," she whispered.

He blew out a steadying breath. At least Eve was talking now. "And?"

"What you saw was exceptionally strong magic. They spelled the entire ground floor with a trigger warning, like the magic I did at your house. And I think ... maybe ... it was another Watcher. But I didn't recognize the musclemen with her."

"Another Watcher?" Raph's gut tightened. Was she finally going to tell him the truth?

"Do you know about us?"

"A little," he said carefully. "Rumors, mostly. They're an

ancient coven based in a giant, old craggy castle in the UK, who do all the Templar's protective spells."

"The giant craggy castle part's right, though we don't do *all* the Templar's protective spells. Some magic needs to be carried out by other lines of witches. But yes, the coven handles most of the spell craft for the Templars. And others."

"And to become a Watcher?"

"That's a long story. But one thing we all have is extraordinarily powerful magic, and most of us have some other-world family tie."

Was that why she'd been able to call the shadows? Was that why the voices of the past went silent when she was around?

"Are you most?" he asked softly.

"That doesn't matter," she said, shaking her head. "What matters is that if I'm right, the other Watcher is the actual thief who took the relic. I just don't know why."

Raph stared at Eve. Fucking hell. If Eve hadn't taken the relic, then Gray was wrong, and Eve was actually trying to get it back.

"Raph? Well, what do you think?"

"Ah, say that again?" He turned his attention back to Eve. Her hair had come out of its twisty thing, and a few wisps caressed her jaw. That stubborn jaw that he'd run his lips over hours ago. Fuck. Just the memory made his damn dick go stiff. *Not the time. Not the bloody time.*

"I said I should put a ward spell on your apartment. We need to sleep at some stage, and I don't know about you, but I won't rest wondering if those buggers could find us."

"Ward spell ... right, yes, of course. And *buggers*? We're way beyond that. Those bastards need to be dealt with.

They can't be allowed to get away with stunning innocent people like that. Okay, so let me guess, salt and crystals?"

"Yes. Any chance you'd have both?"

"Good chance on the salt. Not so good on the crystals." Raph stood up and headed to the kitchen. From the pantry, he grabbed his rock salt grinder and a small refill bag. "I've got this right now. I can go to the twenty-four-hour shop and grab more salt. But we'll have to wait until morning to get any crystals."

Eve followed him to the kitchen island and regarded the salt for a moment. "Okay, I need to ward all the entry points —at least you're high up, so the windows shouldn't be an issue. So the front door is a must. Any other external doors? Balconies?"

"Nope. Just the one entry point."

"Then yes, that salt will be enough. But energy is the problem." Eve sat on one of the stools at the island. "I tapped out the crystals and used everything I had back at the farm."

"You said earlier you need a day to recharge? Is that for the crystals too?"

"For me, food and sleep will help. From completely tapped out, I can be back to full strength within a day. The crystals need time and exposure to the sun or moon or something to help them charge. Any chance you have a selenite charging bowl handy?"

"Yeah, that would be a *no* to any selenite. What about your necklace? Does that crystal have to go through that too?"

"It helps." Eve picked it up. "But it's also tuned in to me."

"Tuned? As in a frequency?"

"Yes, I spent a very long time working with the amethyst to the point where the crystal frequency resonates with me.

The pendant enhances my power and lets me channel energy in a specific direction. So we're a package deal, different from other crystals like the ones you got at the farm. Those ones, I'm basically drawing on their energy to help me feed the spell."

"Okay. So you draw on the pendant's energy. Can you draw on other sources—like, maybe me?"

Eve dropped her pendant. The amethyst brushed against her chest, warm and comforting. But all her attention was on the man on the other side of the kitchen island.

Draw from him?

She'd have to touch him ... take his essence into her ... Heat pooled low in her belly. Yes, it was technically possible. But it went against Watcher rules to draw on another's magic—especially without their knowledge.

And look what had happened to her mother. A chill raced up her neck.

"Well?" Raph asked as he braced his muscular forearms on the counter.

"In theory, yes, it can be done. But I don't think it's a good idea."

"Why not?"

"I haven't done it before. Have no idea how it'll work. I don't know how you'll react. You might pass out if I take too much. And you're tired—"

"Uh-uh, right now, I'm more wired than tired. Look—I even made a rhyme."

She stared at him. Was he taking this seriously?

"Come on, that was a joke."

"I know. And that's the problem. I'm serious here, Raph. I don't know how taking your energy will impact you. There's also this rule Watchers adhere to—never steal another's magic."

"Okay, if you want serious, I've got a few things to point out. One, I'm not a witch, so you're not taking my magic. Two, you're not stealing—I'm offering. And three, your own fucking coven are stunning random civilians. I think you can do this under the circumstances."

Goddess, he was right. This was the most unusual circumstance she could imagine. And what good would sticking to the coven's rules be if she ended up kicked out anyway because she didn't return the relic? Or worse ... if the relic fell into the hands of someone who knew what its true power was.

"Okay. We'll give it a go. But you need to let me know if you start to feel giddy at all." She stared at him hard. "I'm serious. You have to promise me—the moment you feel lightheaded, you say something."

"Right, like a safe word."

She held in a groan—what she wouldn't give to need a safe word with this man. She cleared her throat loudly. "This isn't sexual. Strictly me taking your energy to feed a spell."

"Got it. But I still like the idea of a safe word. I'm going with ... succubus."

"Raph. We have a missing relic. We're casting a spell to stay safe while we get some sleep because I'm being chased by a very dangerous witch, and you're about to place your well-being into my hands. This is—"

"Serious. Yeah, yeah, you've said that. I deal with stress through humor. Sue me. But I'm keeping my word."

"Fine. Succubus." *Do not laugh, Eve.* "But one day, I'm introducing you to an actual succubus and then see if you're laughing."

"Whoa. Now that sounds fun."

"Enough. Now bring the salt and come with me."

"Yes, madam. Coming now."

Eve regarded him for a moment. His bright eyes were glittering, but his expression was serious, and those delicious lips were straight.

She blew out a surreptitious breath. This sexual banter was no good for her concentration.

She stomped to the door and then stood still and closed her eyes. Calm, focus. Calm, focus. She picked up her crystal, letting the warm tingle in her palm.

"Salt." She held out her hand. "I'll see how far I can go."

She quickly cast the salt circle and handed the container back to Raph. She closed her eyes, focusing on the energy of her crystal.

"Um, is this it?" Raph asked.

"No." Her eyes snapped open. Ugh. Raph was zero good at calming her down. "This is me trying to get centered so I can do the spell."

But clearly, that wasn't happening. She picked up her crystal and gentle tingles tickled her palm. Crap. She bit her lip. Not enough energy for a standard ward. But maybe she'd get through a temp ward—a day max. At least that would let them get some sleep.

And then a yawn overtook her, so big she wobbled on her feet for a moment.

"Hey." Raph grabbed her arm. "Are you okay?"

She stiffened. "Raph, never touch a witch in a circle until they give you the all clear."

He dropped his hands, but his lips pursed, and he didn't back away. "What, I should just let you fall over?"

"Yes. You don't know what spell has been cast—and some of them can be deadly."

"Fine. But since I didn't implode or explode or anything else nasty, do you need a hand now? You were shaky there."

"No, I'm good now. Just tired." She eyed Raph. His hands were on his hips, but genuine concern tightened the skin around his eyes. Ugh. This was what came with working with others. "Don't do it again, though."

"Gee, you're welcome." He rolled his eyes. "So, magic time? What do you need?"

Goddess, all the things she needed ... Eve clenched her jaw. Not the time for that. "Just do what I say. You and I need to be inside the salt circle, but you don't have a ton of salt here, and I need to spread it around us both, so we'll have to be close. Then I'll place the candles. They must be in a precise formation, so once they're set, you can't move them. At all."

Raph stepped so near their toes were touching. If she looked up, she'd be staring at his face. If she took a deep breath, her breasts would graze his chest.

"Close enough?" His voice rumbled in her ears.

"Yes." She scattered a fine line of salt around their feet.

"Now what?" Raph asked.

Eve swallowed the lump that thickened in her throat. Goddess, but he was hot. And not just the whole sex-on-a-stick thing. His body poured off waves of heat. If she was back in Rome, they wouldn't need a blanket to keep warm in bed ...

Crap. She yanked her mind away from the image of Raph in a bed. By Hades, she needed to get a grip.

She didn't risk looking into his eyes—no way did she

need that temptation. Instead, she closed hers and took a deep, slow breath. That was just as bad. His scent heated her on the inside too.

Oh, this was bad ... so very, very bad. She had to do this spell now; otherwise, she was going to combust any second.

"I'm going to grab your hand," Eve said in a rush. "Like this. Now, I have no idea what this will feel like for you—but if there's any pain or any—"

"Succubus. I've got this. You've got this." His hand tightened around hers.

Goddess, she hoped so.

Eve took hold of her pendant and then gathered her energy and sent it into the crystal. From where their hands met, tingles gathered against her skin. A warm, delicious heat began to grow. She channeled that heat along with hers into the crystal.

Raph hissed. She tightened her eyes against the urge to check him out. But damn it, had she hurt—?

"I'm good," he whispered. "Don't stop."

"Okay. Here goes." The heat where their palms met grew stronger, and he squeezed hers. She tightened her grip back and then began. "Step across those who may, if no license, keep at bay. Hold the line, pause in time. As I will, make it so."

Over and over, she chanted the incantation as she channeled her—their—energy into the crystal, and from there, into the spell.

All the while, the heat slid through their hands, through her, swirled around and around. The hairs on the back of her neck stood up.

The spell culminated in a burst of energy; heat flooded her, and she gasped, dropped Raph's hand. Only he didn't drop hers.

"Raph …" She opened her eyes. His deep green gaze glittered back at her. She licked her lips. His tightened.

"Yes?" he whispered.

"Are you okay?" Eve asked.

"Okay … no. No, I'm so much better than that."

"Then why are you still holding my hand?"

"Because I want to do this." His sinful lips touched the center of her palm. An arrow of heat arced to her core.

His gaze held hers. A question in them. She knew what he was asking. And, by the goddess, she was in total agreement.

"And this." He pulled into the solid wall of his chest. And then his lips were on hers, melding and shaping.

"Wait—" she gasped and pulled back.

A growl rumbled through him.

"Step—carefully—out of the circle. Don't disrupt it."

"Hell." Raph looked down at the floor, shaking his head, then stepped over the salt. "Do you still—?"

"Goddess, yes." She followed him and launched back into his arms. Fitted herself against his chest, his hips, his cock. She almost whimpered. He was absolutely perfect. She wrapped her arms around his shoulders and pulled him into her.

A low chuckle escaped him, and she silenced his laugh with her mouth. His taste was rich and heady, like wine and chocolate. A moan escaped her.

And then he widened his mouth on hers, and his tongue stroked inside. And his phone rang.

13

———

Raph dragged himself away from Eve. Every part of his body rebelled—wanted to dive back into their kiss. Into Eve. Unable to resist, he leaned back down and nipped her lips.

But the phone kept ringing.

"They're not stopping," Eve whispered. "You'd better answer it."

"Hell." He shoved a hand through his hair. "Okay. But, Eve ..." He drank in the sight of her—hair rioting around her face, lips puffy.

"Go. Answer it." Eve pulled her shirt down and smoothed her hair.

He blew out a hard breath and adjusted his pants. He was so fricking hard a diamond couldn't scratch him right now. Grabbing his phone, he checked the display and only just held back a groan.

"This is about another job—I'll take it in my bedroom." Raph thumbed the answer button as he closed the door behind him. "Gray, what the hell do you want?"

"Why are you whispering?"

"Because I'm not alone and you keep ringing. This better be important. Now, what's up?"

"Me. I'm downstairs. Buzz me through."

"Shit, you're here? You were in Boston a day ago."

"And now I'm here. Come on, Raphael, I've been on a plane for close to twenty-four hours. I'm tired. And it's fucking hot here. Get rid of whoever's there and let me in."

"I can't get rid of her." Raph blew out a hard breath. "Listen. You're a client. That's it, okay? It's the truth so just stick to that. But first, is there anyone else around?"

"A few people. Why? What the hell's going on, Raph?"

"You mean other than the fucked-up situation we're in? Just come up to level three. And make sure no one follows you. I'm in 307."

Well, wasn't this just great. Shit. The spell!

Raph raced back into the living room. Eve was eating a bowl of cereal at the kitchen island. One of those perfect brows rose as she looked at him.

"You need to release the ward at the front door. I've got someone coming up."

She stopped, spoon midway to her mouth. "Now?"

"Yes."

"Raphael, I just warded that door. If I remove the spell, it has to be cast all over again." She dropped the spoon into the bowl with a clang. "You really need to make your mind up. Stun people or not."

"Hey, it's not like I was expecting a midnight visitor. But it's a client. And I'm a PI. You aren't my only customer, you know? So please, can you remove the ward?"

She huffed and shook her head. But she got off the stool, muttering something under her breath all the way to the door, then she stood back inside the circle. She picked up her crystal pendant—was the stone glowing?—and murmured something over and over.

A pulse of energy similar to when she'd made the spell swept over him, and the hairs along the backs of his arms prickled. And then she toed the salt circle, scattering the fine stuff everywhere.

She lifted her chin, dark eyes mysterious, and stared back at him.

And his body responded. Damn, but he wanted more of her. He stepped closer. "I'm happy to redo the spell with you."

Eve's gaze dipped to his lips and then back to his eyes before she rose on her tiptoes. His dick rose too.

"No need," Eve said against his lips." I've got all the energy I need now." She ducked around him and sauntered back to her bowl of cereal.

He held in a groan. She was going to kill him.

Only the hard knock at the door stopped him from stalking back and picking up their kiss right there against the kitchen island.

Damn Gray. Raph hauled the door open. And there was the bastard himself. With his blue eyes, short-trimmed beard and dark hair. Looking like a young George Clooney and way too awake for this time of night, let alone after flying from the other side of the world. Gray held a tan leather overnight bag in one hand, and a satchel crossed his shoulders. He wore a white polo with blue jeans and leather shoes. The whole ensemble was probably worth more than Raph's entire apartment.

"Hey," Raph muttered.

"And hello to you too. I know it's late, but you look ready to kill."

"Yeah, yeah." Raph let Gray pass. "Get in here. We need

to ward the door again. And drop your bags over by the couch."

"*We?*" Eve said from behind him.

"Fine, you. Eve, this is Grayson—call him Gray. Gray, Eve."

"Raph's witch. Hello."

"I'm not his witch. And hello to you too. You're American?"

"Yep. From New York. What about you?" Gray asked easily.

"English. From Cheshire."

While they were sizing each other up, Raph rolled his eyes. "All right, you two, it's almost 1:00 fucking a.m. We—Eve—needs to ward the door."

"Again." Eve slanted Raph a look.

"And then you need to tell me why you're warding the door," Gray said as he took a seat at the island.

"You know about wards?" Eve asked as she picked up the salt again.

"Some. I'm an investigator back home in America, and I come across witchcraft every now and again."

"Raph said you were a client."

"Subcontracting," Raph cut in. "Gray needs some help with a job, and he's called in a favor. Plus, he's paying, so he definitely meets client status."

"Well, this is the last circle I'm casting until I get more salt. Just saying. And, Raph—since it's 1:00 fucking a.m., as you put it, where can I sleep?"

"Spare bedroom and bath are through the door at the end there. Gray can have the couch."

An hour later, Eve turned out the light in Raph's spare bedroom, once again wearing someone else's clothes—this time one of Raph's T-shirts in a soft cotton. She dropped onto the big bed. It was too hot to get under the covers, so she lay there in the dark on top of the quilt. Raph and Gray must have gone to sleep because the low murmur of their voices had stopped at least ten minutes ago, and now there was nothing but her thoughts and the dark view of the night sky outside the window.

But adrenaline still rushed through her veins. Eve had tried a warm shower to calm her pulse, but nada. Her heart was still racing.

She let her body sink into the mattress and closed her eyes, trying a series of deep breaths. Nope. Her senses were so damned alive.

It had to be that spell. Ever since she'd taken Raph's energy, she'd been on such a high she could've warded the entire apartment complex.

Was that normal? But since Watchers didn't practice sharing magic, let alone taking energy from a nonwitch, it had never come up in her training. Well, there was one person she could ask. But surely the coven would be watching her mother. There were the other Watchers she'd gone through training with, but competition had been fierce between the witches, and Eve had been an outsider from day one. No way would any of them go against the coven to help Eve.

No. Eve was on her own still.

She rolled onto her side and stared into the night. Her relic was somewhere out there. In the hands of someone who shouldn't have it.

But why? Was it really about the monetary value? Or was it worse? Was it someone who knew its true potential? That knowledge was locked down to a few key individuals, so surely not. And none of them would ever risk the relic rejoining its sister relics.

Her gut tightened. No, that could *never* be allowed to happen.

Eve rolled to her back, stared at the ceiling. Could she have failed in crafting her ward so badly? Yes, it was her very first ward as an active Watcher. But that spell had been handed down through the generations of Watchers for close to two thousand years. She'd studied the ward for almost a year before leaving Cheshire.

She knew every syllable of every word. The precise mathematical grid layout of the crystals. The build of magic, the pressure release as the incantation let loose, the pulse of energy when the spell completed. And it had all happened. Every single word and step was exactly as she'd trained.

Yet the relic had indeed been stolen. And by the Frinecki crime family based on them having it now. But that part didn't sit right.

Eve tossed to her side again. Shut her eyes and tried to calm her mind ... but her thoughts raced off once more. *The echo of her boots across the Vatican corridors. The relic alone in the dark vault. Raph's sinful smile. Raph's enticing scent.*

Damn it. Her eyes pinged open.

Maybe a cup of tea would help. Surely Raph had something decaffeinated. Eve slipped out of bed and padded barefoot out of the bedroom, leaving the lights off. Soft, even breathing sounded from the couch.

As quietly as possible, she opened one cupboard after another.

"Looking for something, princess?" Raph asked.

"Crap!" She grabbed her chest and whirled.

"Sh! Not so loud." Raph stood from the couch, shirtless and in boxer briefs riding low on his lean hips. "You'll wake Gray."

Her mouth went dry. Goddess. All that smooth, tanned skin. The ridged abs. The lines of his pecs. Every single muscle was defined in the mellow light. She even made out tatts on his bicep and shoulder.

"I thought *you* were Gray." She dragged her gaze up to his face. Busted. A knowing gleam entered his eyes, and Eve ruthlessly shut down the teeny-tiny burst of desire coiling in her belly. "What—you gave up your bedroom? Let me guess, you sold your bed for the night?"

"I'm wounded you'd think that lowly of me. Now, are you looking for something?"

"My system's still on hyperdrive. All the adrenaline from tonight, I guess. Do you have any tea?"

"Yeah, I keep chamomile on hand. Take a seat; I'll bring one over."

"I can make it."

"Nah, you'd just make a heap of noise and wake up Gray. I'll do it."

Man, he was hot. She took a seat at the opposite end of the couch from where the pillows indicated he'd been lying. A T-shirt was draped over one of the cushions, but the night was so warm it wasn't a surprise he was shirtless. If she was alone, she'd probably be wearing a tank top and undies, max.

"Here you go," Raph said when he came back. She curled her feet under herself and took the mug he held out.

"Thanks."

"No worries. Figured I might as well have one too." He sat down but placed his mug on the coffee table.

"I like the tatts." She nodded at this shoulder. "That one's a Celtic knot?"

"Yeah, it's a shield design—meant to be for protection. A few of us got them the night we graduated from the police academy."

"And the one on your arm?" She peered closer. "It's ... odd. Familiar, but I can't place the design. Is it Celtic too?"

"Similar origins." He picked up the T-shirt and pulled it over his head. "So, you really can't sleep?"

"Nope. You neither?" Eve asked into her tea. And she was *not* disappointed that he'd covered up.

"Not easily, no. I called a contact with the cops and gave them a heads-up about the hotel. But I'm seriously pissed about what happened to those people."

Eve rested her mug on her knee and considered him for a moment. His jaw was rigid; his lips pulled tight.

"You really mean that, don't you?"

"Of course. They're innocents. I don't like seeing people get hurt at any time. But that kind of shit is not on," Raph said.

"Is that why you became a private investigator? To help people?"

"Sort of."

"Come on. I've told you my secret." Most of it, anyway. "Your turn. And I already know you're otherworld and your sister sees the future. What about you?"

"Okay, here it is. No big sob story or anything, but I was a cop. And yeah, I have this ... need to help people." Raph held up his hand when she opened her mouth. "That's a story for another time."

Damn.

"But my ... heritage comes with some side effects. And that made it hard to fit into the team environment you need in the police force. I stuck it out for a few years, but it was really hard for others to work with me. So I decided to head into the private sector. But my police background has been helpful."

"So, what is it?" Eve asked.

Raph grimaced. "You want to know what my curse is, right?"

"Wait—Isa has a gift and you have a curse?"

"No, that's just Isa putting her positive spin on things. We're both afflicted with an ability not of this world. I'm a realist, though, and as much as Isa says her ability to see the future is a gift, it's caused her a hell of a lot of pain." His features tightened. "So yeah, I call it a curse."

"You don't have to talk about it if you'd prefer not to." Eve bit her lip to stop from demanding he tell her right there what his curse was. "Seeing the future must be ..."

"No." Raph sighed. His hands tightened around the mug. "I don't see the future. I see—and that's not even the right word; I *experience* things from the past. That's why I'm good at finding lost people—that and plain good detective work."

"Wow." Eve sat up in the chair. He could see the past?

"You don't have to worry," Raph said quietly. "For some reason, I can't see anything about you. I'm wondering if it's got to do with how powerful your magic is."

"Ah, thanks. Good to know. Odd, but good."

"Yeah."

A shiver raced down her spine. Exactly who was her PI? Well, right now, he was the man helping her find her relic.

That was all that mattered. And she needed sleep at some stage if she was going to tackle tomorrow with a clear head.

"Do you, um, think we could maybe put something on television? Anything really, just to stop my mind from racing?"

"Sure. How about a Christmas flick?"

Moments later, a classic action movie took over the screen.

"Uh, how is this a Christmas movie?" Not that she minded; *Die Hard* was one of her all-time favorite films.

"Think about it—the music. The time of year. The fact that it's set *during* a Christmas party. Of course, it's a Christmas movie. And the best one ever."

"Huh." Eve regarded Raph for a moment. "You're right." She took another sip of tea and settled into the couch.

14

———

Warm prickles teased at Eve's nipple, and a coil of heat wound deep in her belly. She pressed back into the embrace spooning her. Against the hard length pressing into her back. A moan fell from her lips, and her hips shifted, seeking more of that rigid …

Eve's eyes snapped open. But every other part of her stayed still.

That had been some dream … except … the pressure on her breast tightened, and a stroke on the sensitive nub of her nipple had her arch her back.

Oh goddess. She and Raph had fallen asleep on the couch. And now they were spooning—well, he was spooning her. His tanned arm wrapped around her waist, his hand snaked under her shirt and cupping her breast. And his thumb. Hades, his thumb rubbed the tight pebble of her nipple over and over.

The coil in her belly tightened. Her core clenched, wanting more of that pressure not just on her breast but between her legs.

Eve bit back another moan. She was so damned close,

one touch to her clit and she'd be coming.

Was he awake? Goddess—did he know he turned her on so much?

She licked her lips and turned her head a fraction. Early morning sunlight shone around the edges of the window blinds, casting enough light to make out Raph's head pillowed on a cushion behind her, his eyes closed. Sinful lips relaxed. Even breathing, warm and deep.

Well crap. She was about to combust, and he was asleep?

His thumb strummed her breast again. She almost let out a whimper. Okay, she had to get out of there *now*.

She eased his hand from her breast, a chill following as soon as his heated touch was gone. She grabbed a cushion, tucked it into Raph's chest, and carefully laid his arm over it.

And then Eve stared at him. Soaking in all his gorgeousness with the rumpled hair, his long frame, the bulge in his shorts ... okay. No more perving. But she couldn't stop one last glance before she padded to the spare bedroom.

Flinging off her clothes, she headed straight for the shower.

The water was hot and firm on her back, and she adjusted the nozzle so the spray was in a tight circle. The showerhead was attached to a long cord, and she ran the spray over her shoulders, down her side, along the backs of her calves, and then back up her legs. The hot spray hit between her thighs, and she moaned, body already so sensitized that the burst of water made her knees tremble.

Eve swept the water back again. Let it hit right on her clit. As if it was Raph's hand between her legs. Raph's thumb rubbing, caressing, stroking. And then he'd drop to his knees, his expression rapt as he eyed her core. He'd lean in, and with one hand, part her folds, and then he'd feast ... his wicked tongue lapping her up, delving inside ...

Pressure gathered, stacked. Eve wobbled on her feet—braced herself against the tiles as the tension crested ... yes, yes, *yes!* She gasped. Her body sent her flying.

Raph woke up with the biggest hard-on he'd had in forever, alone on the couch and dry humping a bloody cushion. Fuck ... that had been one hot dream. And so damned real his palm still itched as if he'd actually had silky flesh in his grasp ... And not just anyone's flesh. Eve's. Then the dream had shifted, and he'd been in a shower with her, his tongue inside her flesh, her taste ambrosia, her scent filling his nostrils, her moans and cries in his ears.

In fact, that dream was so damn real her flavor still tingled on his lips.

Yeah, no wonder he had a raging hard-on.

Raph groaned and stretched his back and shoulders. His muscles groaned back at him. Well, that's what you get for being all nice and giving your bed to an old friend because they'd been sleeping on an airplane for a day.

"Morning," Gray called out way too cheerfully from the kitchen. "Have a good sleep?"

"Speak of the bloody devil," Raph muttered.

"Talking from experience?"

"Not going there." Raph sat up, keeping the cushion on his lap. "So, can I have my room back now?"

"All yours. I had a shower. Towel's in your laundry. You keep a neat place here, Raph. Didn't think you were that type."

"I have no idea what the fuck you think about. But if

you're making coffee, make me one too. And remember the door's warded—so don't answer it, no matter what. Don't need anyone accidentally frozen on my doorstep."

In the shower, Raph closed the glass door and let the hot water drum into his shoulders. He dropped his neck forward. God, that felt good.

He reached down and cupped his balls. Fuck they were tight. No wonder. He'd had a hard-on for Eve pretty much solid for the last three days, let alone after this morning's dream.

A growl rumbled through him. Man, that dream had been so hot he was surprised he hadn't blown a load off against the cushion.

But here in the shower ... the memory of her dream-taste had his mouth watering. The feel of her under him on the couch from their kiss last night. He grabbed the body wash and lathered it up, spreading the spicy-scented bubbles over his chest, under his arms, down his torso to his dick.

And fuck ... this was what he needed. Take the edge off the clawing need he had to get close to Eve.

Closing his eyes, Raph grabbed his dick—but it wasn't his hand he saw behind his eyelids. It was Eve's. Her wet hair plastered to her face, water spiking her lashes. Her high and tight breasts gleamed under the bathroom lights as water ran in rivulets down their swells. Her grip tight and hot as she swept up his shaft, the tip so fucking sensitive he hissed when she ran her thumb over the slit in the head.

And then she slid her hand back down to the base—up, down. She kept the momentum strong and fast, just like he loved it, and then his balls tightened. Sensation prickled up his shaft. And his body erupted, his hips thrusting into her hold.

Raph slowly let his dick go—the bloody thing was still semi-erect—and he reluctantly opened his eyes, panting. Only the musk of his semen and the spice of the body wash remained of the fantasy.

And even after he'd hopped out of the shower and was drying off, his semi wouldn't go down. He eyed his dick. Really? The bloody thing still wasn't satisfied. Well, to give it its due, a hand job was up there, but nothing compared to the reality of Eve just in their kisses. If they ever did get together ... man, that would be some ride.

And there was the question. Would they? He still didn't know for sure if she was involved in the theft up to her delicious eyebrows or not. And then the other problem. He was lying to her. And in six days or less, he was handing over the relic she was hell-bent on retrieving for herself. Not that he had a choice. But he'd be a prick to have sex with her, given what he was doing.

Goddamn it. How had this all gotten so stuffed up?

Raph's phone beeped with an incoming message, the screen filling with the name of an antique store Frinecki was apparently a silent partner in. That was exactly the type of information he needed.

After pulling on navy chinos and a white short-sleeved polo—perfect for pretending to be antique shopping—Raph headed into the kitchen.

Eve and Gray sat at opposite ends of the island, drinking coffee. Eve was back in her clothes from yesterday, and her hair once again pulled into a sleek dark coil. But her cheeks were rosy, and her mouth soft. The tight expression he'd come to know tempered.

The sensation of her breast in his grasp from the morning's dream made his palm itch, and he clenched his fist.

"So, what's on the cards for today?" Gray asked as he passed Raph a mug.

Eve stiffened, and her mouth turned into an O. What was that all about?

"Thanks," Raph murmured, still eyeing Eve. "I just got a message from my contact. She suggested we check out a particular antique shop. And we need to research Saturday's gala event."

"And I need to go shopping," Eve said. "Gray just gave me an idea—I need to get a deck of tarot cards. And obviously, I need some clothes since I can't go back to the hotel. While I doubt the cov—ah, the witch from last night will have put another trap out, she had a lot of power and could've laid a delayed snare."

"I can go," Gray offered. "Give me your room number and the details, and I'll grab what you need."

"You? Why would you help me?" Eve pursed her mouth, distrust clear in her expression.

Because the Templar wanted to check her room for incriminating evidence or information about where the relic was.

But all Raph said was, "It's a good option since you can't go back." Raph took a seat beside Eve. Tried not to focus on the curve of her lips. "And why do you need the tarot deck?"

"I'm a witch, remember? I can still do magic to help find the relic, and the tarot deck is one way. Plus, I need crystals. But the answer is still no to Gray. You two don't know what a witch is capable of if they don't care about hurting others. No. What I need is to get the right tools and then to cleanse the lobby, the lifts and the corridors all the way to my hotel room—in case they figured out my room number too."

"You're not such a bad witch, you know that?" Raph said.

"No, it's just as possible Gray would pick up a tracking

spell and bring it back to me here. So let's just give the hotel a miss for now."

"Right." And there she was—focused, bossy Eve. Raph bit back a sigh. "Clothes, crystals, salt and a tarot deck. Got it."

"Yes, and then I'm coming with you to the antique shop. If we find my ... item"—Eve cut Gray a glance—"then I can get out of here."

"What item are you looking for?" Gray took a relaxed sip of his coffee, seemingly oblivious to the suspicious look she sent him. "Maybe I can help?"

"Nothing you need to help with," Eve replied. "So tell me about you? Did you really fly to the other side of the world without a hotel booking? What if Raph hadn't been here?"

Raph hid a grin. Eve was sharp; she'd pick up Gray's interest in no time. And, in fact—that was bad. Any thought of smiling was whisked away. Shit, if she got too scared, would she run?

Then he'd be forced to find the relic *and* worry about Eve getting to it as well. And now she knew where it was going to be come Saturday night—if she didn't use her magic to find it before then. Although given how accurate Isa's visions were, he gave any other outcome about a half-a-percent chance of actually happening. He had to act now.

"Gray said there was a mix-up with his check-in dates," he blurted. "They had him down for today instead of yesterday."

"And what, they couldn't just rebook him?"

"They were full. But you'll be out of here today, right, Gray?" Raph gave Gray a smile and held his gaze.

"Right, that's what they said." Gray returned his smile.

Eve settled back in the seat, her body relaxing. Okay, so they'd dodged a bullet there.

15

———

EVE LED Raph out of the clothing shop on an inner-city street in Fortitude Valley. She was dressed in three-quarter length pants and a loose top. If she had to run for any reason, she didn't want to have to worry about tripping over a skirt. And the top would hide her tools once she restocked. Which was their next destination.

She only had one problem. Zero funds. Luckily, Raph had agreed to pay her potion bill—the potion she had yet to make—in purchases. And he'd believed her when she'd said her credit cards were back with her passport in the hotel room. Only the passport was the truth there.

But she would do the spell, so it was a fair exchange in her mind, even with the lie about her credit cards.

Not that she'd gone overboard. She'd bought a full change of clothes so she could wear one set and wash the other. That would be enough. It wasn't like she was going to be falling into any more piles of cow dung. Plus, quality implements and supplies for her witchcraft were not going to be cheap. And those were far more important right now.

"The shop is just around the corner," Eve said over her

shoulder, recalling the directions from her internet search. "It's called Southern Moon."

The sidewalk was filled with people out and about, even in the sticky morning heat, but she wove through them all easily enough. And Raph stayed right on her heels. Not that she needed to look to know where he was. The prickling sensation along the back of her neck when he was near had only strengthened since the spell at the farm—and their kisses since.

And there it was, a little shop front among a row of many, tucked into an even smaller side street. The front glass door was painted with a tree of life in deep greens, and through the shop window, row after row of dark timber shelves held jars and canisters and tools.

"Come on," she called out to Raph, picking up her pace. "That's it."

Eve pushed through the door. Frankincense scented the air, tempted her to stroll down the aisles, amble around tables. Linger over myrrh and sandalwood.

Her heart calmed and the tension in her shoulders eased.

The shop was one large room. Paintings and woven creations adorned deep turquoise walls. Two men, one dark-haired and one blond, stood behind a counter tucked into the far corner. A closed door at the back of the shop presumably led to a storage area or maybe a reading room. Sometimes shops like this would even have a space where they kept light-sensitive—and dangerous—goods.

Throughout the shop, every surface was covered with everything a witch could dream of.

"Blessings be," the dark-haired man behind the counter called out.

"Welcome to Southern Moon," Blondie said with a smile. "How can we help?"

"I'm looking for some tools, plus supplies for a spell-amendment potion that can be administered without a witch present."

"Ooh, so you want some lavender and rosemary. Plus, you'll need eucalypt for the spell to bind."

"Eucalypt? I haven't used that before."

"Haven't been making potions in Oz, then?" Blondie grinned.

"Well, no. No potions anyway. In fact, back home, I'd be prepping for winter solstice—so this is all different to what I've been working with in recent months."

"Summer solstice here, hon. If you're looking for solstice ritual supplies, check out the table along the wall, and feel free to have a good look around. And if you need any help, call out."

Eve took him at his word and carefully checked through every item they had.

Oh goddess, they had crystals—and they were quality. Malachite and azurite. Quartz and lapis. Amethyst. Black obsidian. She almost cried. They were expensive, though—but as soon as she held her hand over the minerals, the tingle that shimmied through her palm told her all she needed to know. They'd been charged under both moon and sun.

The next shelf held ritual implements.

One row was dedicated to jars and boxes filled with herbs and roots and elements for spell work. She was in paradise.

Then she found the summer solstice ritual table. Eve couldn't hold back a smile as she picked through the supplies and tools. She might've been looking forward to the winter solstice a week ago, but this was where the goddess had brought her, so this was where she'd celebrate. She picked out an assortment of interesting stones—they'd make the perfect sun wheel arrangement.

"You look ... happy," Raph said.

"How could I not be? My mom used to own a shop just like this in Glastonbury. I used to love helping out in the shop, at least until ..." She snapped her mouth shut. That had been years ago. And she hadn't been back since. She checked her phone screen. Crap! She'd been poring over the shelves for an hour. No wonder she'd lost track of time here —this was one place guaranteed to capture her attention. "Right, well, I know what I need."

Thirty minutes after they'd left the witchcraft shop, with so many bags of implements that Eve's potion spell was almost entirely paid for, Raph drove back into the city. He parked near the main outdoor shopping mall.

"Wait, what's that?" Eve grabbed his arm as they walked past a glass shopfront painted with a Christmas scene.

"Uh, Santa and a sleigh?"

"Those aren't reindeers."

"Yeah, they're kangaroos."

"I get that. But why? What, Australia doesn't like reindeers?"

"Don't you know? Santa switches to kangaroos when he gets to the Southern Hemisphere."

Eve laughed. "Let me guess, reindeers can't handle the heat? They're not alone."

Raph couldn't stop a chuckle. "It's an Aussie thing. Now, we're almost there. Game time."

He led Eve into an expensive shopping arcade in the middle of Brisbane city. This was the place Raph's contact had said Frinecki had been doing business lately, so it was worth checking out.

He held the door open to a high-end antiquities boutique for Eve and tried not to inhale her scent as she walked past him.

"Remember," Raph murmured, "you're my girlfriend, and I'm looking for something for your birthday. I'm besotted, so will buy you anything."

Eve cut him a glance, her gaze serious. "Why does this sound like we're playing some kind of game?"

"Who's the investigator here? Just go with me."

"Fine. Besotted. Of course you are."

Raph's gut sank. Uh, yeah, he was. And that wasn't a good thing. But he had a job to do—and the consequences if he fucked-up were bad. So he forced the easygoing grin and made a mock bow. "You're such a besotting creature, after all."

Eve snorted and kept walking, only to pull up short. "This place looks more like a museum than an antique shop," she whispered.

A woman with sleek blonde hair, maybe in her fifties, appeared from a doorway at the rear of the little store.

"Hello, how may I help you?" she asked.

Her eyes dipped to Eve's shorts and then to Raph's polo. She kept her expression blank, but that zero warmth gave away her impression of them easily enough. Raph was going to have to make it clear he was there to buy—and that he had money to make sure she showed him the good stuff, especially if she kept the real valuables out of sight.

"I'm looking for a gift for my"—Raph picked up Eve's hand—"darling's birthday. She keeps saying she wants something *old*. Well, older than the fancy new sports car I bought her. And I said to her, darling, if there's anything all my family's money can do to make you happy, then that thing is yours. And so here we are."

Eve tightened her grasp on his hand. Raph held in a wince but managed to extricate his fingers before she broke them and tucked them into his pockets. Man, she had some grip. And for some reason, that turned him on all over again.

Hell, was there ever going to be a time he didn't have a semihard-on for this woman?

"Oh, well, yes. Welcome to Eleanor's. I'm Eleanor. We certainly have a selection of the finest ... er, old items money can buy."

Raph let the woman lead him and Eve around the shop, and when the time was right, opened his questioning about something *more* old. *More* special. Maybe a keepsake box of some type that his darling could store all the diamond rings he planned on buying her.

Eleanor showed them a few trinket boxes but not their relic. She was trying for all her worth to get a sale when Eve started to stare at Eleanor with the same look as when she'd stunned the musclemen back at the hotel. Uh-oh.

Raph risked his fingers again and grabbed Eve's hand and pulled her into his side.

"I've heard about an auction this weekend," Raph interrupted Eleanor. "Maybe we can get something there."

"Oh, I'm sorry," Eleanor replied without missing a beat. "I do think that the event is booked out for the night already."

As soon as they left the shop and its stuffy owner behind, Eve flipped her grip of Raph's hand—suppressing a chuckle when his brows rose in alarm—and pulled him toward the café at the end of the arcade.

"Don't be a wuss," Eve said over her shoulder. "I'm not going to break your hand."

"Not for lack of trying anyway." He wriggled his fingers in her grip, and as much as she was battling disappointment that the relic hadn't been at the shop, she couldn't stop a grin.

"That's what you get for calling me darling and making out that I'm some bimbo who's only with you for your money."

"And my good looks."

"Hmm ... no, that didn't come to mind."

Raph laughed, and Eve had the insane urge to laugh with him. What was it about this man? Somehow he was getting under all her barriers and making her ... happy. Which was the last fricking thing she should possibly be.

Focus. The relic.

She walked faster—almost jogged—and forced Raph to keep pace all the way to the café, where she stalked to the farthest table in the corner of the building.

The café looked like an old-fashioned tearoom with stenciled artwork on the glass-paned doors and old lamps scattered through the room.

She let Raph order them both a coffee, and as soon as

they were on their own, she took the tarot deck from her bag of goods from Southern Moon.

"What are you doing?" Raph asked from across the table.

"I need to do this quickly," she muttered. "No time to explain."

She opened the deck and split the major and minor arcana. From there, she shuffled the major deck. *Goddess, please let this work.*

"Does the woman in the antique shop speak the truth about the gala event?" she whispered.

Eve dealt the twelve cards all facedown, then let her hand hover from left to right. An invisible tug in her belly made her pause midway through the deck. She completed the run and started again. The tug happened again. She stopped this time and turned the card over.

"The sun," she murmured.

"So?"

Eve looked up at Raph. His green eyes were locked on hers. This was the serious Raph, the one she liked—but didn't know exactly how real he was. "The sun is a sign of positivity. In a reading like this, I'm taking it as confirmation Eleanor's telling the truth. The gala is sold out."

"Damn it."

"Yep. She might be a bitch, but she was being honest."

"You think?"

"Yep, takes one to know one. So I can see that easily enough."

"Hey, you're not a bitch."

"That's pretty much what every trainee in the coven called me, behind my back *and* to my face."

"They sound like a sucky group of trainees."

"Not really." Eve cut Raph a look and shrugged. "I was ...

distant. Focused on being the best, and nothing and no one else got my time. In their eyes, I *was* a bitch."

"How old were you when you started?"

"Sixteen. Basically, as soon as my magic manifested strongly enough that the coven felt my presence."

"I have no idea what that means."

"My magic was sending little shock waves through the energies of the world. It's natural. It just means I have highly functioning power. Which is what the coven looks for."

"Is that how they found you here in Brisbane? They can sense where your magic is?"

"Not exactly. One of the first things they teach trainees is to control their magic when it's not being used. But they can trace me if I perform a spell outside a salt circle. Which is why I only use magic like that when it's life or death. That type of thing."

"What about the tarot just there—wasn't that magic?"

"That was me trusting my intuition and the cards to steer me right. I could've used a spell to help reveal the truth, but we know the coven is here now. Makes sense not to do anything major outside of a circle unless ..."

"Absolutely necessary," Raph said. "Got it. Okay, so you joined the coven at sixteen. Then what?"

"I graduated top of my class and became a Watcher."

"And do you like it?"

"Like it?"

"Yeah, as in, are you happy doing it? Like when you do something that makes you so content, you'd give up everything else for it and never have any regrets. That thing you do that doesn't feel like work, but something you were made for."

Eve opened her mouth to reply, "sure" on the tip of her tongue. But that little voice in her gut pinged. *Was* it all worthwhile? She'd dedicated every waking moment to being the best. Yes, there had been a payment for that. She hadn't seen her mother in over a decade. She didn't have any friendships. The only relationship that lasted longer than one night was with her vibrator. Eve didn't have a life other than being a Watcher.

But she knew going in what was coming. And she wasn't any victim to sit here with a bleeding heart feeling sorry for herself about those decisions. And no way was she having anyone else question that either.

"There have been some ... sacrifices, sure," Eve said. "But that was what I signed up for. Of course, I'm happy. Or will be once I'm actually doing the job. Technically, I'd only just started as a Watcher when this whole shit show started."

"Wow. So you're new to being out in the world. But then, how long were you studying for?"

"Ten years."

Raph whistled. "That's ... intense. I had no idea there was some kind of lifelong training program like that."

"Magic is a serious business," Eve said. "What I can do is serious. The spells that need to be cast are deadly serious. And they take years to master. Most familial witches learn spells handed down through their ancestors from the cradle. When you join the coven, you're joining an entirely new family and learning spells dedicated only to that familial line."

Raph's expression clouded over. "Like the shadows?"

"Yes." She searched his face. "Why does the Spell of Shadows trouble you so much?"

"What do you know about it?"

"Well, I know I never actually called it before the other day. It takes tremendous power to wield and will drain you fast. Plus, if the shadows get out of control, it can become dangerous. It's classed a category vertex—only use in extreme circumstances and not even in training."

"Vertex? As in the tip of a triangle?"

"That's right. The coven teaches spells in an inverted triangle. At the top are everyday-use spells; in the middle are the more complicated, challenging spells and at the bottom are complicated, rarely used spells. And at the very, very end point are the vertex spells. That's where the Spell of Shadows is kept."

"Hell, that's bloody dangerous. Who else has access to it?"

"I think I'm the only one among my trainee cohort who got to look at the spell book that held that incantation. None of the others had enough power to call it."

"That's because the shadows aren't of this world."

"What? I thought I was enhancing the shadows of the room—making it look like it was nighttime, but a dark that no light can get through."

"That's the effect you get to start with. But the shadows are daemons. You're calling up the daemons from the first gate of Hell and pulling them into this world through the shadows of the room, so that's the form they take initially."

"What does *at first* mean? You said that twice."

Raph took a deep breath—but then the waiter came over with their coffees. They both sat back until they were alone again.

"So?" Eve asked.

Raph drained his coffee, then glanced around the fussy little café. Not the kind of place he'd usually pick to grab a hot drink. And not the place to reveal something about himself he'd never told anyone. Ever.

But for some reason, he was contemplating telling Eve the one thing that would make her lose all trust in him. An oily slick washed through his gut.

"Nothing," he muttered. "Listen, since we're in the city, why don't we check in on Arthur? See what he knows about the auction event. Plus, we should check in on him."

He stood and turned to leave.

"Raph ..."

Damn. She wasn't going to let this go. He forced a calm expression before he turned back to her. She still sat at the table. Her dark eyes locked on his. Mystery swirled in the depths of her gaze. Along with steel and grit and an icy disdain for any other option than what she wanted.

And fuck if he didn't admire that. But admiration didn't mean jack shit when so much was at stake.

"This isn't the time, Eve. And definitely not the place." That much was the truth.

"Fine. Right time and right place, all that jazz." Her lips tightened. "But you'll tell me."

"Of course." Maybe.

The shopping arcade was close enough to Arthur's antique store that they could walk there in under fifteen minutes. Somehow, Eve barely looked to be affected by the heat—although, given she'd come from the middle of fricking winter, surely she had to be hot? Maybe she was an ice queen. Except their kisses had said otherwise ...

Raph shut that thought down. Not the place for a hard-on. Every single time he'd remembered that dream, or their kiss, or glanced at her lips, or at the curves of her breasts beneath that floaty top, or the way her skin gleamed under the sun, his dick had been at half-mast.

They reached Arthur's shop, and Raph practically ran to get into the air-con filled space. Hell, he'd take on a room full of things screaming at him right now if it meant getting out of the stinking heat. As the bell tinkled above the door, Raph braced for the items to call to him ... but nada.

He couldn't help but cut Eve a look. Coincidence was pretty much out the door now. Although, there was one way to tell for sure. But he rapidly parked that thought. Arthur was talking to them.

"And it's delightful to see you both again, too," Arthur said. Luckily both Eve and Arthur seemed oblivious to Raph missing out on the conversation up till that point. "So, Mr. Smith, have you returned for that gift for your sister?"

"Absolutely. And it's Raph."

"Lovely. And you, Eve?" Arthur's sharp gaze landed on Eve.

"I'm with him," Eve said. "Looking for something for his sister."

"Oh. I didn't realize you knew each before ..."

"We didn't."

Raph just resisted the urge to roll his eyes. Small talk wasn't one of Eve's strengths. He cleared his throat.

"We've gotten to know each other since the ... incident. Turns out we both love antiques, and when I told Eve about coming back here, she wanted to come too. Plus, we wanted to see how you're going."

Raph steered the conversation quickly around to the gift for his sister and got that out of the way—picking up a present that was way too expensive, but what the hell. His third client was paying the bills right now, and their bank balance was enough to run a small country.

Once he'd paid for the trinket box at the counter, Raph picked up Eve's hand purposefully. Her eyes narrowed, but he flashed her a look.

"Arthur," Raph said, "I've heard about a fancy event in the antique world coming up this weekend. I was thinking maybe I could take Eve to it."

"Ah, you're talking about the gala auction. There are going to be some spectacular pieces under the hammer. And a portion of the night's proceeds go to one of our local charities. A very worthy cause."

"That's the one. Is it true it's sold out?"

"I imagine so," Arthur said. "It's an institution in our circles. New tickets go on sale the day after the event for the following ear, and they typically sell out within the week. I won't be bidding, of course, but I'm looking forward to seeing what they have."

"Is there a catalog or something?" Eve asked.

"Some pieces are cataloged, yes. But there's always at least one precious item that no one knows about—I suppose they do that to build the interest in securing a ticket to the night. But in past years, those items have been priceless, one-off pieces. There are usually buyers who come in from all over the world just for this one event."

"Wow. Sounds amazing. I would've paid a lot of money to get a ticket to that." Raph pretended to give Eve a sad smile. "Maybe next year."

"Um, Mr. Smith—Raphael, that is. If I may?" Arthur tilted his head toward the side of the shop.

"Sure. What's up?" Raph hid his unease behind a casual smile.

"While I certainly appreciated the support with your purchase today and what happened earlier in the week, I can't help but sense something else is going on here."

Arthur eyed Eve and Raph's joined hands. "Perhaps if there *was* something else going on here, and you were able to tell me more about it, I could assist ... after all, you have proven yourselves invaluable as both friends and customers. It would be my honor to help if I can."

Raph glanced at Eve. Her dark gaze was locked on Arthur, but then she squeezed his hand and nodded.

Right. Looked like some time for the truth—or at least a cut-down version of it. Raph explained that the item Frinecki's man had stolen from Arthur's shop did actually belong to Eve, and now Raph was helping her retrieve it. And that they thought the item might be at the auction.

"Well, I'm sorry to hear that, Evangeline. My sincere wishes for the return of your property. But, well, the person who sent his goons here to take your item—I can only strongly recommend you bring in the police, my dear. Getting involved with the likes of him is dangerous business."

"Thank you, Arthur." Eve let go of Raph's hand and touched Arthur's sleeve. "I can see you really do mean what you say. However, there are other reasons, some that I can't in good conscience share, that means I can't bring the police into this matter."

"What about this? I have one ticket. Perhaps one of you can go to the gala event and at least see if your property is there?"

"Arthur, are you sure? If this is an important opportunity for your business—"

"No, no. It's mostly for me to stickybeak, and after all these years, I think my contact network is good enough. However, I'm afraid the ticket is strictly non-transferrable. One of you will have to be err, Arthur Stanley for the night. I completely understand if you'd prefer not to take the offer."

Eight hundred dollars and one invitation to the event later, Raph and Eve left the antique shop. Eve abruptly stopped as soon as the door closed.

"What's up?" Raph asked.

"I'm going to need a dress, aren't I?"

"What? No—more like I'm going to need to dust off my tux."

"No." Eve scowled. "My relic. My time to get it back."

"Yeah, except you're dealing with a crime family here. And the ticket is in Arthur's name, remember? Plus, you still don't know who else might be around—like a certain witch on the hunt for you. Much better that you stay hidden and I go to the event."

Eve crossed her arms, and her chin rose. Hell. This was an Eve he recognized.

"Come on, be reasonable," he tried. "I'm the pro here, right?"

"And I'm the witch who can stun you and leave you in your apartment."

"Fine. You get the ticket *if* we can somehow change it into your name. But I'm going to get one for myself. Somehow."

"Then I do need something to wear," Eve said.

He bit back a groan. More shopping.

16

———

"I HATE DRESS SHOPPING," Eve muttered from inside the changing room of the formal wear shop.

"What was that?" he asked.

She stuck her head past the heavy drape that curtained the changing room.

Raph reclined into the deep green velvet of a plush sofa, obviously designed for those not trying on gowns. He sipped a coffee the fawning shop assistant had handed him as if he were a god deigning to visit the land of the mortals.

And damned if he didn't look like one. A dark, sinful god made for pleasure and adoration from all those who served him.

"Nothing." Eve ducked back behind the drape. If she complained, he'd just say fine, and he'd take the ticket. And that wasn't happening—surely there was a way they could change the ticket to Eve's name.

Which was why she to go through with this and get a bloody dress.

But really, why such a large space for one person to get changed? Maybe the regulars of the shop had entourages?

Going by the price tag on the dress hanging opposite her, they probably did.

Eve blew out a sigh. Raph had insisted she could pay him back—but this was going to cost her half a year's worth of spells.

And hadn't Raph said he needed the payday from this job? His credit must run long. Like the rest of him.

Ugh, no. No more thoughts of Raph and his long body bits. Not until she saw her relic again. And anyway, Raph had insisted he pay for the gown, and she was going to be at that gala event no matter what. She was getting her relic back.

All Eve had to do was evade the coven for the next five days. And then ... then she'd take her life back. Everything she'd worked for and sacrificed for. And make sure the relic was safe under a ward no one else could ever cross.

That was the other thing she'd do before the gala event. Work on a spell so intricate, so strong, no one else, not even another Watcher, could cross it unless they knew her ward. And she'd make damn well sure that spell only stayed in hands that were after the well-being of the relic.

Eve regarded her reflection in the mirror, the dark-eyed, dark-haired woman whose peers considered her unfit to take on the Watcher role because of an event that happened before she was even born.

Well, they could all go to Hades. She wasn't proving herself to them anymore. *She could do this. She would do this.* She'd return to her Watcher life pre the missing relic because she was the strongest witch the Watchers had.

Eve quickly stripped and folded her clothes on one of the chairs before contorting to get into the one-shouldered dress. Huh. It was heavy—must be the weight of all the sequins. And tight.

But it would do. And the gold complemented her skin tone.

"How are you going in there?" the polished voice of the shop assistant called out.

"It'll do."

"May we see?" she asked.

"See?" Eve frowned at the drape. Why did anyone need to see her now? She was perfectly capable of making sure she looked presentable.

"Eve," Raph said. "Let Sienna see the dress. She can make sure it's the right fit."

Of course he knew the shop assistant by name. "Well, if it gets any fitter, I won't be breathing."

"I can come in if you prefer," the too-helpful Sienna added.

Eve sighed. Why all this fuss, she'd never understand. But no. She knew herself. She knew her body. And if Raph was prepared to add the gown to her ledger, so be it.

"Not needed. I'll be out shortly."

Once she was back in her day clothes, Eve shoved the drape aside and handed the dress to the waiting Sienna.

Raph cocked one of his brows. "So?"

"It'll do."

He stared at her. "Thousands of dollars and *it'll do*?"

"Yes." Eve shrugged. "What else do you want me to say? It's so tight I'll have to be naked underneath? I can say that if you want."

The shop assistant gave a choked cough and backed away.

But Raph ... his eyes darkened. And those lips, oh goddess, they turned up at the corners. "Well, in that case, darling, I could've come in ... helped you out of it."

A coil of heat pulsed between Eve's legs, and she squeezed her thighs. Damn. This man was hotter than fire.

"Not this time, sweetcakes."

"Sweetcakes?"

"You called me darling. I get to call you sweetcakes. It's only fair."

Raph stared at her for one more moment, and then he tipped that gorgeous head back and laughed. And her lady bits began to tingle.

By the goddess, the moment she had her relic, she and Raphael Smith were on.

Raph and Eve grabbed lunch to go from Raph's favorite Thai restaurant and had just arrived back at his apartment when his phone beeped with a message from Isa.

"I'll just take this in the bedroom," Raph said after he deposited their takeaway containers on the kitchen island. "Help yourself."

As soon as the door closed behind him, he dialed Isa back. "What's up?"

"I'm downstairs. Let me up."

"What the hell? Why are you here? Someone's threatening to kidnap and fucking hurt you to make you do their dirty work, remember? You're meant to be staying up at the farm where no one can get to you."

"Sorry. No can do," Isa said. "I have to see you and Eve and ... never mind. Just buzz me up."

"Shit, you'll have to wait. Eve's warded the door to stop anyone from coming through. Give me five minutes."

Eve scowled at him as soon as he asked her to remove the ward, but when he mentioned it was Isa, her face brightened, and she didn't argue any further.

And then Isa was there. Shit, she hadn't been to his apartment in forever. She hugged him, and he hugged her back just as hard.

"All right," Raph said. "So what's so important that you drove all the way here—especially when ..."

"When what?" Eve asked over a mouthful of pad thai.

"When she's had issues with past clients, making her prefer to stay away from crowded, known places." Raph cut Isa a look. "And she's not meant to drive."

Isa rolled her eyes at him but at least didn't add in the fact about Parsons.

"If you're in danger," Eve said, "I can put stronger wards out. They can hurt—"

"No," Raph said. "No stronger wards or hurting people." Although shit, maybe that's just what he needed to keep Isa safe. Maybe. If they could guarantee no innocent bystanders would get hurt ... but that was a pretty tall order. "Not yet, anyway. Isa won't be staying. Right?"

Eve blinked at him and turned to Isa. "Don't listen to him. If you want a ward, I can do some spell work and see if it's possible. I've never warded a person, though, so it'll take time."

Raph resisted the urge to growl. Just. "Okay, simmer down on the magic, princess. Now, Isa, what's going on?"

"I had another vision—this time with me in it. And I rarely have visions of myself, so I know it's important. I was doing a piece of art."

"Hey, I love your art and all, you know that. But art's not an important—"

"Yes, yes, it's important." Isa reached into her handbag

and pulled out a piece of paper. "I sketched this as soon as the vision left me. This is what I'm going to do for you. So I'm going to be here for a while. Apparently, Eve needs this to get into the gala event this weekend."

Raph turned the paper over. His gut dropped. Drawn in lead pencil was a carbon copy of the invitation Arthur Stanley had given them earlier in the day.

"Oh crap," Eve breathed over his shoulder.

"You drew this?" Raph hadn't even heard Eve move, but she stared at the paper and then at Isa.

"Yep, and in my vision, I was making this for Eve."

"Me? Did you see any reason in your vision why I was getting the invite?"

"Sorry, no." Isa shrugged. "All I can tell you is that I handed this to you, and someone else was in the vision ..." Isa's face paled.

"You okay, Issi? Damn it, you shouldn't have driven so soon after a vision."

"No, no. I'm okay. It was something else. Anyway, this man, he was accessing some kind of computer system to have your details added to a registration list to match the invitation that I'm going to make for you."

"Oh, shit." Raph shoved a hand through his hair. "Of course, the event will have names on a database. Eve, given who else is there, we don't want to go by our real names. That's too big a—"

The doorbell buzzing interrupted him, and Raph scowled at his door.

"Who else is coming today?" Eve threw her hands in the air. "Really, Mr. Smith, you need to think long and hard about this ward business. The next time I stop someone from entering, that is it. No one else but you, me, Grayson and Isa. Got it?"

"*Mr. Smith*?" Isa's lips twitched.

"*Princess* here forgets I'm not her damn employee every time she gets mad."

"You are! I'm paying you, remember?"

"What, with spells?"

"Yes. They're a perfectly valuable, tradeable commodity. And you know it."

The buzzer rang again. And again.

Eve met Raph's gaze with her standard icy disdain.

"Fine." He stomped to the intercom. "Bloody loco witch."

"What was that?" Eve said.

"Nothing. What?" he said into the receiver.

"And hello to you too, sunshine," Gray's voice rumbled on the other end of the line. "So I'm all set at the hotel but wanted to work on our ... job. Let me up."

Raph jabbed the door release and ground his teeth as Eve started to fill the top of the kitchen island with all her purchases.

"Okay, so where can I set up my workspace?" Isa asked.

"Set up a—?" He whirled back to Isa. "What do you mean?"

"The invite. I'm forging you an invitation. I have the skills to recreate one exactly like the real thing—and according to my vision, this is the only way both you and Eve get to go to the gala."

"Isa. We need to talk." He glanced at Eve. Her head was bent over her items—was she counting leaves from a bunch of herbs? "Hey, Eve, I need to have a chat with Isa. We'll be in my room. Gray will be here in a moment."

Eve waved a hand at him but didn't speak or look up from her task, so Raph dragged his sister into his bedroom.

"Isa." He took a deep breath and lowered his voice. "I'm

not joking. There's a serious sicko out there who's threatening to kidnap you. Kidnap! And you've come right here to where he knows I am. This is the last place you should be."

Isa crossed her arms. "I had the vision, Raph. I know I'm going to forge this invitation and hand it over to Eve. After that, I'll go home. But clearly, I'm not getting kidnapped before I do that invite, right?"

"Fuck!" He dropped to the bed. "You're meant to be in hiding, remember?"

"That was from Liam and his goons, who are now half a country away. Now, no more arguments. I need to get to work. Can I see the invite?"

Raph somehow resisted grinding his teeth. Why were all the women in his world so bloody stubborn?

"Raph? You in there?" Gray's voice echoed through the door, followed by a hard knock.

"Yeah, yeah," he called out. "Be there in one minute." Raph blew out a hard breath and eyed his sister. "But you stay right here in the apartment—you don't go out at all. Deal?"

"Deal. Now, I want to see Eve." She spun and opened his bedroom door, only to pull up fast, her back stiffening. Gray's fist was raised as if he was about to knock again.

"Hi." Gray stared at Isa; then, his gaze flew to Raph. Raph scowled. What the fuck was wrong with the man?

"You're ... Grayson?" Isa whispered. All color drained from her face, and she stared at Gray as if he was a fucking ghost or something.

"Just Gray. And you're Isa?" The big man moved back with all the grace of an elephant. Which was not him. What the fuck was up with that? Raph followed Isa out.

"You're him!"

"What?" Gray took another awkward step back.

"Gray is who?" Eve stopped counting herbs or whatever the hell she was doing and looked over.

But Isa ignored them all and stalked closer to Gray. And for the first time ever, Raph swore fear crossed over Gray's face.

"Issi, what's going on?"

Finally, color flooded back into Isa's cheeks, and she whirled to face away from them all.

"Isadora. What is going on?" Raph eyed his sister's tense back. "Who is Gray? What are you—"

"He's the one ..." Isa turned back to Gray and stared at him, her eyes going vacant as if she was having a vision. Then she visibly collected herself, so that couldn't be the case. "In my vision, Gray was the one who got your name onto the guest list or whatever you call it."

"Okay, you need to step back." Gray looked at Raph. "Can you please tell your sister to move?"

"Who, me? I'm not doing anything. But sure." Isa spun to Raph with her usual energy. Raph eyed her closely.

"Are you okay?" he lowered his voice.

"Totally. Just surprised to see someone else from one of my visions. That doesn't happen often. Trust me, Raph, I'm okay. So, where's the invite?"

"Over here." Raph picked the invitation up from the kitchen island but kept an eye on Isa and Gray. What the hell was going on with them? He handed the thick black envelope over to his sister.

She carefully opened it and slid a single piece of black card out. Fancy gold lettering covered most of the front, along with a crest of some sort.

"Wow."

"What?" Raph asked.

"This is beautiful." She turned the invitation over. "Look

at the calligraphy—it's hand done. Huh. No wonder you need me. You can't mass produce this. You need someone who can copy that particular type of copperplate."

"What's copperplate?" Eve asked, coming over too.

"A type of font that calligraphers use. Hmm. Okay, I'm going to need a very specific type of nib—that's the point of the pen that forms the letters—and ink. And card. And now it's a *really* good thing I came when I did. I'll need to practice on the same quality card to get a feel for how the ink runs."

"You need all that?" Raph asked. "Listen, we still might be able to buy one more ..."

"But what if we can't?" Eve said. "We know the event is sold out. And the only reason we've even got one ticket is that Arthur's such a gentleman. Come on, Raph. If we're both going to the gala, you know this is the best backup plan we have."

"Can't you magic our way in or something?"

"Depends. Can I cast a circle to hide my magic? And exactly what type of spell will I need? It's not like there's a catch-all spell just to go poof—'make this thing I want to happen, happen.'"

This time Raph did grind his teeth. Damn it to hell. Having Isa here in the city was the absolute last thing they should be doing.

"Hey," Isa said, "I know you're worried about me, Raph. But I'm serious. I'll stay right here in the apartment the entire time. And let's face it. Do you want your invitation?"

Bloody fucking hell. He shoved a hand through his hair. He didn't want the invitation. He *needed* it.

"Raph," Eve said, "perhaps if you could tell me who this guy is that's hassling Isa, I can do a spell specifically for him."

"Oh, wow. Is that possible?" Isa's eyes widened.

"Maybe," Eve replied. "I'd need to do some work on it, though, maybe a poppet."

Eve turned to Raph; genuine concern shone from her eyes. His gut curdled. Sure, Isa had an old client who'd gotten too pushy. But he wasn't the real risk here. The real risk was Parsons. But he couldn't tell Eve that. Without question, Eve would ask why—and he wasn't having that conversation.

Raph cut Isa a look. She knew the truth—and why they couldn't tell Eve anything more.

"It's okay, Raph." Isa put her hand on his arm. "I know what I saw. I'm supposed to do this. Although there is one thing."

"What?

"I brought my art bag, but there's a lot of equipment we still need. Since I'm not leaving the apartment, you'll need to pick it up for me."

This time Raph couldn't stop his groan. More shopping.

17

———

Midmorning on Wednesday, Eve carefully set the last of her tools on the kitchen island and took a seat on one of the stools. Isa had taken over the dining table for her art station and was practicing her calligraphy. Raph was out working—he was going to talk to the event company who were managing the gala auction.

So Eve finally had a long enough period of silence where she could craft and refine the spells. Two wards and one potion, to be precise.

Since neither Eve nor Isa liked air-con while they worked, they'd agreed to open the windows, leaving the flywire screens to keep the bugs out. But that meant it was warm, so Eve had stripped down to a black tank top and running shorts.

She arranged her crystals in a neat line and then took the precisely counted bowl of herbs—Raph had a set of little porcelain sauce dishes that had turned out to be perfect receptacles—and arranged them in alphabetical order. Then Eve picked up the athame. The silver handle of the knife fit her palm flawlessly, and the scrollwork inlaid into the five-inch blade depicting the phases of the moon had the quality only a master crafter could affect.

"Those crystals look so pretty," Isa said as she came over to the sink with her ink bottle. "Are they arranged in a rainbow for a reason?"

"It's how the coven train us to lay them out. This way, I know exactly which crystal is where and I don't have to pause or risk selecting the wrong stone—which can make the magic weaker or, in some cases, completely derail the spell."

"So, how does magic work? You didn't have all this at the house when you made the ward there."

"Well, you need two things to make magic. Power and a spell. The power can come from you or from things like these crystals."

"Or herbs, fire, water, things like that too, right?"

"Absolutely. You know about magic."

"A little," Isa said. "But I'd like to know more."

"Well," Eve said, "every living or natural thing carries an element of power. You can think of it as energy. What differs is how strong an item's energy is and its natural properties. Then we have the spell. The spell is the intent to make something happen. Some spells can be simple; you whisper one word and add some power, and wham, you have magic. Others require a lot of power and a more complicated spell, one that's learned and practiced. I've had close to ten years practicing ward spells."

"Wow. That's a long time. I had no idea."

"Yep. But the wards I've set so far are spells I've learned from others. What I'm doing now is making my own spell. Something I've never done before. So it's taking a lot of trial and error, using what I know already, plus adding in more power, more intent, and more elements to make the spell harder for anyone else to break."

"Oh." Isa's eyes, so much like Raph's, widened. "You think someone broke your wards before?"

"Yes. Yes, I do." Eve picked up her pendant and ran her thumb over the fracture. "And that puts all the spells that Watchers have learned over the last two thousand years at risk. I think we need new spells."

"Can someone break through the ones here, now?"

"I added an extra element in there already, so not likely. And I don't think the people after me will be coming to your farmhouse, at least as long as I'm not there. So you don't need to worry about your place when you go home."

"Good to know," Isa said. "And thank you for telling me about the magic."

"You're welcome. So how did you come by your knowledge so far?"

"I like to read, plus back in ... well, where I'm from, there were some lovely practitioners I worked with for a while when I was trying to get control of my Sight."

"Did they help?"

"A little. But then the problem with my boss got worse, and I had to leave."

"And there isn't anyone up where you live who can help?"

"There's the local coven, but from what the witches who helped in the past said, it takes strong magic to help shape my gift. Plus"—Isa shrugged—"I'm meant to be keeping a low profile and all that."

"Well, maybe once this thing with my missing item is sorted, maybe I could ..."

"Really? You'd help me learn to control my visions?"

Eve's stomach seesawed. Helping others wasn't her gig.

And how would she do that from a whole other country? But the hope in Isa's eyes was impossible to douse. "Uh, sure. We'll figure something out."

"Thank you, thank you, thank you." Isa picked up Eve's hand and did a little dance. Eve couldn't stop her lips from twitching.

"Okay, okay. Enough of that. I need to get back to the spell. And aren't you meant to be working on an invitation or something?"

"Actually, I had an idea. If my invitation isn't good enough to fool anyone, I wondered if you could add a spell to your jewelry so that someone would look intently at those rather than you or the card. If you get into a hot spot, it might help."

"Huh." Eve regarded Isa for a moment. "That's not a bad idea. But I can see how good you are. Your invitation will be perfect. Mind you, I'm still hoping we find the relic before Saturday."

"It's not likely." Isa sighed. "My visions are solid in that way."

"Well, it can't hurt, that's for sure. Okay, adding one more spell into the mix. I'm going to be at this for days."

"Just as well it's Tuesday, then."

And it looked more and more like Eve and Raph were *both* going to the gala. Something, maybe anticipation, zinged through her.

Ten hours later, Eve rolled her neck and shoulders and stood back from her new boundary spell. Well, she'd done it. But would it work?

All she needed was someone to try it on. The hairs on the back of her neck prickled, and then the front door opened. Raph and Gray stomped into the apartment; their expressions were tired and frustrated.

Raph regarded her for one moment before his eyes tightened further.

"Didn't go well then?" Eve asked from the kitchen island as she noted in her book the placement and timing for each element of the spell she'd just completed.

"No." Raph tunneled a hand through his hair and stalked past her. He did that hair thing a lot when he was frustrated. And why was that sexy as hell?

Raph pulled up in the middle of the apartment. "What happened to my place?"

"What do you mean?" Eve shared a look with Isa, who shrugged. Ink smudged across Isa's cheek, and the messy bun she'd piled her hair into earlier was coming undone.

"There's stuff ... everywhere! You've taken over the kitchen. Isa's taken over the dining table. I need space to work, too, you know."

"There's the coffee table," Eve said.

Raph's jaw ticked, then he pivoted toward his room. Uh-oh. He was looking bloody prickly. Maybe she shouldn't—

Raph rebounded as if hitting a solid wall. "Eve." His voice lowered. "Why can't I get into my bedroom?"

"Oh. It worked. Perfect!" Eve said.

"No, not perfect. I can't get into my bedroom!"

"I needed a doorway to try the spell on. Your bedroom door's closest to the kitchen, so it's easiest for me to reach with the new spell."

"*New* spell?"

"Yes. New." Eve hopped off the stool and joined Raph.

"Now, try it again. Actually, let me see. I should be able to pass but not you." She walked through the doorway. Nothing stopped her. She stepped fully into his bedroom and turned to face Raph. "Try again now."

Raph's lips tightened, and his eyes glittered, but he slowly held out a hand—like he was expecting to meet the resistance of her spell—only nothing stopped him.

Eve's stomach dropped. What had gone wrong?

"Well, thank the stars for that," Raph said, entering his room and gesturing for Eve to leave. "Now, can I please have some privacy?"

"Pfft, you're in a grouchy mood, aren't you?"

"You know what? I've been hunting leads all day with zero fucking success. So yeah, I'm pissed."

"And I've been working on this bloody spell all day. And it just failed. But I'm not getting—"

"Hey, hey, you two," Isa called out from the living room. "Enough already. We're all tired and hungry. Eve, we barely ate lunch, so please—let's eat and then regroup."

"Fine." Eve glared at Raph and marched into a solid but invisible wall blocking the doorway of Raph's bedroom. "Oh goddess."

"Eve." Raph's voice was calm. Too calm.

She turned around. "Yes?"

"Why aren't you leaving my bedroom?"

"Well, it looks as if ... that is, the spell seems to be working again. Kind of."

"Are you guys coming out?" Isa appeared on the other side of the doorway, hands on her hips.

"What's up?" Gray came into view next, although standing several feet back from Isa.

"Eve?" Raph asked in that same deceptively cool voice.

"Let me try one more time." Eve reached out—and met

the invisible wall of her spell. She spread her fingers wide. Tried her other hand.

"What's with the stunned-mime act?" Gray asked.

"Well," Eve said, "the stunned part is because there might as well be a solid barrier right here. This is my first time creating a new spell from scratch. This is a big deal. Do you realize how many other ways this can help—?"

"Eve. Focus." Raph joined her. "The spell's working. Great. Now you need to remove it."

She resisted the urge to bite her lip. Damn it. She eyed the salt just through the doorway, maybe five steps away, sitting on the kitchen counter.

"Well, I can remove the magic, of course. But because I didn't know the spell was working, I, uh, left one very important ingredient out there."

"Where?" Isa asked.

"In the kitchen. The salt."

Isa and Gray both turned to the island bench.

"So, no removal spell, then." Raph sighed and crossed his arms.

"Not unless you want me to bring the ... you know who here," Eve said.

"Care to share what you're talking about?" Gray asked.

"Not really." Eve raised her chin.

"How long will it last?" Raph said.

"Not too long. A few hours. Give or take a few minutes. I only crafted a temporary spell given I wasn't sure of the outcome."

"Hallelujah for that."

"So what? You two are stuck in there?" Isa asked and chewed on her lip.

"Looks like it." Raph cut Eve a look. "Unless you've got a better option?"

Eve sniffed. "Clearly not."

"Sorry, Issi; you and Gray are doing dinner on your own. Gray, Isa isn't going out, so can you grab takeaway?"

"On it. What about you guys?"

Eve met Raph's gaze and shook her head. She ignored the rumble in her stomach. A growling belly wasn't a life-or-death situation, certainly not worth risking the coven finding her. She checked out Raph's bedroom—he had a television opposite the bed, which was big enough for the two of them to sit comfortably. And he had an en suite. They were fine.

"Looks like we're eating later," was all Raph said.

Raph showered and, still in the bathroom, changed into shorts and an old tee. At least the tee was long enough to mostly cover his hard-on. A state he'd been in for days now. But he'd given up on expecting anything else with Eve around.

From the moment he'd come back to the apartment and found her sitting at his kitchen island, looking like she belonged exactly there, something in his chest had clicked. A deadlock engaging. Raph could see her sitting there, an array of instruments laid precisely before her, dark hair gleaming, mysterious eyes meeting his, when he walked through the door, every single fucking day for the rest of his life.

Except that was loco. Eve was from another country, and she was a client—quasi, anyway. She'd be gone when this was over, and he'd probably never see her again.

Four days to hand the relic over.

Raph's gut churned like a washing machine filled with acid sloshing around his insides.

He frowned at his reflection in the bathroom mirror. And then he'd gone and chucked a hissy fit because his space had been invaded. Hell. Eve was getting to him. *Really* getting to him. He needed to get some distance.

"Are you done in there?" Her voice filtered through the door.

Raph bit back a groan. Space was impossible right now unless he planned on staying in the bathroom all night. He eyed the toilet seat.

"Seriously, I need to go to the loo."

And there went that idea.

Raph swapped rooms with Eve, and minutes later, she returned to the bedroom. In a tank top and running shorts, with her hair pulled back into a high ponytail instead of the usual twisty-bun thing, she looked ... sexy. Stunning. Powerful.

And Eve sat on the edge of the bed. His mouth went dry. His dick went even stiffer.

"So ..." Raph turned to the open doorway, desperate for something else to look at. "Where are Isa and Gray?"

"Isa's in the shower. Gray's grabbing Thai. What did you find out today about the relic?"

Business. Of course.

"The meeting with the event company went well—Gray was handy to have along there. He checked out their computer system while I pretended to be interested in holding a black-tie event. I've arranged a second meeting with them up at the lookout restaurant on Friday to view their options."

"What? Why?"

"They're keen to impress a potential future client by showing off a venue they're setting up right now. And I'm keen to get a look at the layout of the site."

"Clever. What about the tickets?"

"No luck. Apparently being sold out months in advance adds to the exclusivity or some bullshit."

"Well, you said Isa's visions were always right."

Raph scowled. "I was hoping this might be the first time they weren't."

"Raph, don't worry. Isa'll be okay. She's staying right here in the apartment, and the wards are up. This old client won't get her."

"Yeah." Unfortunately, Parsons knew where Raph lived. He'd have to figure out a safe way to get Isa home again. But Eve was right about one thing, Isa was safe with the wards on the apartment.

Hours later, long after Isa had gone to bed and Gray had gone back to his hotel, Raph tried to concentrate on the evening news. But the only sounds that filled his ears were the even breaths coming from Eve where she lay on her side, back to him.

Was she finally asleep?

Raph unkinked his stiff muscles and eased to his feet. Really, why didn't they make king-size beds bigger?

He tiptoed around to Eve. And his breath halted in his chest.

Eve was deprickled in her sleep. And in his bed, lips softly parted, eyelashes sweeping over her gleaming cheeks ... she was perfect. Several strands of her dark hair wrapped over the sleek curve of her breast where it rose above her tank top.

He took a step back, and back, and back—right into the

living room. Well, thank the stars for that. The ward was down.

And not a fucking moment too soon. Raph had been about to do something totally stupid. He blew out a long, slow breath. At least he could eat now. He grabbed the take-away containers from the fridge, the golden light spilling into the kitchen, and opened them. The crack of the plastic lids disturbed the quiet, and he winced. Damn. He didn't want to wake—

"Oh, thank the goddess. I'm starving."

And there Eve was. And he wasn't only hungry for Thai.

In silence, they ate straight from the containers on either side of the kitchen island. And it was ... comfortable. Right. Again. Raph snuck a look at Eve's lips as she finished off her pad thai.

"That was delicious." Eve placed her rubbish in the bin. "You're so lucky to have restaurants like that close by. Right, well, I need to work out what went wrong with the spell. I'll do that here, and when I'm done, I'll sleep on the couch."

"No," Raph said, "I'll take the couch. You take my bed."

"No. You slept on the couch two nights in a row. I'll take the couch. Plus, I really do need to review my spell and work out what went wrong."

"Now? It's like, midnight."

"Yes, now. Especially now while the ward's still fresh in my mind."

"It's a new spell? Yours?"

"Yes. Of course. I said it was."

"All right, don't get tetchy."

"I'm not tetchy. And don't doubt my ability."

"Not tetchy, got it. And I'm not doubting your ability. I don't have a clue what it means to make new spells." But Raph wanted to. And more, he wanted to know about Eve.

18

———————

Two days after the failed ward spell, Eve stood within a salt circle in front of Raph's bedroom doorway and crossed the athame over her palm, not so deep as to break the skin but deep enough to leave a red groove. She whispered the shock and stun spell for the last time and let her power and the words combine.

Power curled low in her belly and swooshed through her veins. The magic was done.

"All right, try the door one more time." Eve waved the athame toward Raph and then at the doorway.

Raph cut her a look.

"Go on, Raph," Isa called out from the dining room table. "I want to see the look on your face when you get zapped again."

"And why do we need a shock and stun?"

"I'll be able to separate them eventually, which means you can have a deterrent when I dial the shock up to cause real pain. Or if you want to buy yourself time to get away, we use the stun."

"Fine. But why do you have to electrocute *me* again? Why not Gray? He's not doing anything."

"Am too." Gray's head bobbed up from where he sat on the couch in front of his laptop. "I'm almost in."

"It's a mere buzz. Don't be a wuss," Eve said.

"Don't see you getting buzzed."

"Little do you know. I tried it on myself first. Now, come on, it's only the third time. I've made one tweak which should mean you get the buzz and then can't move—but it'll be temporary. Trust me."

"Fine." Raph rolled his eyes. "I must be deluded."

Eve couldn't contain her laugh.

"That wicked laugh isn't helping, princess."

"Wicked? Me? Now, now, I only take *mild* delight in your pain, Mr. Smith."

"Mild. Right." Raph's lips curved. "Well, here goes." He cut her one look before he reached out and stuck his hand into the doorway. "Shi—!" His mouth went tight, his eyes narrowed, and then he stilled.

"Wow. Eve, that's impressive," Isa said, grinning. "I've never seen that look of sustained pain before."

"Thank you, Isa," Eve said as she set the timer on her watch. "That's a lovely compliment. Although I've made sure the pain is mild—not much more than a bee sting and won't last. The stun, however, captures him in that moment of pain and ensures he can't move until the magic dies."

"Can he hear us?"

"Yes." Eve stepped out of the salt circle and slowly walked around Raph. "He's totally aware of everything that's going on. But the spell won't last long, so get your fill of his face while you can."

"Can you bottle that type of magic?"

"Maybe. I've only just created this one now, so to bottle it would take a lot more time and effort. If it's possible at all. I'd have to consider the use, though. It's one thing to throw the spell myself, but an entirely other matter to give someone else the power."

"Yes!" Gray shouted from the couch. He tapped a few more times on the keyboard. "And that, baby, is it. I'm in. And now ... you and Raph are officially attending the ball."

Isa clapped her hands. "Perfect. I've got one invitation ready to go with it."

Eve surveyed Gray and Isa—both pleased with themselves and their actions, but they had nothing on the blood rushing through her veins. She was one step closer to getting her relic. And the gala was two days away.

She was almost home.

"Mmm ... mmm ..."

"Looks like Raph's starting to move again," Isa said.

Eve checked the time. "Right. That was exactly five minutes for it to begin to wane." She tapped the athame against her lips. "Raph, I need you to keep trying to move. I'm timing you until you get your full range of movement back."

"Mmm ... never trust ... mmm ..."

"That's right, keep trying to talk. Speech is another movement the stun restricts. Try to say that again."

"You ... mmm-mmm-menace."

When Raph finally got all his feeling back and the fog completely lifted from his brain two hours later, instead of focusing on the relic he was meant to be handing over to

Parsons in two days, he eyed Eve as she wrote something in her notebook.

"You look ... happy." *For the first time since I've known you,* he wanted to say. She'd let her guard down a few times, sure, but that was it.

Eve stopped writing, her eyes widening. "I guess that's because I am."

"And why is that such a surprise?"

"I'm a Watcher." Her face grew serious. "That comes with responsibilities around magic that shouldn't be taken lightly. I guess I've been serious for most of my life. And using magic for anything other than training and for protecting relics, it's actually a pleasure. I never saw magic like that before now."

"Then I'm glad you have," Raph said.

Eve snorted.

"I'm serious. Why is that such an issue?"

She stared at the notebook for one moment, then closed it with a snap and swiveled to face him. "Because you don't know me. We're not longtime friends or even family," she said matter-of-factly. "So why would you care about what makes me happy?"

"So what if I haven't known you for an age? You're still a human being, aren't you?"

"I fail to see why it matters to you," Eve said.

"Seems a shame to spend your entire existence—and Watcher's live long lives, right?—never doing something just to make you happy." Raph regarded her carefully. A tug of something, maybe sympathy, had him lean forward. "You're allowed to be happy, Eve."

"But I have a purpose. A reason for being what I am, who I am."

"So? Look at Isa and me. We've both got this"—he

glanced at Isa, who was deeply absorbed in painting—"curse, but we both do our best to manage that part of our lives and be happy."

"I get the sense you make the most of enjoying life."

"When the time's right, sure." Raph grinned. "But I found a way to do something useful with my life *and* be happy. Just saying."

"Finally." Isa groaned from the dining table and pushed her seat back, rolling her neck and shoulders. Then she stood up and peered down at her work. "Well, you now have a second invitation."

Raph glanced at Eve. Her eyes darkened, and something inside him quickened. Two days to go.

"Well, you two? Why are you just gazing into each other's eyes when you should be over here checking out my amazing artwork?"

"Coming," Eve murmured, still staring into his eyes.

Well, hell, he wanted that word on her lips as she lay under him—or over him. The pulse leaped at the base of her throat. Was she thinking the exact same thought?

"Leave your coffees there, though," Isa continued. "Don't want anything coming near my masterpiece."

"We'd better go," Eve whispered. She looked at his mouth. His lips bloody well tingled like it was her tongue and not that hot gaze touching them. She smiled, and a wicked light entered her eyes before she turned away.

Raph bit back a groan. He was going to be drooling for her if this kept up.

"Wow. Isa, this is amazing. *You* are amazing," Eve said.

He forced his body to behave and went around to the other side of the table. Bloody hell. He shot a look at Isa. "You *are* amazing. It's absolutely the same."

"Thank you," Isa said. "And yes, it is."

"You're a wonderful forger," Eve said. "Thank you."

"Yeah, not sure forger's up there on the desirable skill list." Raph cut Eve a glance.

"Well, it should be," Eve said with a sniff. "It's an art form."

"Thanks for the support, Eve." Isa smiled.

Eve looked down her nose at Raph and nodded. "See, your sister appreciates my recognition of her forgery skills. She's an artist."

"Right, well, it's time for the *artist* to head home." Raph slipped his hand into his pocket and considered his sister. "We just have to work out how to get you out of the city and back up to Maleny safely."

"Raph, I'll be fine. I drove here myself. I can drive home myself."

"No, Isa. I'm dead serious about this. You—*we*—know the dangers here. But Gray's offered to drive you home. You can hide out in his car until you leave the city."

"And how am I going to get around when I'm home?"

"I'll follow Gray afterward in your car. Plus, you know how dangerous driving is. It's meant to be only if you absolutely need to, right?"

"Why?" Eve asked.

"Because of the visions." Isa grimaced as she packed away her supplies. "You've seen how ... encompassing they can be."

"Oh. I do see."

Raph didn't bother to hide his scowl. "Isa had a vision once while she was driving. It could've gone badly. For her and anyone else nearby. She hardly ever drives anymore. Which is why I was not expecting to see her down here."

Isa sighed. "An hour and a half with Gray? The man can't stand to be around me. Don't think he'll agree to that."

"He already has," Raph said. "So he can't not stand you that much, hey?"

"Isa." Eve began to help his sister pack up. "When this is all over, I'll find a way to help you control your gift."

Raph eyed Eve. Could she really help his sister?

Saturday morning, Eve set her alarm to wake up before sunrise and gathered her solstice supplies. The window in Raph's living room faced east, which was perfect, so she sat on the floor and laid the stones from Southern Moon in a sun wheel pattern.

As dawn broke and the first rays of light shone through the window, she said a blessing to the goddess for connectedness. For Raph and Isa and their dad, for Gray, for her mom.

A warm buzz hummed through her hands as she ran them over each stone. And then she sat still and let the solstice sunrise fill her up.

Once the sun had fully risen, she uncrossed her legs and stood. Anticipation zinged in her veins. What a perfect day to finally get her relic back.

After everyone else had woken up and Raph and Gray were preparing for their drive, Eve found Isa packing her bag in the spare room.

"Do you need a hand with anything?" Eve asked.

"No, this is it. I've got my art supplies packed already." Suddenly the smaller woman launched herself at Eve and hugged her tight.

"Oh. Touchy-feely, right?" Eve awkwardly hugged Isa back.

"Good luck finding your ... thing," Isa said. "I really hope you find it and that everything works out perfectly for you."

"Thank you. And thanks for your help. And for putting yourself in danger to come down here."

Isa teared up. "Oh no. I want to thank you—I haven't used my gift for a good purpose in such a long time."

Eve hugged Isa one more time, then Raph joined them, looking perfectly put together in those pants that hugged his backside and a casual tee. Casual, sexy and delicious. "Okay, Gray's downstairs and ready to go. Remember, I'll be back early afternoon. I'm going to visit Arthur first to get as much background on the world of antiquities dealers as possible, and then I'll drive Isa's car completely in the other direction to well and truly lose any tail. I'll be gone for several hours at the least I'm guessing."

"Got it," Eve said.

"Now, the limo's booked for five thirty."

"Why do we need that?"

"Part of the story we're telling. We need to arrive like we belong. But Gray's going to park down the road from the event center, so we have a confirmed getaway option. And I booked the car under Arthur's name," Raph said. "Just in case. I'll let him know when I see him—again, just in case."

"So you're A. Stanley tonight?"

"That I am. See you later, princess."

As the door closed behind Raph and Isa, a shiver swept through Eve. Their plan was falling into place.

19

———————

CLOSE TO THREE hours since leaving his apartment, Raph reached the turnoff for the Gold Coast, the tourist mecca of hotels and miles of golden beaches. Perfect.

He'd met Arthur at his shop and stayed there for a good two hours, giving Gray and Isa plenty of time to drive up to Maleny, and anyone looking for Isa plenty of time to spot her car in the city.

And the plan had worked perfectly. He'd spotted the tail as soon as he'd turned onto the main highway and had let them stay with him, on his bumper, the entire hour's drive. Damn, he was happy he and Gray had gone with this idea.

Now it was time to lose the car following him.

At the next roundabout, he flicked on his indicator and moved into the exit he was supposed to take; but at the last moment he spotted a tiny gap in traffic and veered out of his lane, back into the roundabout, and doubled back. Sure enough, the tail had followed him into the exit lane, but with the heavy traffic they had no choice but to leave the highway.

After thirty minutes of zigzagging to make sure the tail stayed lost, he took a final turn north to head up to the farm.

His phone buzzing had Raph glance at the screen, and his gut tightened. Why was Gray calling?

Checking his rearview mirror, he pulled into the next service station, parked in the farthest parking space from the building and hit redial.

"What?" he said as soon as Gray picked up.

"Change in the plan."

"Fuck off there's a change in the—"

"No time to explain. But Isa's safe. I can't be there tonight. That means you need to do this, Raph. Get the relic. Keep it safe. I'll be in touch."

"What—?"

"Here, speak to Isa." A fumbling sound echoed through the phone.

"Raph?"

"Isa? You're still with Gray? Where are you?"

"No time to talk, Raphael. But listen, you have to keep close to Eve, right? Whatever you do, stay close to Eve. And when the time comes, embrace the dark."

Raphael? She'd used his full name. The lead weight in his gut hardened. "Isadora, what the fuck is going on?"

"Got to go now. Love you. Talk soon. Close and dark, remember, Raph? Stay close!"

The line went dead.

Raph hit redial, but the line rang out. He tried again— nothing. "Damn it!" He banged his phone on the steering wheel. Then he dialed Isa's number.

It rang and rang and rang. Hell. Maybe Dad knew what was going on? He quickly called him, but he didn't know anything either. Raph took a moment to reassure his father that Isa was okay. And that better well be the case.

But what in the hell was going on?

Another car pulled in beside Raph on the right. Followed by another on his left. Oh hell. He quickly started the engine, jammed the gearshift into reverse, and was just pressing the gas pedal and checking the rearview mirror when he noticed the van parking behind him. Raph hit the brakes, jerking to a halt. And the bollards in front of his vehicle meant he wasn't going anywhere.

Bloody hell.

Four huge men piled out of the cars on either side of him; the nearest rested one hand on his roof and knocked politely on his window.

Raph lowered the window a fraction.

"Hey, boys. What's up?"

"Mr. Smith," the goon said. "Mr. Parsons wishes to talk with you in person. You need to come with us."

Raph glanced at the clock. It was close to eleven, and he had to be back in town within a couple of hours. "Tell you what, I've got some pressing business today, boys. How about I call Parsons instead?"

"No can do. We have very strict instructions." The lead goon nodded at the others, and they surrounded Isa's car. "We're here to make sure our boss gets what he wants."

"Right." Raph sighed. "Well, it looks like I'm seeing your boss today, then." Raph opened the door. "Why don't I follow you to wherever this meeting is meant to take place?"

"No, the boss prefers you to travel in our vehicle. We'll bring you back to your car after."

Okay, so at least they planned on letting him drive himself home. That was encouraging.

As he got out of the car, Raph took a deep breath and touched the car roof where the lead goon had placed his hand. With a whoosh, Raph was taken into a sepia-toned vision.

The lead goon was emerging from the mouth of a hellgate. Seven dark stone pillars rose to sharp points surrounding the gate, each column marked with a glyph of the seven levels of Hell.

Raph's blood iced over. This was no goon.

Fuck. No wonder Parsons had inside information on Raph. He had seventh-gate daemons working for him. Raph didn't need to see anymore, and the risk of something else coming through to the present from the past grew higher the longer he spent there, so he snipped the vision off.

"And so if you'll come this way, Mr. Smith," the lead daemon said.

Raph blinked as the real world came back into view. Bloody hell, what did Parsons have to do with a seventh-gate daemon?

Well, there was one way to find out. And it involved going to see Parsons. Right now.

As Raph locked Isa's car, the lead daemon slid the van's door open, revealing two more goons—were they daemons too?—sitting in the back seat.

"Quite a crew you've got here," Raph said mildly as he hopped inside.

"The boss says we gotta make sure you don't see nothing on the drive." The lead daemon threw a punch at Raph's jaw. Raph ducked and reacted with a swing of his own. Jabbed the guy in the gut.

"Drug him!" another goon snarled. Something jabbed into his arm, and Raph swung around—grabbed the person behind him.

Then a fist hit him in the cheek, and the lights went out.

Raph groaned as the world swam into clarity. A hammer was pounding away solidly across his temple, and cotton coated his mouth. He gingerly touched his cheek and hissed. Fuck, his head hurt everywhere. He blinked, and the spinning eased.

He was sitting on a long gray sofa opposite a wall-mounted television. He blinked again, and the rest of the room came into focus. A bed to one side. Block-out curtains along one wall. Was he in a hotel? And how long since they'd knocked him out?

Suddenly the television turned on, and Parsons appeared on the screen, looking like a shark sizing up its next meal. His pale hair was perfectly combed back from his face, and his predatory blue eyes coolly regarded Raph. His smile showed his teeth but with zero warmth.

"Welcome, Mr. Smith. My apologies about the unfortunate greeting my men provided."

"Not my usual way of saying hi." Raph scanned the room again. He was on his own—for now. "What did they give me?"

"Just a little concoction—mostly based on doxylamine. You should have little to no side effects."

"A simple blindfold would've done the trick."

"Rest assured, that's what will happen after our visit is over."

"So I will be leaving?" Raph said.

"Of course. I have hired you to do a job, Mr. Smith. That job is still a vital requirement."

"And I've still got one day left to get it to you, remember?"

"Well, you may find this interesting as my men were not looking for you. The room you're in now was meant for your sister."

"Why?" Ice trickled down Raph's spine.

"I felt your motivation to deliver on the contract in a timely manner might be waning. I assumed with your sister's influence, though, you'd be motivated enough to treat finding my property with the urgency the situation demands."

"We have a binding contract," Raph said. "You know there's no need for this, right?"

"Oh, of course, of course. I'm just so passionate about ensuring I get my property *quickly*; I don't want to miss any opportunity to have it returned speedily. And since my men found you instead of your sister, I've taken this opportunity to make clear how far my reach extends."

"I'm beginning to see exactly how far that reach goes. You have quite a few ... unusual resources. Who takes care of your hiring?"

"I like to be hands-on with my employees. It helps keep them ... on target."

Right. So, Parsons was a sixth-gate daemon or higher. Unless someone higher up the pecking order from Hell was pulling the strings and using Parsons? Bloody hell. The only way to know for sure was to see Parsons in the flesh.

"Maybe we could meet in person?" Raph said, forcing his voice to be as mild as possible. "Businessman to businessmen, you know?"

"I can safely say I'll be there to collect your delivery, Mr. Smith. And in the meantime, I'll keep this room ready, just in case your sister resurfaces. Are we clear?"

"Crystal."

"Perfect. I thought that might be the case. My men will now see you back to your sister's vehicle."

"Right." Raph stood—his knees wobbled, and his vision swam for a moment.

"Such a pity about your sister, though," Parsons said. "I had been looking forward to making her acquaintance. I wonder wherever may she be?"

The next moment, the door opened, and Parsons' squad piled into the room.

"Now," Parsons continued smoothly, "blindfold this time, gentlemen. While I appreciate your endeavors to meet my demands, I'm sure our visitor understands the situation."

Raph bit back a curse. Oh yeah, he understood all right. These daemons wanted the relic.

Fuck.

He let the daemon squad blindfold him and get him back into the van. Raph gauged roughly an hour had passed before they pulled to a stop and the engine turned off.

"We're here," the lead daemon said, jerking Raph's blindfold off and sliding open the door.

Raph blinked in the sudden light. But that wasn't bright midday light—this light had the golden tones of late afternoon. His stomach sank.

Head throbbing, Raph got into Isa's car as the daemon squad left the car park. He fumbled for his phone.

Bloody hell. It was five o'clock. And the phone had one percent battery left, and of course there wasn't a charger in Isa's car. But he got one message off to Eve to say he was running late and would meet her at the event.

The city of Brisbane lit the summer night sky far below Mount Coot-tha's summit, but after the rented limousine disappeared down the dark mountain road, Eve ignored the stunning view —and the butterflies rampaging in her stomach—and kept her gaze on the guards lining the entry to the event center.

She'd had the limo stop by Southern Moon so she could strengthen the spell on her bracelet, and that had taken some time, making her late for the auction. But given Raph's cryptic message, it had seemed like a good idea.

And now she was here. She'd had a tiny hope that Raph would be there when she arrived.

After Raph not phoning or answering her calls all after-noon, Eve assumed something bad had happened. But finally, Raph had texted to say something had happened that had held him up, and he'd fill her in later.

Fill her in? He'd better have a damned good reason for going AWOL.

Well, right now, Eve was on her own. And she was fine with that. She always had been in the past, so this would be no different. Time to use her forged invitation and Gray's hacking to lie her way into this auction and take her relic back.

In her too-tall heels, she strode to the building clutching her invitation in one hand and holding the crazy-tiny purse in the other. Pfft. The bag wasn't even big enough to hold her ceremonial knife, but Raph had gone all fashion connoisseur, as apparently nothing else would do.

Three security guards in black suits and curly-wire earpieces scanned the entrance, their gazes roving over everyone coming and going. Another security guard stood beside a glamorous woman who was focused on a laptop.

Eve joined the queue and, following the people ahead of her, handed her invite to the tuxedoed guard when it was her turn. He stared at her, then at the invitation. Then he murmured her name to the woman.

With her heart pounding—surely, they could hear it—Eve forced a smile and sharpened her accent to cut glass. "Good evening."

"And good evening, madam." The woman typed something into her laptop. "Welcome. And may I say, your dress is divine. And that bracelet ..." She stared for a long moment. "Why, it's stunning." She gave an elegant wave of one hand, and another guard behind her released a red velvet rope.

Well, at least one thing had worked. That boded well, right?

Heart still hammering, Eve kept her chin high and forced herself to walk calmly down the red-carpeted stairs toward a double entryway.

As she approached, ushers opened the doors, and then she was inside.

By the goddess.

The entry landing was several steps above a large circular room. Christmas trees covered in tiny shimmering gold lights ringed the walls, and chandeliers hung from the high ceiling, casting more golden light upon the people filling the room, beautiful in their suits and stunning dresses. Their laughs and voices high on champagne and glam.

But Eve ignored them all. Tonight was about one thing only.

Fake smile firmly in place, she grabbed a flute of frosty champagne from a passing waiter to keep her hands from tugging at the clinging material of her dress, and pretending to sip her drink, she leaned on the landing balustrade.

The auction items ringed the room, with spotlights shining down on each. Only a gold braided rope separated the throng of people from the precious goods. She frowned. What kind of security was that?

Pedestals held many unique items, a set of jewelry with green stones sparkling under the lights, a porcelain urn decorated in red-and-blue dragons, and next to that, something covered by a black cloth.

Eve's pulse quickened. Was that it? It would make sense if the relic was hidden. She strode down the steps, handed the champagne to a waiter and—

Ran into a hard wall of muscled masculinity encased in a sleek black tux. Her breath whooshed out. But there was no need to look up to know who it was. Raph's scent wrapped around her.

"Oops," Raph said.

Her legs trembled for one moment, and something hot and heady crashed and tumbled through her. Like the bubbles from her champagne were dancing in her belly. And lower.

Focus, Eve. The relic. The one way she could prove her innocence and stop the world from falling apart. And it was right there. Three more steps and she'd have it.

In fact, it was so close; she could take it now—

Raph took her arm and steered her toward the porcelain urn. "How clumsy of me," he said loudly, then pressed his face against her hair. "Get a grip. You can't just take it."

"It's right there," she whispered back. "Protected by a stupid-ass rope!"

"And the place is surrounded by guards and filled with innocent people. You take it now and all hell will break loose. Stick to the plan."

"Fine. But it's not leaving my sight."

"You can't stay here all night."

She arched one brow.

"Good evening," a cultured voice said from behind her. "They are beautiful pieces, aren't they now? They'd all make a truly perfect Christmas gift."

Eve eased around. *Francisco Frinecki*. After studying him and his business over the past week, she'd recognize his face anywhere. Her blood iced. She could stun the bastard right now—

"Yes," Raph said. He squeezed her arm, and she reluctantly dropped the spell. Crapola. *Not the place. Not the place.* "We're admiring the urn."

"It is a stunning piece indeed."

"Yuan dynasty, right?" Raph asked. "Made from white china clay."

Eve kept her gaze on Frinecki—never turn your back on a shark and all that—but she wanted to gape at Raph. He made this shit up so easily.

"You know your porcelain," Frinecki replied.

Really? Raph had been right? Lucky guess or yet another side to the more and more mysterious Raphael Smith? Her gut said the latter.

"It's a pastime of mine," Raph murmured. "I love beautiful things."

"As do I." Frinecki's gaze roved down Eve's dress, and something crawled inside her. "The urn is from my personal collection. I've donated it tonight to help raise funds for children in need. Such a worthy cause."

The crawlies congealed into outright disgust. How dare he sound so pleased with himself when he was—?

"You're a truly generous person," Raph said, his voice sycophantic. His grip stayed firm on her arm, although he pulled Eve into his side as if they were meant to hold on to each other. "And it's your stunning piece that brought my wife and me here tonight."

Wife? Being married wasn't part of the plan. She couldn't help it this time and turned to him—a series of scratches marred his cheek, the surrounding skin red and purple and angry. What, by the goddess, had happened to Raph? Was this why he'd disappeared?

"And I have to say the urn isn't the only stunning thing here tonight," Frinecki continued. "You ... your dress is perfection, my dear. Just seeing you has made my evening."

"That's ... lovely of you to say." Eve forced her attention back to the relic-stealing bastard whose men had stabbed her. She somehow held in her grimace. What were you meant to say to bullshit like that?

"The truth is always easy." Frinecki waved a hand in the air. "Is it not?"

"Mm," she murmured under her breath. No way she could make up anything coherent to that line. Time to do away with the crap. She had a mission to accomplish. "So, do you know what's under the black cloth?" Eve nodded toward her relic. "Is it from another patron such as you who's donated something amazing to the auction?"

"Ah, that's a secret item. And one of mine. But I can assure you it'll be worthwhile for anyone who has the means to purchase it. And of course, the children will be the ones who benefit."

"Oh, of course." Eve held in a snort. She had no idea what percentage of the auction sales actually went to the cause they were championing, but everything she knew about this asshole screamed he was getting way more out of this event than they were.

"There will be dancing later as well. Perhaps you could save me a dance Ms. ...?" Frinecki raised one brow.

Eve stared at his face. Was he for real?

"Stanley," Raph cut in. "Sarah. And I'm Andrew Stanley."

"Sarah and Andrew Stanley," Frinecki said. "How lovely to meet you both."

"And you, too. We're very fortunate to meet such a giving benefactor to the community. Now, *darling*," Raph said easily, "I heard the view of the city is stunning from the terrace. Why don't we take a look before the auction starts?"

20

Raph plastered a fake smile on his face and guided Eve through the throng of event goers and waitstaff—battling the urge to have a pissing contest with every single person who looked at Eve like she was the most fucking delicious thing there.

Because damn, she was.

Raph had just come inside from the terrace when an itch teased the skin at the back of his neck. He'd stopped in the shadow of the doorway. Looked around. And then his gaze had been drawn up like it was being reeled in.

His breath had whooshed away. His chest had gone all tight and tingly.

Eve was magnificent.

And yeah, the gold dress was hot—the sequins shining under the chandeliers making her look like a golden statue. But that hadn't been it. Her mysterious eyes had surveyed the room. Her skin glowed. Her dark hair was out, falling in tamed waves down her back like a 1940s Hollywood star.

No wonder Frinecki had made a beeline for her. The bastard.

But then Eve had gone all mission critical and practically run for what she thought was the relic. He had his doubts. And he'd had no choice but to intercept her to stop her stuffing this up. Now he just needed a quiet place—as quiet as they were going to get in the middle of a bloody gala event—to bring her up to speed.

"Over here," Raph murmured, pretending to smile into Eve's hair. "The view is stunning."

Finally, he led Eve over to the railing, ignoring the stunning view of the city skyline lit up below them.

"Raph!" The shadows on the terrace darkened Eve's eyes as she looked over his face. "What, by the goddess, happened?"

"Yeah, sorry about the late thing."

"And that?" She nodded at his cheek.

Raph quickly filled her in about Parsons still wanting the relic. Left out the one little part she might've taken objection to, the fact Raph *had* to deliver on the contract. Tomorrow.

"So this ex-client really wants the relic?" Eve went stiff in his arms. "Why didn't you mention that before now?"

"I didn't want to worry you—and I honestly didn't know the whole story until today."

"Well, it's not your choice about whether or not to 'worry me.' Goddess, we need to get the relic. Now."

"I'm sorry—I should have said something sooner about my client. But I agree, we need to find the relic quickly."

"So let's head inside and take it."

"I don't think it's under the cloth. That's way too public for a stolen item. Trust me, the relic is somewhere else. But I have an idea about that. And we need to regroup re getting out of here. Gray's gone. Isa too."

"What? Do you mean still up at the farm?"

"No. As in gone—they never made it to the farm. And Isa's with Gray. I have no idea—" A group of event goers wandered over to them, laughing and sipping on their drinks. "How amazing is this view?" Raph said loudly. Then he leaned in even closer to Eve. "There's an office on the lower level that's guarded by one of Frinecki's people," he whispered into Eve's neck. He pretended to nuzzle the skin right there. "Can you stun them if we need to?"

A shiver trembled through Eve, and she shifted, her lips almost touching his.

"Of course. But without a salt circle, the coven will find me with a spell that strong in no time."

"Then we leave the stun until the last moment—if needed—before we get the hell out of here. Did your bracelet spell work?"

"Yes," she whispered. "And it's strong. The woman at the front door couldn't take her eyes off it."

Raph couldn't stop his gaze from dipping down to her lips. So close. So lush. Right there. Heat built in his gut, in his veins. In his dick.

A growl sat low in his throat. Bloody hell, he wanted her. His body tightened. He dipped his head—

He stopped himself just in time.

"Come on." Pulse hammering, Raph tucked Eve's arm in his. "We need to go."

Otherwise, he was going to blow the plan completely out of the water and make a spectacle right here on the terrace. Thankfully she didn't argue—a first—and even leaned into him as if they were a couple.

A pang of something almost ... wishful hit him in the gut. Even though he was nearly certain she wasn't involved in the original theft of the relic; she was not what he wished for. Eve was leaving after this relic business. And no question, she wouldn't want to speak to him ever again once she knew all the truths he hadn't shared.

"So," Raph said, "between my recce the other day—"

"Recce?"

"Reconnaissance." Raph snagged them each a glass of champagne. "Here, pretend to drink this. Now, the other day when I came up here to meet with the event company, I got a quick look at the back-of-house areas. There's an entire section that you need a staff card to enter."

"Well, that's going to make it hard."

"And that's why I'm the PI here." He took a pretend sip of the bubbly and surveyed the crowd between them and the staff door. Then he withdrew a staff card from the inner pocket of his jacket. "Something I appropriated the other day."

"Oh, well done," Eve said.

"Be prepared. It's a PI motto."

"Isn't that the Boy Scouts?"

Raph shrugged. "Not the point. The point is that we have it."

"Will it still work?"

"Let's hope. Otherwise, I'll need to get another. See the door with the security guard out front? Through there is a corridor leading to all the staff rooms. There's at least one large office that I saw last time. Frinecki's come and gone from that corridor on multiple occasions, so I'd bet the relic is somewhere there."

"Why don't you think it's right here under the black drape?"

"Because none of Frinecki's henchmen—"

"Henchpeople. He's got women on the payroll too."

"Fine. None of his hench*people* are watching that item. But they're coming and going from this corridor. That tells me there's something special in there. Not up here. And they're not putting the relic up for auction. No way. It's too risky."

"Then why is it here at all if it's not going up for auction?"

"Good question. Don't know the answer to that yet. Okay, here we go—one of Frinecki's henchpeople is heading our way now. Quick, dance with me."

"No one else is dancing."

"Doesn't matter." Raph pulled Eve in and began to sway with her to the croony music coming from the singer and band. She fit him perfectly—she was tall enough that every curve and hollow met exactly the right angle of his body. And for one minute, everything else drifted away, and his world narrowed to dancing with Eve in his arms.

"What next?" Eve whispered into his neck.

He forced his attention back to the task. "We watch that door." Moments later, Frinecki's henchpeople swapped places. Raph checked the time.

Bingo.

"They're rotating the watch every fifteen minutes. They'd only do that for something important," Raph muttered into Eve's hair. "We need to get into that corridor on the next swap over. I've got the swipe card—but we need to get rid of the henchperson. How long does your bracelet spell last?"

"I've got it up to thirty seconds," Eve said. "I can drop it. If the beads scatter, their attention might go to more than one. Probably better than having them stare at my wrist anyway."

"No, it still needs to look real. Can you fall over— pretend to be drunk, maybe?"

"Fine. But I never get drunk. I'll pretend I tripped over your giant ego."

"There's something else big you could fall over. But my ego will do for a backup option."

She snorted. "Your feet?"

He laughed and brought her closer.

"Hey, why so tight?"

"Making it look real," he responded. Which was a total lie. She just made him so bloody … happy that he'd reacted like she really was his wife.

And then her arms tightened around him too, and he let the fantasy roll.

In the background, the laughs were getting louder, and the MC announced the auction would start soon.

And eventually, the next changeover happened.

"This is it." Raph reluctantly let Eve go. "Make sure you fall right in front of the henchperson. I'll be over there."

Eve tripped and fell. Her bracelet broke apart, the large glass beads rolling over the floor, and she started to moan and groan about her ankle.

"Don't overdo it," he mouthed. But apparently, Eve's moan was the right amount of groan because the hench-person helped Eve up, right as one of the bespelled beads rolled past.

Raph had complete trust in Eve's spell and didn't stick around to see any more. He swiped the stolen staff card against the reader. Eve was backing toward him, watching the hench-woman, so he grabbed her arm and yanked her after him.

The corridor was empty, but Raph still ran to the only door there with a card swipe attached and used the staff card again. This time, Eve was right there with him.

The office had a large desk in the corner and two smaller

pods of workstations nearer to him. One wall had a closed door in the middle, and the rest were covered in shelves. A whiteboard with what looked like the layout of the auction sat in the middle of the room.

"You take the desk. I'll check through there." Raph waved toward the internal door.

Eve nodded and slipped off her high heels.

Raph strode to the other side of the room. The handle had a standard lock, but luckily, he had something that would take care of that easily enough. He took out his toolkit from his inside pocket. The slimline black case looked like a vanity kit, but its utensils could do more than just snip or clean a fingernail.

Raph picked the lock in no time.

A flick of the light switch revealed a large walk-in storage space, half-full of office furniture and filing cabinets.

"Raph!" Eve furiously whispered.

"What?" he mouthed, joining her.

She jabbed a finger toward the corridor outside the office. Oh shit—multiple voices were coming from right there.

Raph grabbed Eve's arm and pulled her into the storage space. It was a bit tight in the room, but he and Eve fit comfortably enough among the stored furniture and cabinets. He flicked the light switch off and closed the door as quietly as possible.

In the pitch black, he dropped to his knees and searched for the handle. Shit. He had to set the lock now. With fast, precise movements, Raph reengaged the lock from his side, using touch only. *Come on, baby. Come on, baby. Yes!* The lock clicked.

"This way," one voice—masculine—said. He heard a

combination of footsteps, the slap of flats and the click of heels crossing the room.

Raph winced. Stilled. Didn't even breathe.

"I thought we might have our own toast," the masculine voice continued. Frinecki. No question. Raph finally exhaled —controlling his breath so he didn't make a sound. Shit, that had been close.

"Well, I do love a celebration, Frankie," a muffled feminine voice, heavy with a British accent. "But here?"

"The package will be arriving within the hour," Frinecki said. "And I thought you might like to see where the sale will take place."

"Why here, Frankie? The event is so much ... nicer."

"Ah, but up there, you have so many eyes. Here we have complete privacy."

Still on his knees, Raph plastered his ear to the door to make out as much of the conversation as possible. Moments later, Eve's shoulders and hips grazed his as she knelt beside him. He sensed her pressing her ear to the door too.

And she had to be facing him because her breath whispered over him.

It was so dark Raph couldn't see a bloody thing, but holy hell, he could feel her. Smell her. Breathe her in.

Desire surged through his veins, and he closed his eyes. Not that it mattered. His senses were filled with her.

Not the place. Not the place. But his dick was having absolutely fucking zero of that.

"I do love the way you say my name, my dear Caterina," said Frinecki.

Eve gasped. Raph grabbed her shoulder—shit, she was so tense she was shaking—and whispered into her ear, "Sh!"

In the office, Frinecki continued, "Plus, this was the only room where we can be assured of privacy. Part of my arrangement with the event company is to have private space for my ... respite."

"Rest?" asked the woman. "Is that what you want?"

"No. Since our business won't occur until the end of the night, what I want is more of that pussy you gave me a taste of in Rome."

"Well, since the deal doesn't go down for a while, how about you do?"

"With pleasure. Although once we've kicked the celebration off, I need to rejoin the party."

"And I need to circulate. Keep an eye out for our meddlesome Watcher. Really, Frankie, why your men haven't managed to get rid of her is beyond me."

"You did say this would be handled back in Europe, dearest. Remember?"

"Turns out our little miss perfect was hiding a streak of rebellion a mile wide. But never mind. The coven is actively tracing her magic. They'll call me the moment they track anything."

"They trust you that much?"

"Of course." Then the slide of a zipper, followed by the swoosh of fabric, whispered through the door. "Well, what are you waiting for? We don't have long. And don't mess my hair."

"In that case, let me do this."

The woman gasped, then moaned. "Well, that was a good starter," the woman said. "Now give me the main meal."

Raph recoiled. Oh shit. They were going to go for it— right there?

21

Kneeling with Raph in the pitch black, as Caterina and Frinecki moaned and groaned and flesh slapped on the other side of the door, Eve bared her teeth in a silent snarl. She could stun Frinecki and that fucking traitor Caterina—right fucking now.

How dare the red-haired trainer pretend to be the perfect fucking Watcher and then steal the very thing their magic protected?

And given the slaps and groans and gasps coming from the office—ew—Eve could take them both out with no challenge. Stunned naked traitorous ass sounded like a plan—

Raph cupped her cheek. The vitality of his palm on her skin made her blink. Then he whispered, "Wait. The relic's coming here. We just have to *wait*. Stun them now and you'll reveal your magic while we have to delay for an hour until the relic arrives."

How did Raph know what she was thinking? She silently gnashed her teeth at having to hold back. But damn it, he was right.

And now they knew for sure the relic—*her* relic—would

be in that room in one hour's time. And they were in the perfect position to take it back.

Eve bit her lip to suppress the urge to shout out. Thank the goddess, all their effort—Isa's, Gray's, Raph's—everything they'd done to help her, it had worked.

"Okay," she breathed. "No stun."

In the office, slaps and groans and the slide of flesh on flesh continued. Frinecki's grunts quickened.

"He sounds like a quick fire. This'll be over soon," Raph whispered so quietly the words touched her lips more than her ears.

On the other side of the door, Caterina's moans grew louder. Goddess, she clearly didn't care about the henchpeople outside hearing anything. "Yes, yes, yes," Caterina cried out. Frinecki groaned in unison with Caterina's gasps.

Eve took a deep, slow breath—and inhaled Raph's scent. Heat bloomed in her belly. Her nipples pebbled. He was so close, *they* were so close, but goddess, she wanted to be closer. She shifted forward. His body stiffened.

His breathing shortened, and where their knees touched, he pressed into her.

And there in the dark with Raph, everyone else disappeared.

Eve rose on her knees. Raph did too, and their thighs and hips met. Inhaling a rasping breath, she reached for his arm. His muscles tensed beneath her touch, then she felt her way down his forearm, his wrist, to his palm.

His fingers interlaced with hers. The skin between her fingers tingled, and an answering tingle quivered through her core.

She drew his hand to her thigh, dragged his palm up, the fabric of her dress bunching beneath his grip. Higher, higher, she pulled him until, finally, his palm met her skin.

He grasped her thigh, clenching so tight she'd wear his fingerprints, then she pulled his hand farther, higher. His fingertips grazed below her tiny panties.

Raph paused, fingers dallying.

Oh no. No, no, no, no, no. He had to keep going. Eve tugged him higher, and a soundless growl vibrated through his chest. Heat drenched her core.

Finally, goddess finally, he swept beneath her panties, traced her and then dipped between her folds. Found her clit.

Oh, sweet goddess, yes. *Yes.* Eve bit back a whimper. Then he ran his finger back and forth until her flesh throbbed and her core clenched. He dipped inside and stroked deep, and her nerve endings screamed, gathered. His wicked fingers moved faster ... firmer ... faster still ... She gasped, and his mouth suddenly covered hers, and then she convulsed as her orgasm slammed through her.

Outside, muted laughter and footsteps once more echoed through the door. "How's my dress?" Caterina asked.

"Perfect. Now, after you, my dear," Frinecki said.

Eve should've been relieved as the door clicked shut, but in the darkness, with her core still throbbing for Raph's touch, his lips on hers, his hand on her flesh, nothing else mattered.

"They're gone," Raph whispered against her lips. "But fuck, Eve ... do you know how much I've dreamed of hearing you cry out? Every time I close my eyes, I see you shivering in my arms. I hear *your* cries. *Your* gasps. *Your* breath hitching when I lick you up."

Oh goddess, yes, she wanted that too. No, *needed* that. Eve's body clenched. Heat flooded her core again. Her nipples tightened. How could whispered words be so damned sexy?

"More," she breathed back over him. "Tell me more."

"I want to lay you down right here. Want to devour you and breathe you in. Want your scent all around me. Part of me. Inside me. I want to pinch your nipples as you come," his decadent voice continued through the dark. "And then I want to bury myself inside you."

A shiver shook through Raph. Answering wetness drenched her. Oh, goddess, Eve needed this. And wasn't her relic practically in sight? She widened her mouth and claimed him right there with her tongue.

"Raph," she whispered into their kiss and grabbed his cock through his pants. "I need to touch you, too."

"Yes," Raph growled. "Yes, yes, yes."

He thrust into her grip. She couldn't contain a smile.

"Sh," she cautioned him. "Henchpeople are still outside."

"I don't care," he bit out. "They could storm in here with an army, and as long as you get a hand on my dick, I'll die happy."

Oh goddess, Raph delighted her. Eve fumbled with his belt buckle, tugged the leather free, then yanked his pants and underwear down. His cock brushed against her.

Damn, but she wished she could see it. At least his hard, thick length filled her grip. She ran her palm over the satiny tip. Her mouth went dry.

"Raph," Eve whispered, "you've been keeping this away from me?" He let out a strangled moan, hips surging back and forth.

"Hell, I don't have a condom. Any chance you have one in that bag?" he whispered.

"The tiny bag you insisted went with this dress? No." She stroked up his shaft. Reveled in the way his body trembled at her touch. "But I can think of something else we can do. Stand up."

She stayed on her knees as he rose to his feet, then she dipped her head, blew a breath over his flesh. "I'm about to enjoy this. A lot."

He groaned. "Same here. But are you sure?"

"My panties are soaked right now just thinking about tasting you." She swirled her tongue around him. "Drinking you down when you come in my mouth."

A growl vibrated through his chest. "Gods, witch, you are going to be the death of me."

"Maybe just the little death, huh?" She smiled and took him into her mouth.

A moan hummed through him.

"Sh," she whispered around his cock. And then she tasted him deeply, ran her tongue down his length.

He cupped her head, and his hands clenched in her hair as, again and again, she moved up and down his length, taking him as far as she could, then releasing him all the way to the tip.

Raph's hum grew louder, and his hips thrust forward—his grip on her hair tightened—she ran a hand over the delicate skin beneath his cock.

And then he stiffened. Musk and salt flooded her mouth as he came and came and came.

She licked her lips and settled back on her knees.

"You taste amazing," she whispered.

"Come here," he whispered back and pulled her to her feet. In the dark, his lips met hers, and he kissed her deeply, his tongue dancing with hers.

"Now it's my turn. Stand still." She felt him sink to his knees in front of her.

And just like that, her body responded. Aching. Weeping. For him.

He bunched her dress back up again, the cool air drifting over the back of her knees, her thighs, then to her core when he pulled her panties aside.

He leaned in; his hot breath washed over her folds, then his mouth was on her. Nerve endings coiled and pressure gathered in her core. Oh goddess—more, more of that touch. She jammed her palms flat against the wall to hold her up and couldn't stop the gasp that escaped her.

"Sh," he whispered against her.

"I know." She wiggled to create her own friction. "More!"

"Always so bossy. Can you handle it?" His wicked tongue did crazy things to her flesh again. "Silently."

"The next sound will be your shout of pain when I hex you if you don't bloody finish me."

She dug her fingers into his hair and held him where she needed him. Yes, more of that pressure, right here.

Raph's groan vibrated through the dark.

"Princess—"

"More!"

"Yes, madam."

His mouth moved on her flesh again. The pressure deepened. The coil tightened. She flung her head back. Bit her lip. And then she went flying.

When she returned to earth, she sank to her knees in front of him, and this time, *she* kissed him.

Raph cupped Eve's jaw and worshipped her lips exactly like she deserved. Her mouth ... holy gods, he hadn't expected what she'd done to him.

Finally, he lifted his head. "Baby, next time we do this, I need to see you. Like all of you."

Eve hauled in a breath, the sound stuttering through the dark. "Baby? Think I prefer princess."

"Seriously, we need to do this again. I've had you in my dreams. And now for real, in the dark. But I need to do this with you in the light. When I can make you scream your lungs out."

"Huh. What about you? I want to lick every inch of that chest. I want to sit on top and make you beg for more."

"So what, a competition to see who makes the other beg the loudest?"

Her low chuckle made the hairs on the back of his arms rise. Fuck, but he wished he could see her now.

"Eve, would you mind if I did something?"

"What—more than going down on each other?"

"Uh, yeah. It'll sound weird, but I need to touch you."

Raph had to know she was real. Right now, this experience was just so bloody surreal—and so bloody amazing—it could be another dream. The sounds of her breathing filled the storage space before she picked up his hand.

"I'm right here," she whispered. "Touch away."

He followed the line of her arm, up to her shoulder, to her collarbone, and up to her neck and her face. He cupped her jaw and ran a thumb over the full curve of her lower lip. Eve didn't move; she seemed to understand this was necessary for him.

He didn't examine the need too closely. Could hardly put it into words for himself. But everything in him had to know her right here. And if he couldn't see her, he'd do it this way instead.

22

———

An hour later, sounds echoed again from the office—numerous voices and footsteps. Raph stilled. At his side, Eve stilled too. Together they eased toward the door and pressed their ears close.

"And here it is, the real rarity of the night," Frinecki's voice said.

"Frinecki," Raph whispered. Eve squeezed his hand.

"Safe and sound," another masculine voice said. "Where do you want me to put it?" The voice was familiar ... Raph mentally clicked his fingers. Michael Frinecki—the head baddie from the day at Arthur Stanley's antique shop. And the man who'd stabbed Eve.

Raph barely restrained a growl. That guy was going down. Only Eve's hand tightening on his again had him stop from doing something rash. *Focus. Get the job done.* Don't blow this because you're angry.

And angry wasn't even close to describing how he felt.

"On the desk. But keep it in its case. And then stand guard outside the door. Wait for our buyer. No one else comes in here until my business is complete."

"So, I finally get to see my redemption again." It was the woman from earlier.

"It would seem so, my dear," Frinecki said. "Now, where's our buyer?"

"All in good time. They'll be here soon enough. Now please, may I see it again? One last time?"

"For you, of course. After all, if you hadn't cleared the wards, I wouldn't be about to make more money in one deal than I ever have before."

"Always about the money, Frankie."

"You may have your witchcraft, but my power comes from money. Pure and simple."

"Don't you even want to know what this little box can do, though?"

"No, I told you. Money is my god. You can take the rest."

"If you insist. Now, perhaps one kiss for old times' sake?" asked the woman.

"The buyer is due any moment, my dear. As much as I enjoy our ... time together, this is business."

"Tsk, tsk, like I said, always about the money. Oh well, you won't get one last taste."

Eve squeezed Raph's hand twice. He squeezed back. That line had sounded ... permanent.

"Once our buyer has departed," Frinecki said, "then I'm all yours."

"Oh, Frankie. So blinded by the money that you missed one small, itsy-bitsy detail. The only one departing right now is you."

"Why do you have a knife? Why are you cutting yourself?"

"This is my athame," the woman replied. "A ritual knife. But don't worry—I'd never sully the blade with actually stabbing you. But I do need my blood for a spell." The woman fired off the words to the same spell Eve had first used back in the antique shop.

"Caterin—" Frinecki's voice stopped midword.

A surge of electricity that made the hairs on the back of Raph's neck stand up washed through the storage room.

"Ooh, that face is perfect," the woman continued in the office. "Just perfect. I call it stunned mullet. You do it quite well, Frankie. And now for something more permanent. Strike once and mount the knife. Strike twice and raise the strife. Strike thrice and end the life. Mark my words and make it so."

"The door!" Eve said. "Open the door now."

"What the fuck?" Raph felt around for the lockpick. There. He jabbed the pins back in the lock. "Wait—"

"Caterina's alone," Eve said. I'll take her; you get the relic. And stay low." Eve barreled into the office.

Oh shit.

Eve's gut tightened as she leaped into the office. She was too late. Frinecki's horrified ashen face was turned toward Caterina, his entire body frozen in motion.

"I knew it was you." Eve shook her head at herself. "Who else could've gotten through the ward and just happened to be in Rome?"

"Yes, you should have," Caterina said. "But alas, you were entirely too trusting."

"And yet here I am."

"Yes, I suppose you've proven not to be so blindly trusting after all. Not that it matters."

"Why?"

"Why did I steal the gift of gold?"

"Why all of it? You're a Watcher."

"Because of the likes of you. Because all I ever got were the training gigs. The real deal? The prestige of casting the wards to keep everything safe? Oh no, they had to go only to the best of the best." Caterina's lip curled. "You. As if."

"You did all this out of your pathetic jealousy and ego over me?" Eve said.

"No! I did all this for *me*. I'm going to take the relic now that Frankie here has done the deed of bringing it to me. I know its power. I know how to use it."

"So you used Frinecki to steal the relic? And then what? He was useless?"

"A little sex and the lure of a fortune, and Frankie was putty in my hands—or pussy if you like. He had the contacts to smuggle the relic out of Italy, so he was necessary. But yes, tonight was always going to be his last night on this earth. At least he had a good time."

"You're a fucking praying mantis," Eve said.

Caterina threw her head back and laughed. "Oh, I do like that. Praying mantis indeed. Think I'll keep that one. Along with the relic."

"My relic will be coming with me."

"I'll give you one chance—since you've proven to be so resourceful. Join me. With the power of the three gifts, we can rule these pitiful excuses for life-forms," Caterina said.

"You're kidding, right? You know what I think? I think you've used all your magic to stun and kill Frinecki. You don't have anything left—unless you've got a source you can tap into?"

"I've got something else." Caterina's eyes lit up. "Guards!" she screamed.

The outer door crashed open. Michael Frinecki and another henchman ran inside, drawing guns from within their jackets. They skidded to a stop, heads swiveling from Frinecki to Caterina to Eve and back again.

"What the fuck's going on?" Michael yelled.

"She killed him!" Caterina pointed at Eve. "And they're trying to steal the relic. Stop her now!"

"Raph, you've got it?" Eve shouted, keeping her gaze on the advancing henchmen. "I'll get Caterina."

"Got it!" Raph yelled from the back of the office. "But don't worry about her. Worry about the guns."

"I can spell—"

"Not enough time. Listen, boys, we're at a party. Put the guns—"

"Shut up!" Michael waved his weapon at Raph. "And stay right here. Don't fucking move."

Caterina ran out through the door. Eve went to chase her—

"Stop!" Michael said. "One more step and you're both goners, party or not. Now hand it over. Again."

Eve gnashed her teeth as the door swung shut. Damn it. She couldn't call two stun spells, not without a lot of backup power. And Raph was on the other side of the office, so she couldn't borrow his power. But no way was she giving the relic up this time. She had to do something—even if Raph had cautioned her against it.

Eve grabbed her pendant and, under her breath, muttered the Spell of Shadows. *Come on. Come on. Come on.* At the last moment, she let the crystal channel the power, but this time she kept a tight hold on the spell. The shadows grew from the corners of the room, from beneath the desk, from behind the men.

"Put your guns down. Now," Eve said.

"You're loopy, right?" Michael Frinecki laughed. "We've got the guns. You've got nothing."

"You see what happened to your boss? Look at what's coming for you next."

"Eve," Raph said, "what are you—?"

She let the spell fly, and the shadows roared to life. They streamed into the room. An endless torrent of dark.

Michael Frinecki's eyes bugged out—right as shadows swallowed him. He screamed and something crashed to the floor.

"Eve, you have to stop them," Raph yelled as he ran to her. "Now!"

The shadows reached the other henchman, and he too screamed before the shadows engulfed him.

"I've got this." Goddess, please let that be right. "*Clear the path, stave the night, show the dark, bring the light.*" But Eve couldn't let go of the crystal. It was like last time—the gemstone bonded to her skin.

And the shadows didn't clear. They grew and grew and grew. A lump suddenly stuck fast in her throat. She cleared it and said the spell again.

Nothing.

"Eve, don't move!" Raph said.

The shadows. Had the pressure in the room intensified? Why couldn't she breathe? Raph's hand clutched hers.

"Eve, whatever you do, do not let go of me. Got it?" Raph's voice echoed through the thick air, right at her ear.

She nodded as the shadows encroached farther, surrounding her and Raph. Oh goddess, what had she done?

Raph went still. She whirled to him, still trying to wrench her hand from the crystal. *Let go. Let go. Let go.*

"Raph! I can't let g—!"

"Sh," Raph whispered. He drew her hand to his lips, and in his glittering gaze, flames began to burn ... richer ... deeper. Then his lips tightened. Those beautiful, decadent, sinful lips ...

Suddenly the heaviness in the air dwindled, and the crystal fell away from Eve's grip as if she'd never begun the spell. The shadows disappeared, revealing chairs upended, tables on their sides, papers strewn everywhere, and the bodies of the henchmen lying on the floor, their faces withered shells—cheeks hollow, eyes sunken. Oh goddess, no.

"I killed them," Eve said.

"You didn't," Raph said. "The shadows did."

Eve cradled the box with the relic to her chest as she got out of the taxi in front of Raph's building. Her stomach was a mass of jitters, and even with the relic in hand, she couldn't relax until they were in Raph's apartment and behind the safety of her ward.

"Are you sure I can't help you—?" Raph asked.

"No." Eve elbowed Raph's attempt to take the box away as he came around from the other side of the car. "This is my responsibility. Let's get inside. Quickly."

"Okay, okay." Raph strode to the foyer, carrying Eve's shoes and her stupid purse, and keyed them into the lobby.

What, by the goddess, had just happened? Heart still pounding, she cut Raph another glance. His lips were still tight, and his jaw clenched. What did he know about the shadows? Well, he was about to tell her everything he knew.

And she wasn't calling the Spell of Shadows—was it even a spell?—ever again.

Inside the apartment, Eve checked the ward on the front door as soon as Raph closed it behind him. The spell was intact, but she added another layer just in case.

"So what next?" Raph asked once she was done.

"I need to get back to Rome and get the relic to safety. Then I can clear my name and get the coven onto Caterina."

"You really mean that, don't you?" His eyes glittered brighter than ever—and something in his voice made her stop.

Eve scowled at Raph. "Why do you think I've been doing all this? For shits and giggles? Of course I mean that. The relic needs to be safe."

"Uh, yeah. It's just—never mind. So how will you convince the coven ... and others ... that you weren't involved? What if they say you're just bringing it back because you got caught?"

"Now I know Caterina was involved; I'll let them do a truth spell on me and use the relic as leverage to make them do a truth spell on her."

"Maybe." Raph shrugged. "Just let me think on it and see if I can come up with any other options."

"Thanks, but I'm not waiting."

"At least let me see if I can get some help through Gray —he has contacts in some unlikely places. Plus, like you said, we need to get your passport and get you on a plane. None of which is happening this second."

He was right, damn it. Eve reluctantly nodded.

"Do you want me to put it somewhere safe for tonight?" Raph nodded at the relic. "After what happened back at the ..."

At the event. Where the shadows Eve had called had killed two people. Not that she minded killing them—but that hadn't been her plan. And *that* was the concern.

"Raphael, what are they?"

"The shadows?"

"Yes. What happened? How did they—what did you do—?"

"Eve, you don't know what you're dealing with there. The shadows aren't ..." Raph tunneled a hand through his hair, frustration pouring off him in waves. "I can't tell you what they are. But I told you last time—never *ever* call the shadows. Especially never near me."

Eve slid the box closer to her chest. What did that mean, never near him? "Raph. Raphael. Look at me."

He turned to her; jaw clenched so hard it ticked. The iridescent flames in his eyes had lowered to a simmer, but they still lurked in his gaze.

"Who are you?" she breathed.

"Me? How about this—who are *you*? How can you command the shadows?"

"Command? That was the opposite of what I had there."

"Eve, you have more control than any witch I have ever known." He stalked to her, heat and grace and danger in motion. "Tell me."

Her mouth went dry. And moisture drenched her core. Goddess, but she wanted that body again. Now.

"I don't want to say another word until after."

"After what?" he rasped.

Eve lifted her chin and challenged his stare. Her nipples tightened as her breasts grazed his chest.

"You and I." She hooked her finger beneath the waistband of his pants and tugged him tight against her. The proof of how much he wanted her jabbed her in the belly. "Finish what we started. As in sex. You and me. In the light. On this kitchen bench. In your bed. In the shower. Every single way possible."

23

———

RAPH'S GLITTERING gaze locked on her lips. Eve licked them, mouth suddenly parched. His jaw clenched, and a feminine thrill raced through her.

"About fucking time," Raph growled.

"Well," she murmured, "it's certainly time to get to the fu—"

His lips swooped on hers, swallowing the rest of her words. His arms went around her, and he pulled her even tighter. His cock pressed between her legs, his chest against her breasts, and his tongue surged into her mouth, stroking, demanding, owning.

Oh yes, Eve was into this.

She tasted him back, branded him, marked him as hers, even if only for one night. She pressed harder into him, against that wonderful thickness right where she needed it. But there were still too many layers between them.

She fumbled for his pants—

"Uh-uh," Raph whispered into her mouth. "I've had this fantasy ... for days now ... of feasting on you right here."

Eve looked around in a daze. "Here?"

His lips pulled back in a feral grin. "You said it." He nodded at the long expanse of the kitchen counter. Then he picked her up and set her on the counter as if she weighed nothing. He stepped between Eve's thighs and gathered the material of her dress, pushing it up her legs as he moved closer.

"I'm going to eat you up." Raph's gaze locked on her core as he pushed the material past her panties.

Oh goddess, he was sin walking. The tilt of his lips. The hard planes of his jaw. Dark hair falling over his brow. And his eyes—the way he looked at her like she was a feast and he was starving ... her body clenched.

Raph grasped her hips and slid her farther up the counter. The granite was cool beneath her—the exact opposite of his hot breath as he kissed her through her panties.

Electricity shot through her, and she pushed herself up as he yanked the scrap of material down her legs and threw them away. And then he was back.

Eve gasped as he gripped her thighs, held her open, dipped his head.

"Evangeline," he said against her flesh. "I've been wanting to whisper your name—feel how it rolls off my lips." He licked her up. Her back arched. "Say it as I kiss you right here." He stroked her again. Her core clenched. "Make you come. E ... van ... geline."

Then his wicked, heavenly tongue flicked her clit, over and over, until she was a ball of screaming nerves, and then he tongued her deeply, hotly, and the pressure crested. She cried out, held his head to her as he drank her in. Feasted. Even as the tremors in her thighs subsided, he licked her one last time.

Eve dropped back to the counter, caught her breath.

Then levered herself up on one elbow. "Wow. Just wow. You can say my name any time you want."

"You liked?" Raph straightened, still in his black pants and white shirt, bow tie hanging from his neck. Lips gleaming.

"Oh, you know, just another orgasm." Like the third-best orgasm of her life. But Raph was already way too cocky for her to give him any more of an ego boost.

Raph's eyes narrowed. "Well, that sounds like a challenge."

She tipped her head back and laughed. "And why do I think you're up for it?"

He glanced down at the tent in his pants, and one side of his lips turned up.

"Let me see," she purred as she slid off the counter and down past Raph until her feet met the floor. "Yep, definitely up for it."

This time it was Raph who threw his head back and laughed. Delight twirled through Eve's chest. Seeing him like this was ... devastating. How was he so frigging gorgeous? Her breath caught.

"What?" He stopped laughing and stared at her.

And damn it, how was he so attuned to her that he picked up on every little detail? But this was one detail she wasn't ready to share—wasn't ready to even examine. Instead, she did the next thing she wanted. "Raph, it's my turn to see the goods. Those buttons have to go."

"Well, if those buttons are going, how about you lose the dress?"

"I've already lost my panties. Trust me—you have way more to go than me. And I want to see all this sexiness."

"You think I'm sexy?" Raph said.

She shot him a look through her lashes as she unbuttoned and spread his shirt open; his tanned chest and ridged stomach contrasted against the white material, then she pushed the fabric off his massive shoulders.

Sexy? No. Sexy was something you'd enjoy, make a moment of. He was an orgasm for the eyes. So frigging hot she was a puddle just looking at him.

But she managed to roll her tongue up and take a step back.

Oh, sweet goddess. And he was all hers for the night. She mentally fist bumped the energies of the universe that had given her this masterpiece.

"Looked enough yet?" Raph said.

"Not quite. I'm still wearing more than you." She feigned a sad face and dipped her gaze to his pants.

"Are you sure? I mean, I know you felt it earlier. But I want you to be ready for what's coming next ..."

"What? Or who?"

He leaned down and whispered into the curve of her neck, behind her ear. "Both."

And just like that, Eve's nipples pebbled into tight peaks. But she crossed her arms to hide that fact from him. He didn't need any more encouragement. "Promises, promises."

"This is one promise I'm looking forward to delivering." Raph undid his belt and pushed his pants to his hips—holy goddess, how did she get so lucky to be on the receiving end of a strip tease this good?

His pants dropped to the floor.

She had to stop her jaw from dropping too. "Tighty-whiteys?"

"What? They're comfortable, give me room to ... move. I take it by that husky tone that you like them?"

A laugh escaped her—it was either that or a moan. She was so, so, *so* close to getting that hands-down, *slam you on the bed and go for the ride of your life* cock inside her. "I can safely say 'like' is a whole world away from what I'm thinking."

"You're not going to say it, are you?" His eyes darkened, and his lips curved.

Eve locked her gaze on his cock. Licked her lower lip. "That I think you're sexy?"

"Yes," he growled. If it was possible, that tent in his tighty-whiteys grew even bigger. She almost whimpered. She wasn't going to hold out for much longer.

"So how about this? I'll turn around, and you unzip me." She spun and gave him her back. "Then I'll turn around, and you finish the ... rest."

For a long moment, only Raph's harsh, rapid breathing echoed through the apartment. Then he stepped right to her, whispered into her ear, "Yes, boss."

"That does have a ring to it." Eve tilted her neck and gave him even more access. And he didn't need any other encouragement. His lips trailed over the edge of her ear. A shiver worked through her, and then he yanked her zipper down.

She caught the material with her arms just before it fell to the floor. Raph stood so close that with every breath, his chest brushed the skin along her spine. She turned around.

His eyes were alight, their green fire back, but this time that was all locked on her.

"Well, Mr. Smith? I'm waiting."

Raphael couldn't stop a growl rumbling through his chest. She was absolute fucking perfection. And if he didn't get inside her soon, he was going to explode.

But she was such a boss, and the enjoyment on her face made his chest hurt as much as his dick was hard. So he reined in the urge to haul her off her feet, carry her into his bedroom and toss her into the bed. Instead, he hooked his thumbs under the waistband of his jocks and drew them down.

Eve's gaze locked on his dick, her pupils dilated, and fuck if a drop of precum didn't seep out.

Oh hell, just her gaze on him, and he was ready to blow.

"Princess. If you keep looking at me like that, I'm going to last all of two seconds."

Her eyebrows shot up, and mischief glinted in her dark eyes. What was she up to now? "So if I do this"—she let the dress fall to the floor—"you'll go all caveman?"

Holy. Fucking. Shite. Strength in her proud chin. Power in the curves of her arms and abs and thighs. Sensual grace in her curved breasts tipped with dusky nipples. Glory in her gleaming skin and hair. His breath stalled. His balls went tight.

"Witch," he breathed, "you're so fucking in for it now."

"Like I said, promises, promises." Eve shrugged one shoulder. "Now make good on them."

"Are you sure you can handle it?"

She planted her fists on her hips. "Raphael Smith. You better fucking believe I'll give as good as I get. And *that's* a promise."

A growl tore from Raph's throat, and he lunged for her, hauled her body into his arms, her mouth up to his. She wrapped her legs around him, and her wet heat grazed his cock. He hissed, but then she bit his lip, and he kissed her back with every ounce of fury and need and passion that raged through him.

With their mouths fused and their tongues tangling, tasting, stroking, he walked them to his bedroom and spun, dropping her to the bed and following her down, never letting their lips separate.

As soon as they landed, Eve wrapped her legs tight around his waist, and his dick slid home like he was meant to be right here.

Stars shot to the edge of his vision, and his eyes practically rolled back in his head.

Eve gasped and arched, the tight beads of her nipples pressing against his chest. Shivers worked up the base of his dick, and his balls tightened even farther.

"Oh, shit." He stopped. "Condom."

"Damn." Eve's eyes flew open. "Tell me you have something?"

He cut her a look.

"Of course you do."

"I just have to ... resist ..." Raph pulled out with a hiss. "Shit, that was close. You don't know how good you feel, Eve." He blew out a harsh breath. "Don't move an inch."

He lunged across the bed and yanked open a drawer. Scrambled around ... "Yes!"

"Hurrying much?" Eve said.

"Hell yes. Don't want you to change your mind."

He rolled over, tearing the foil packet open, and stopped. Eve was on her knees, and she reached back to do something with her hair, pushing the tight tips of her breasts into the air. Then the thick mass fell around her shoulders and hid those mouthwatering nipples from his view.

"I'm not changing my mind," Eve said, shaking her hair and giving him another peek at her nipples. Fuck, he wanted to latch on to those—

"Why don't you let me do that?" She took the condom

from him and pressed him onto his back. "My turn for a close-up inspection."

"I'm totally at your disposal, but, princess, maybe you can do the inspecting later—" She grabbed his dick, and he hissed at her firm hold. "Okay, I can get on board with this."

Every move of her hands on his dick was excruciatingly hot, and he was trembling by the time she sat back and eyed him. Her gaze was locked on his body, and a red tint highlighted her cheeks. Her breathing was shallow.

"Please tell me you're not planning on inspecting me now?" Raph couldn't stop himself from reaching out and cupping her breasts.

Silken skin. The velvety nub of her nipple. He thumbed the peaks, and as they tightened farther, a groan tore through him.

"Inspections are overrated," Eve muttered and crawled over him until her wet heat hovered right above him.

"Totally agree," he rasped, the need to bury himself high and deep inside her overwhelming. "Eve, I need to—" He surged upward.

"Raph, I need—" She slammed down.

Stars exploded behind his eyes. Scorching fire. Tight, silky clasp.

Eve gasped and then ground hard on him, pushing him to the very hilt. "Yes! Yes, yes, yes. Yes!"

"Holy fuck," he said between gritted teeth, battling the urge to let loose, determined to watch Eve—her mouth parted, head tipped back, the long line of her neck, breasts tilted upward, hair swinging. The ripple of her orgasm clenched him over and over, and he couldn't hold out.

With a shout, Raph grabbed her hips and held her to him, then thrust upward, over and over, as he fucked her harder than anyone he'd ever done before. And as the stars blasted white-hot behind his eyes, Eve's hoarse cries matched his as she came again.

After Raph and Eve showered, they dressed as lightly as possible, given the heat. He pulled her back into his arms, and they practically toppled to his bed. He pulled the white cotton sheet up and over them. Satisfaction rolled through him.

"Why did I say in the shower too?" Eve said with a groan into his chest. "How many orgasms have I had now?"

"Let me count. Once when I went down on you in the shower, then another one up against the tiles. Twice in the bed. Once in the kitchen." The image of her splayed on his granite counter replayed through his mind. Her scent. Her feel. Her taste. He tightened his arm around her. "So five in total?"

"Seven for the day," Eve said. "You forgot the T and H in the storage space. Two more there."

"T and what?"

"H. You know, tug and head?"

"What? No way. You just made that up."

"Did not."

"Did so," Raph said. "But either way, you're right. Can't forget those."

"Raph, this was ... well, I don't want to feed your ego anymore here, but by the goddess, seven? Like, that's got to be a record."

"Maybe it's you who shouldn't have their ego fed. I've had a permanent hard-on for you for days."

"Well, it was your tongue and hand and cock doing the work ... so I'm giving you the kudos for this one."

Raph smiled into her hair. And something warm spread in his chest. But he pushed that soft sensation away before it seemed too important. They'd had amazing, mind-blowing sex. Of course he was happy. Although there was one thing about Eve that he couldn't figure out.

She was drawing lazy patterns in his chest hair, and he inhaled deeply. Breathed in her scent and everything about this moment.

"Eve, there's something about you ... that's different."

"What do you mean?" She kept drawing those circles. "Like my pussy is a super-orgasm-maker?"

"Well, it did come seven times today, so that too. But this is more ... you know what I said about my curse?"

She stopped her patternmaking and met his gaze. "The voices from the past?"

"Yeah, those. Usually, they're with me all the time. They get stronger around things that have more of a past to share."

"Like antiques?"

"Exactly. But when you're there, it's like those voices are muted, nothing more than white noise in the background that I can disengage from—detach from—in a way I've never been able to do before."

Raph opened his mouth to say more, to say he wanted to know about Eve—what were her likes and dislikes, and what made her laugh, made her cry.

Evangeline was more than just a body who made the things in the room go quiet. She was fast becoming the air that he breathed. The fucking beat of his heart.

But he stopped himself from going that far. How in the hell had such a deep ... *connection*—was the only word he could describe it as—happened within one week was a total mystery.

"I'm glad." Eve curved one arm over his chest and held him tight. "You've given me my relic back. And a gazillion orgasms. Nice to think I've done something for you too."

"So what's the whole Watcher deal? You said you grew up in a witchcraft shop?"

Eve took a deep breath, pushing the curve of her breast into his side. He twirled one of her curls around his finger. Let it go. Smiled when it sprang back into a corkscrew.

"My mother used to be in the coven, but they, uh, kicked her out when she was eighteen."

"That sounds pretty harsh."

"Well, she broke their number one rule. She stole magic from a less powerful witch."

"Is that how it works—you can only steal from someone weaker? So Caterina couldn't have stolen your power from you tonight?"

"Yep. If Caterina had tried it, I could've sent the spell in the other direction and taken hers, especially since I would have been aware it was happening. She wouldn't have had a chance. But my mom, well, she did it by accident. But the coven has their rules, and you can't ever cross them."

Raph tightened his arm around her. "That must have been rough."

"She had me shortly after they kicked her out. So rough is an understatement. But when I turned sixteen, well, the coven basically came calling. Apparently, my magic had been causing some of their spells to go haywire, so they knew a strong witch had come into her power, and they tracked the power to me."

"And you just went with them? After what happened with your mother?"

"Mom was the one who helped me make up my mind. An untrained witch with my powers would be dangerous. She was strong—had been training for a couple of years before the ... transgression, so she taught me the basics, but she knew I needed more help. Plus, her power wasn't as strong as mine, and if anything went wrong, she wouldn't be strong enough to contain it—and me."

"And what was it like?"

"There was still a lot of resentment over me being there. Mom had really caused an issue for the coven with her actions, and those witches have long memories. So I made sure that I was the best at every test, every time, so no one could ever question my right to be there. And I never made a mistake."

"That must have been hard to do."

"It worked," Eve said with a shrug. "I came out on top. And look, I'm here right now with the hottest PI ever."

"So the whole all-work-no-play persona?"

"It's not a persona. It's how I had to be to get to where I am."

"You're not such a bitch, really, are you?"

"And you're not such a self-obsessed asshole. We made a good team tonight." She pressed a soft kiss to his bicep and then yawned.

"Yeah, we did." He couldn't contain a yawn either.

"And I have to say," she whispered sleepily. "I love your tatts. The Celtic knot shield on your shoulder is very cool."

"Thanks," he murmured, his eyes drifting shut.

"And the circle-triangle thingy, too."

Raph's chest went tight. His eyes shot open, and he stared at the ceiling. Hell. How was he going to tell her the truth?

24

———

THREE THINGS WOKE Eve up the next morning. First was the urge to check the relic. The box sat on the bedside table closest to her. Her breath whooshed out.

Second was the absence of the hot, rangy body that had been her pillow all night.

Third was the murmur of Raph's voice from the living room. Who was he talking to? Maybe Isa?

Eve sat up and peered into the cardboard box. Nestled inside was her relic, gold glowing in the dim morning light filtering through the bedroom curtains.

Right before they'd gone to sleep, she'd started to get out of Raph's bed to bring the relic in with them, but he'd stopped her. He'd told her to stay where she was, and he'd bring it in —that she'd expended a lot of energy and needed rest.

That little act had been one of the most thoughtful things anyone had ever done for her. Maybe that's why the moment stood out even among a night of frigging orgasmic awesomeness.

Goddess, had last night really happened? Eve rolled over

and stretched; twinges pinged in her lady parts. Yep, that had happened.

And she had her relic! For the first time in nearly two weeks, she breathed easy. Finally. And on top of that, this time with Raph ... they'd been a team. Both in and out of bed.

The word had a ring to it. She'd never been part of a team before. Even if she'd been interested—which she hadn't—no one in the coven had been strong enough to keep up with her spell work, so any team would've been *a leader and a follower* type of deal. Not her thing. But Raph, well, he held his own with her in a totally different way. Maybe, one day ... once she was set in her role as a Watcher, she could base herself anywhere in the world.

Dressed only in the tank top and panties, she padded into the living room.

Raph sat at the dining table, cell phone up to his ear, and his gaze cut to her. "Yeah, have to go. Catch you later."

"Morning," Eve said. "You didn't have to end the call."

"Morning. It was a client, so I kind of had to. But I think it's almost sorted anyway."

"Not Parsons? Is he still after it? We need to keep an eye out for him if that's the case. Or was it Gray?" She pulled out a seat at the table opposite him. "You've been working so hard on my job that you mustn't have had any time for other clients."

"Your job's certainly been consuming. But it's okay. I've been continuing a couple of inquiries where I can. I just can't, uh, discuss them. Client confidentiality and all that. So, coffee?"

"Do nettles sting?"

Raph blinked and paused midstride. "Never heard coffee

and nettles put together before. But I know the answer, so I'll be right back."

"I'll get dressed."

"No need on my account."

She laughed and quickly dressed in a skirt and top.

"Thanks," she murmured as Raph handed her a mug. "So, I need to book a plane ticket. I also need to work on a glamour spell. I'm not letting the relic out of my sight until it's where it belongs."

"How does a glamour work?" Raph asked.

"A good glamour can make one thing appear like something else, roughly the same shape and size. But the spell is pretty complicated, so I'll need at least a few hours."

"And I have to follow up with my contact at Frinecki's business—want to see what the word is. I've had the news on all morning, and they haven't mentioned anything about dead bodies at the gala."

"What?" Eve paused, cup midway to her mouth. "Nothing about his death?"

Raph shook his head. "Hence I need to talk to my source."

"Well ..." The hairs along the backs of her arms prickled, and she rubbed them.

"What is it?"

"Not sure. But—"

Something bashed once into Raph's front door, and Eve instinctively gathered her magic.

"What the fuck is that?" Raph ran and pressed his eye to the viewer. He jumped back.

"What? What did you see?" Eve asked.

"Ah, someone's there. Like right there. But they're frozen."

"They must've knocked on the door." Yes. Eve pumped a fist in the air. It had worked!

"Uh, Eve. Why are they frozen?"

"I extended the ward to the door itself."

"So no one can even knock? What if it's a neighbor—someone innocent?"

Eve folded her arms. "Raph, no one is stepping foot in this apartment until the relic is safely glamoured and I can build a new ward around it that only I can pass. And don't you PI's have a saying—something about coincidence?"

"That doesn't mean you can just go around stunning anyone," Raph said.

"Why not?" She threw her arms in the air. "I swear, Raphael Smith, I thought you were the one who was all easygoing and wouldn't care if I stunned the entire city. Instead, you're worried about a neighbor?"

"Why yes, yes, I am. They might be *innocent*. And I swear, I thought you'd lost the neurosis over the relic."

"Neurosis? This is my life. And the relic poses a far greater threat than anything else you can imagine; if someone gets a hold of it, who knows what it can do. If you're so all about 'protecting the innocent,' then you should think about that."

Eve stormed to the door and yanked it open, revealing a tall man with deeply tanned skin and yellow eyes, mouth agape, eyes wide. One hand was reaching into his jacket, the fabric still swaying even though his body was frozen.

She gestured at the man. "Do you know him?"

"No."

"Then I'm guessing this is exactly the type of person my ward spells are meant to be keeping out." She grabbed one of the man's arms. "Now help me get him inside. He'll be stunned for at least half an hour, and I want to know why he's here. Maybe he's from Parsons. Or has something to do with Isa or Gray. Either way, we need to find out."

Shit. Eve was going to glamour *and* ward the relic right there? If she made it so only she could get past the spell, he had zero chance of fulfilling his contract. The tatt on his arm burned, and his legs were moving toward the relic before he'd even realized it. Shit. The binding wouldn't let him not hand over the relic.

Okay, so he'd find a way to deliver and make this work for Eve, for Isa, for Gray. As soon as he had that thought, the burning in his arm stopped, and his legs were under his control once more. Thank hell.

And damn it. He *had* to speak with Eve. She'd surprised him—continuously—so maybe she'd be okay with the truth. Except she was bloody single-minded about the relic. Would she see things from his point of view at all?

Eve. Isa. Gray. Fuck it. Eve had proven to be more than just a hot-headed princess. He had to try.

But right now, they had to get the frozen guy inside, and he had to convince Eve to take the ward off the door. He grabbed Frozen Guy's other arm ... oh hell, images of Frozen Guy's recent past ricocheted through Raph.

Traveling from the sixth-hellmouth gate to the seventh. Entering the human world through the seventh-hellmouth gate ... Meeting up with the daemon crew who'd taken Raph from Isa's car ...

Well, fuck. Why would a sixth-gate daemon come *here*?

Bloody hell. Ice surged through his veins. He couldn't let

Eve find out why the frozen daemon was here, not until he'd told her his whole story.

Together they picked up Frozen Daemon and half dragged, half carried him into the apartment.

"Leave him near the door," Raph said. "I want to get him out of here before he unfreezes and don't want to move him for a second time. Hey—how much of this will he hear?"

"Everything."

Fuck. Raph pulled Eve into his room. "I'll check him out," he whispered. "And can you *please* take the ward off the door?"

Eve pursed her lips and stared at him.

"Seriously, a kid could knock on the door. The doorway will do, surely."

"Fine. So who's this, do you think?" Eve asked.

"That's what I'm going to find out."

Raph searched Frozen Daemon's pockets and found a wallet and cell phone. Raph thumbed through the wallet until he found the ID. "Lance Parker. From the US."

No way was that his real name, but Raph didn't say that out loud.

"One of Frinecki's men?" Eve whispered. "Or Parsons?"

"Who knows?" Except, he did know. Raph bit back a curse. He had to tell Eve everything. But Lance Parker, a.k.a. Frozen Daemon, needed to be outside first. This conversation was going to be ... tricky.

"Anything else on him?" Eve asked.

"His cell."

"Can you use his thumb to open it up?"

Shit. Raph could, but what if there was something damning about Raph on the phone? He surreptitiously pressed the power button on Frozen Daemon's phone and turned it off.

"Looks like it's fried," he said to Eve. "Could the stun spell have interfered with the tech?"

"Possible. Or the battery could be dead."

"I'll plug it into my charger. Just in case." Raph jerked his head for Eve to follow him back into his room. "What happens when the stun comes off?"

"This stun will leave him pretty weak at first, disoriented for a little while too."

"Weak and disoriented. Sounds good."

"Okay," Eve said, "let's get him outside. Is there somewhere on this floor we can stash him until the stun wears off?"

"Yeah, at the end of the corridor is the utility area. I'll carry him there—you work on the door spell."

"He's pretty big. Can you handle him on your own?"

"Are you offering to leave the relic here and help me?"

"That would be a no."

"Didn't think so."

Frozen Daemon turned out to be deadweight, but as soon as Raph had him stashed in the least likely place anyone would find him, he jogged back to his apartment. But before he went back inside, he called Isa again. Nothing.

He dialed Gray. Also nothing.

Damn it. Raph smacked the phone against his thigh. Isa needed to know their grandfather's people were here. He quickly sent her a text to fill her in—she needed to be on her guard more than ever. Wherever in the world she was right now.

Raph went to knock to get Eve to let him back in but stopped, fist midair. What were the odds his houseguest had put an even worse ward on the door?

"Eve?" he called out instead. "Can I come in? My keys are in there, and the door automatically locks."

"Fine," she snapped. "Coming."

Okay. That had sounded more pissed off than normal. Moments later, Eve yanked the door open and stormed back into the kitchen. He followed her, keeping his gaze on her the entire time. She stopped at the kitchen island, glaring at her supplies spread out over the counter.

"Uh, what's wrong now?" Raph asked.

"I need rosemary for the glamour spell. It's a key ingredient. And we don't have any."

"Why rosemary?"

"It's the active agent in the spell that triggers memory loss of the item in case someone's seen it before the glamour."

"Will ordinary rosemary do? There's a supermarket on the corner that's open on a Sunday."

"Should do."

"Okay, since you don't want to leave the relic alone, do you want me to get the rosemary while you stay here? Or do you want to come and bring the relic?"

Eve pursed her lips. "I'll stay here. But be quick, please. I want to get this glamour done today, and it takes several hours."

"Fast rosemary. Got it. Just need to check, you've still got the wards on the doorway, right?"

"Correct. No one can cross your threshold."

"What about the walls?"

"Well, if they bash through your walls, then yes, they'll get inside the apartment. But then I'll be here. I'll pit my magic against anyone."

Shit. How would her magic go against a daemon? Mind you, she'd managed to stun Raph and now the sixth-gate daemon, so she had some sway. "Okay, I'll be quick."

Raph showered and dressed quickly, and as soon as he reached his car, he dialed Parsons.

"Good morning, Raphael. I take it my man delivered his message, then? Although I did think you would have called faster given the stakes."

Raph forced his voice to remain calm. "Actually no, can safely say your man never delivered any message. So what's up?"

"What a shame. My man has such a way with words; I'm sure you would've loved to hear him speak. Pity. Well, let me share the news. For some reason, my men couldn't find your sister ... to ensure her well-being, of course. But in a stroke of luck, they did find someone else you might know."

Raph's gut clenched. What the hell was this?

"I'll take your silence for interest in what I've got to say. But here, I'll let my current guest do the talking. Say hello to Mr. Smith."

"Hello?" a weak voice trembled through the phone. "Mr. Smith, is that you?"

Oh shit. Arthur Stanley. A new wave of ice slid through Raph. "It's okay, Arthur. I'll get this sorted."

"Excellent." Parsons' warm voice was back again. "So, do you have my possession? Today is the day, after all. And time is running out for your friend here, Mr. Smith."

Bloody fucking hell. "Yes. Yes, I've got it."

"Perfect. To ensure that Arthur here can return to his business, bring it to me. Now."

"I'm not with the item right now." Raph bit back the urge to snarl at Parsons. Instead, he focused on options. Cool. Calm. Work this through. "But this afternoon will work."

"This afternoon may be good for you, but alas, I don't think Arthur here will agree when my men get to work on him at midday."

"That's not long—"

"Long enough," Parsons said, "I'm sure. And you'd better not be thinking of stalling on our deal now. That would be very bad for your friend here."

"Of course not. You're the client. And I'm the investigator who's going to bring you the item you asked for on the day you asked for it. So, where should I meet you?"

Parsons named the Sound Wave Room, a basement-level bar located in the Carlisle Hotel, one of the city's oldest, nicest buildings.

"Midday, Mr. Smith. Plenty of time for everyone to head home afterward and enjoy a lovely Sunday afternoon."

The phone disconnected.

"Fuck!" Raph slammed his car door shut and drove straight to Arthur's antique store and parked out the front. At 9:00 a.m. on a Sunday, the streets up this end of the city were deserted, and he grabbed a street-side parking spot easily enough.

Please let Parsons be bluffing.

Raph jogged up the steps. The light was on in the shop, but the 'Sorry We Are Closed' sign was turned toward the street. He tried the door handle, and it opened as soon as he pushed it. Shit.

"Hello? Anyone here?" he called, carefully stepping inside.

No answer. If Arthur was here, he'd be rightly pissed off to find Raph in his closed shop. Except the front door had been open ... and that had been Arthur's voice on the phone. But until Raph knew who Parsons really was, which had just shot to the top of his to-do list, he was keeping an open mind about the man's capabilities.

At the back of the shop, a small corridor led to a restroom and a small storage area. Nothing untoward in there. At the very end, an external entry opened into the alleyway behind the building. Raph tried the handle—it opened straightaway. Shit. Both front and back doors were open. Arthur wouldn't do this.

But there was one way to be certain that Parsons had taken him.

Raph blew out a steadying breath, then, in his mind, eased the portal open to his curse. Voices and visions from the past rushed at him—into him, through him and around him—all shouting their history.

Hell. He winced and focused on the one voice he was after—the handle. And there was the last person who'd gripped it ... not Arthur. Raph concentrated, and the face came into view. The daemon who'd punched Raph in the parking lot was pushing Arthur out of the door ahead of him.

Then another voice—a sibilant whisper of darkness came out from the past. A shadow. Ice arrowed down Raph's spine, and he cut the vision.

Bloody hell, that had been close. And even worse, Parsons was telling the truth. He had Arthur.

Raph raced back to his apartment, stopping only for the bloody rosemary, and went straight to the utility room, but the daemon was gone. Fuck. What could he report back to Parsons about Eve and Raph?

What the hell did he do next? The relic. Eve. Isa. Parsons. Gray. Arthur. The bloody contract. Well, there was one thing he had no choice on. And five others he had to do right by. The clock was ticking on them all.

25

———

After booking her airfare, Eve grabbed a coffee and laid out all her tools and prepared as much as she could for the spell. Finished, she stood back from the counter. Everything was ready to go. But no Raph. She rechecked her items and reviewed the spell from her notebook. Everything looked right. Again. All she needed was—

A key turned in the lock of the front door, and Raph entered the apartment. Something in her chest eased, but she ignored the sensation. "About time. I need to get this spell underway."

"Sorry. Something came up while I was out," Raph said.

"What? What is possibly more important than this relic?"

"I got a call about Arthur Stanley. He's missing."

"What? When? What happened?"

"Not exactly sure. Here, have a seat. We need to talk this through, and we need to proceed with caution about moving you and the relic."

"Caution?" Eve sat opposite him at the dining table. "No, I need to get the relic back to Rome, remember?"

"Absolutely. Of course you have to; I'm just saying that Arthur's missing ... and I have a real concern he might've been taken by someone with an agenda tied to your relic."

"Frinecki's people? Parsons? Or Caterina?"

"Could be any of them."

Eve's heart began to pound, and she regarded Raph even as he watched her. His green eyes were dark and serious. Raph was a good man—forever going on about innocents not getting hurt. He loved his family, clearly. And they'd ... connected.

But should she, *could* she, tell him the entire truth?

"Raph, this is serious." She exhaled hard. "No, serious isn't even close. It's not just about my life—this is about the life and death of every human. I need to know you understand that from the outset here."

Raph's eyes narrowed, and he leaned forward. "Tell me."

Eve rubbed her suddenly damp palms together. Damn it, why was this so hard?

"Eve."

"Don't push me," she snapped. "Watchers don't talk about their relics. Rule number two of witch school."

"Okay, okay." Raph raised his hands and sat back. "When you're ready."

"Why do I get the feeling you'll keep pushing at this until you know everything?" She snorted and stared at the relic. Raph had helped her get it this far. And it looked like the relic was going to need all the help possible to get back to safety. But by the goddess, this better be the right thing to do.

"Princess," Raph said, "if you don't want—"

"The relic is the gift of gold," she said in a rush. "You know the Christmas story of the three gifts, right? Gold—"

"Frankincense and Myrrh. Yeah, yeah."

"Do you know what happened after they were delivered?"

"No, I guess they just disappeared into history."

"Not exactly. They did disappear. But for a very good reason. Whoever holds all three gifts controls the bodies, minds and hearts of humankind. The gold represents the physical. The bodies."

Raph's mouth dropped wide, and he stared at her. And stared. Finally blinked. "Wait a goddamn moment. You're saying that your relic—that little gold box right there—can control the bodies of humankind?"

"Yes, that's what I'm saying. But only when it's held along with the other two gifts. For two thousand years, they've been kept apart, each under a separate lock-and-key system. And now, on my watch, the gift of gold was stolen. I can't let it fall into the hands of anyone who knows its true power."

"Holy shit, Eve. You didn't think this was something I should know earlier?"

"No, Raph. No, I didn't. I think it's way more important to make sure the relic is returned to *safety* than telling anyone who doesn't need to know exactly what it represents."

"Just great." Raph laughed, but it was anything but humorous. "You don't trust me, do you?"

"Well, when we first met, you came off as a self—"

"—obsessed asshole," Raph said. "You said that last night. And you meant it, didn't you? You actually think that's me."

"Well, you didn't exactly give me much else to go on at the time, so yes, that's how I felt. Then."

"And now?" Raph asked.

Eve regarded him straight on. How did she feel about him? That was the big question. But she barely knew him.

Sex—even out-of-this-world, multi-orgasmic sex—

wasn't enough to build trust on. She didn't hand her life over to her vibrator, did she?

And sure, Raph had shown himself to be a decent human being, and he seemed to care for her—on occasion—but even that wasn't enough to entrust your life, everyone's life, into someone's hands. No, in every other normal, day-to-day circumstance, trust took time to develop.

Except, this situation was the utter opposite of normal ... and she'd had to make a call. That was all it came down to.

"I don't have a choice," Eve finally said.

Raph's eyes widened for a second, then he shoved his chair back from the table and spun around. "Listen, I need to think this through. Have you had a shower yet?"

"No, I didn't want to be away from the relic—or the door—while you were out." Eve eyed his stiff back as he walked into the kitchen and battled back the stupid-ass urge to go after him and rub the tension out of his shoulders, tell him she'd lied, that she trusted him because he'd proven himself decent and capable and reliable.

"Right, well, while you take a shower, I'll look into who else is in town that would know the truth of the relic."

Raph forced himself to wait one entire moment after the shower had started before he carefully picked up the cardboard box holding the relic, grabbed his car keys and phone, and ran out of the apartment.

As soon as he was in his car, he dialed Gray. Come on. Come on. Come on. Nothing. He left a terse voice message explaining everything that had happened—and what he planned to do—and stabbed the end button.

Damn it, what good was a triple-crossing partner if they didn't answer their bloody phone? Fine. Raph was on his own. He needed to rescue Arthur, fulfill the contract terms, then somehow convince Eve this was the right course of action.

But she didn't trust him—she'd said it herself. She'd only told him about the relic's power because she didn't have a choice. Okay, so he had been lying to her.

But if he told her the truth about having to give the relic to his first client, she'd stun him, take the relic, then he'd never fulfill the binding contract. And the danger to Isa would only intensify. He couldn't let either of those things happen.

Hell, Eve was never going to speak to him again now.

Fuck, fuck, fuck, fuck, *fuck*. He slammed a hand on the steering wheel.

The green lights on the dashboard display blinked, mocking him with their movement. 10:15 a.m. There was no time to second-guess this. He had to be at that bar on time.

The Carlisle was only a couple of blocks away from Arthur's shop. Had Parsons' team been there all along? It made sense. They could use the inner-city alleyways between the buildings to hide their movement between the bar and Arthur's antiquity shop.

Raph did a drive-by, but as the sun rose high over the summer morning, more people were out, mostly tourists in their shorts and sandals. He parked the car the next street over in a public parking lot and took stock.

First thing. Just who was Parsons? He had ties—and deep ties—to the underworld. And he had both seventh- and sixth-gate daemons working with him. Raph knew all too well what that meant. Only a fifth-gate daemon or higher could compel lesser gate daemons to do their bidding. So either Parsons was offering a substantial enough reward to entice those daemons to work with him, or he was a fifth-gate daemon, or worse.

The hairs on the back of Raph's neck prickled.

There was one person he could ask to answer that question, except that was never going to happen.

Okay, so how to deliver the relic and satisfy the contract but not actually let the relic fall into Parsons' hands? Shit a fucking brick. This was close to impossible. Unless ... an image of the other antiques in Arthur's shop raced through his mind. His heart began to pound. Could this work?

Raph ran back to Arthur's shop and let himself in through the back alleyway entry. The place was still empty, exactly as Raph had left it earlier.

He grabbed a brass jewelry box close to the size of the relic, gritting his teeth against the call of the past emanating from the little thing, then picked up a fabric shopping bag with Arthur's shop logo printed across the material.

Raph quickly locked the shop's front door—Arthur didn't deserve to have anyone steal his stuff—then carefully placed the relic and the jewelry box exactly as he needed them in the shopping bag. But he needed something more ... Yes. That was perfect. He took a swathe of deep blue lace from behind the counter.

Perfect. And he was good to go. Please let this work.

Eve tied her hair into a high knot and adjusted the showerhead so the spray hit the back of her neck. For one moment, she just let the hot water stream over her. She might be in a subtropical climate in the middle of summer, but she still wanted a hot shower.

She rolled her shoulders, let the water do its thing and reduce the tightness in her shoulders. Except the opposite happened.

The tension stole down to her chest. Her gut churned.

What was going on? She had the relic. Her flight was booked for that night. The wards were in place here, and no one was coming through them. She took a deep breath, tried to force her pulse to slow, but suddenly adrenaline roared through her, sending her heart racing.

Damn. Something *was* wrong. But what?

Eve turned the shower off and grabbed a towel, wrapping herself in it as she ran into the living room. The dining table was empty.

Her heart stopped. What? Where was the relic? She whirled around—had Raphael moved it?

"Raph?" She raced through his room. "Raph?"

The bathroom. Back into the living room. To the laundry.

Oh goddess, no. Black spots gathered at the edges of Eve's vision. Shit. She forced herself to draw in a breath. Another, until the splotches receded.

Ice-cold and ice-hard fury teemed through her.

Her relic was gone. Raph was gone. Had he been taken with the box? Goddess knew he didn't have much in the way of offensive skills. Although, somehow, he'd handled the shadows last night at the gala event. A shiver trembled down her spine.

But Parsons and Caterina were both still out there—had

either of them gotten across Eve's ward, stunned Raph, then taken him and the box? But why wouldn't they have come for Eve?

By the goddess, whoever had taken her relic—and whatever they'd done to Raph—they would pay.

She quickly dressed in shorts and a tank top. Into her pockets, she put a pouch of salt and her crystals. She slipped the athame in its sheath into her waistband. Secured her pendant around her neck.

Then she grabbed her bag and took off for the parking garage. If Raph's car was there, then he hadn't left of his own accord.

Inside the lift, Eve pressed the button repeatedly. But at the lobby level, the doors slid open, and a massive figure stepped in. The guy that had been frozen in her ward that morning.

"You," Eve snarled. "Where is it? Where's Raph?"

"And good morning to you too. Just who I'm after."

"Ooh, goody. You're just who I'm after too." She whipped out her athame. "And you've got five seconds to tell me exactly what I want to hear before I gut you and feed your soul to the—"

"Hey, no need for that." The big guy's eyes wrinkled. "I'm the messenger. And I have a feeling I can answer both of your questions. The man in your apartment, that's this Raph?"

"Yes, that's him."

"Cool. Okay, well, he's who I'm taking you to see."

"Oh really. Like I'd fall for that." Eve stalled as she readied a stun spell.

"Uh-uh." The big guy rolled up his sleeve and revealed a tattoo high on his bicep. "See this? After your greeting this morning, I visited a high priestess and got a lil' protection.

It's not permanent, sad to say, but at least it means your magic will be useless on me until it wears off."

"Wow." Eve blinked for a moment. Brisbane had a high priestess? She'd love to meet her. Then she stamped the reluctant admiration out. No time for that. "You've got to have good contacts to get a mark like that. Can I see it? Make sure you're not bluffing me."

"Sure. It cost a fortune—as well as something I didn't plan on giving up—so it better be the real deal. But I need this gig, so it was worth it."

Eve peered closer at the black mark. She hovered her pendant over the tattoo, and sure enough, a hum buzzed through the crystal. Now that was impressive. There was magic in the tattoo. Whoever this high priestess was, she was talented.

And it meant she couldn't use her craft on the big guy.

"I could still gut you, though," Eve said. "That'll slow you down until I can get away."

"But then you won't find out where your man is."

"He's not my man."

"I don't give a fuck either way. But here's the thing, the man from your apartment is giving something important to my ... uh, client at the Sound Wave Room. I've been asked to bring you there too. So come with me, and we both get what we want."

Eve's heart jammed in her chest. *Something important* had to be her relic. Hold on. Raph was giving it to someone?

"Why should I trust you?" she said through gritted teeth.

"I don't need to get you to agree to come along with me." The big guy's yellow eyes began to glow. Had his body grown even larger? "I could knock you out right here and haul you there over my shoulder. But I'm not that way inclined."

Right. The big guy wasn't joking. But if he was going to take her to her relic—and to Raph—then she was on board with that plan. Preferably without being knocked unconscious along the way. Plus, the magic-barrier temp tattoo would fade in minutes—they never lasted longer than half an hour at most. And then she could take him down.

"Fine. Take me to this Sound Wave Room."

26

———

AT FIVE MINUTES TO MIDDAY, Raph walked through the light-filled hotel lobby of the Carlisle Hotel and down the marble steps to the basement Sound Wave Room. With every spiraling step, the light dimmed until he was in a dark foyer with sepulchral arches covered in tiny green tiles.

Raph kept a tight rein on his curse, but this room was close to screaming at him. Spaces didn't usually affect him so much. Was that why Parsons had chosen this place as the transfer location?

Raph walked through the foyer and into the main room.

Three people—Parsons' lead daemon and two more of the daemon squad—sat at a long bar. They all swiveled to face Raph.

Against the opposite wall, Frinecki and Arthur occupied a booth each. The rest of the booths were empty. Arthur's cheeks were pale and his eyes glassy. He didn't even glance at Raph. Looked like he was out of it—probably a good thing.

Parsons sipped something from a whiskey glass. He met Raph's gaze and nodded.

"Mr. Smith. How good to make your acquaintance in person after all this time. Please, join me."

"Parsons. And how ... good ... it is to see you, too." Raph made his way to the booth. "So, shall we get this over with?"

"All in good time. Can I offer you a drink?" Parsons flicked a finger, and suddenly one of the goons from the bar was at his side with a silver tray, a bottle of Oban single malt whiskey and a glass with ice. "Let's toast to your success."

A loud gasp had Raph spin around. His stomach dropped. Oh fuck.

Eve stood, staring. Behind her was the sixth-gate daemon.

"Eve, are you okay?" Raph asked. "What happened—?"

"Don't you dare say one single word to me," Eve said.

"Eve—"

"Now, now, Mr. Smith, please, introduce me to your friend. When Stolas here"—Parsons nodded at the sixth-gate daemon—"relayed the surprising news that he'd found a witch in your apartment, I felt it ... prudent to bring her to the party."

"Listen," Raph said, "she's just a witch I met at a party, that's all. We hooked up, you know? You should let her go, though. The last thing you want to do is get on the bad side of a coven here in Australia. They're pretty fierce."

"Is that so?" Parsons considered Eve and then Raph. "I heard rumors of you at a party last night; was that the one?"

"That's right," Raph said calmly. "How did you think I got the relic? The witch was just a bonus."

"Raphael, by the goddess," Eve snarled, "I'll kill you, you fucking—"

"Stolas," Parsons said, "please gag our guest. We don't need any spells being cast now, do we?"

Raph pursed his lips. Pretty sure Eve could call a spell

with her mouth gagged. But he didn't say anything. They might need her magic to get them out of here yet.

Stolas took a necktie from one of the daemon squad and tied it around Eve's head and over her mouth, then nodded at Parsons

But the gag didn't look all that tight. Raph regarded the daemon—was he inept, or was this something else? Once Stolas was done, one of the daemon squad from the bar grasped Eve's upper arms. Was that so she couldn't throw any spells at them?

"Forneous," Stolas said, "I've done my job. Now you do yours. Release me."

Forneous? Raph whirled around.

Parsons was already watching him, his pale eyes filled with mirth. Oh fuck. Parsons was *Forneous*? Even Raph had heard of his grandfather's right-hand man. Or right-hand daemon. Whatever you called it.

This was bad news. Very, very, *very* bad news.

But why the fuck was Forneous after the relic? Was dear old grandpa looking for a scenery change and Forneous doing his dirty work?

"I've done as you bade," Stolas continued. "My end of the deal is honored; therefore, I'm outta here. I've got other matters to ... attend to." The dark-haired daemon left the room.

"Well, Mr. Smith, now that we're all here, I take it you have my goods?" Parsons—*Forneous*—said brightly.

Raph nodded and stepped forward with the bag, aware of Eve's gaze on him like a glacier rolling over him. Ice-cold, unstoppable. Deadly.

Hell, she had to think the absolute worst right now. But he had zero choice about seeing this through.

"I feel it," Forneous whispered. "Finally, after these thousand years, I am in its presence."

"Yes, here it is." Raph lifted the bag and held it open so the cardboard box with the relic inside was visible, then placed the bag in front of Forneous. "The contract is fulfilled. You agree?"

"Agreed." Forneous cackled. "Well done, Raphael. Your grandsire would be most impressed." An electric buzz swept through Raph, the contract fulfilled, and the magical bond released. "But don't worry, he won't hear a word of this. We are all aware of how very little you want to involve your dear grandfather in your life. He's disappointed in you, you know. You and your sister. But that's your choice."

Raph couldn't help the internal bristle at even the mention of his grandfather, but he managed to fake a calm smile. "Well, since our business is done, I'll hand over the box formally and then take my leave."

"Mmm-mmm!" Eve lunged forward.

"Hold her!" Forneous snapped. "And make sure that gag is tight enough."

Forneous licked his lips, and a fervor entered his gaze that made Raph's skin crawl. This next part had to go right.

At his side, Eve struggled against the daemon holding her arms and yelled louder than ever through the gag. Shit, if the daemon held her any tighter, he'd hurt her.

"Eve, be still," he muttered. But she didn't even look at him. Hell, he had to do this now. "Forneous, now I've delivered my part of the bargain, I really must leave. With Arthur and the witch, of course."

Forneous glanced at Arthur and then at Eve. He turned back to his men and nodded at Arthur. "Take him to his shop."

Arthur woodenly rose to his feet.

"Is he okay?" Raph asked.

"He's under sedation," Forneous said. "Will recall little to none of this exchange, or if so, think only of it as a dream."

"And Eve?"

Forneous smiled and motioned for the daemon holding Eve to come closer.

"Shall I leave the bag with the relic? Or just the relic?" Raph asked casually as if he wasn't holding his breath.

"I only require the gift of gold."

Raph's heart started to beat again, and he reached into the bag, withdrew the cardboard box, closed the top flaps over, and placed it carefully in the center of the table.

He backed away, drawing the straps of the antique-shop bag over his shoulder.

"Done. So, I'll take the witch and go?"

Forneous stroked his lower lip while he eyed Eve. "No, I don't think so. This witch has power—I can taste it from here. She stays. I'll accept her as a tithing, if you will. After all, I'm one of the original founders of Hell; it's only fitting you give me some kind of recognition, don't you?"

Eve saw red. *No.* No fucking way was she going to be anyone's *tithing.* And no way in a million solstices for a creepy daemon from Hell.

"Sorry, sweetheart, it was fun and all that," Raph said as he stepped in front of her and met her gaze. He rubbed his sternum slowly, back and forth. And then he turned to Creepy. "Forneous, as much as I respect your position, I can't give the witch over to you. She's not mine to give away. But if you ask her, perhaps she'll agree? She's a bit of a timid thing, though, afraid of her own shadow, you know?"

Raph tapped at his sternum again—right where Eve's pendant rested on her chest.

Shadows. Oh goddess. As if just the thought had conjured them, the crystal pendant hummed between her breasts. Then his other word registered. *Timid?*

"Timid?" Creepy said. "I see more spitfire than mouse so far."

"Maybe she doesn't like being gagged?" Raph shrugged. He rubbed his sternum one more time but kept his gaze on Creepy. "Up to you, though."

"Fine, Mr. Smith, let's see if this mouse is amenable to spending some time with me. You, mouse, know this. There are certain events unfolding in the near future that'll make you a fortunate witch indeed to warm my bed."

Ew. And that was a big ugly fucking *no.*

As the daemon squashing her arms undid the gag, she wanted to shoot daggers at the lying, traitorous Raph, but right now, getting out of there with the relic was the goal.

Just what was the stinking PI up to now? But she didn't have time to work that out.

The gag dropped away, and Eve forced her gaze to the ground, bit back the urge to scream stun spells at Raph and Creepy, and pretended to pick her necklace up in a nervous way, tugging at the crystal.

"Well, my little mouse?" Creepy asked. "What do you say? Will you hand yourself over to me so I may celebrate the glory of this day between your thighs?"

Vomit curdled in her throat. "That would be ..."

Oh, frick it. No way could she pretend this fucker was getting anywhere near her vagina. Eve muttered the Spell of Shadows under her breath and channeled it straight into the crystal. Goddess, let Raph know what he was doing. The last time these had gotten free had been ...

A chill raced down her spine. It was done now. The room was already so dark that the shadows exploded out of the dark spots between tables, around the chairs, from the corners of the room, from beneath the bar. They consumed the air so quickly that she suddenly couldn't breathe.

"Shadows!" Creepy cried. "Portal, now!" He grabbed the cardboard box with her relic and ran for the arches at the far end of the room.

The gift of gold! Eve went to run after Creepy, but Raph grabbed her arm and hauled her off her feet. She landed on her ass, pain shooting up her back.

The rest of the daemons ran for the archway hot on Creepy's heels, but the shadows converged on them, their screams lasting moments before they disappeared into the darkness.

Oh goddess, the relic was gone.

Shadows filled the room—no way could she get through. She tried to yank her hand off the crystal to stop the spell, but it wouldn't come away. Tears burned at her eyes. No, no, no, no, no.

"Eve," Raph shouted. He hauled her up to her feet and into his side. Something hard banged into her elbow. "Don't fucking move!"

"Please, please, goddess," she cried, trying with every-thing she had to take her hand off the crystal.

But nothing. And more shadows poured into the room.

"Eve, watch me. Just me." Raph yelled into her face and said something else.

She blinked. What was he saying? His lips moved, but she couldn't hear anything above the crash of her blood through her veins.

She'd lost it. She'd fucking lost the relic.

Raph grabbed her to him, his brow touching hers. Was he shouting still? His eyes bored into hers—their color darkening, glittering, as he did whatever he did to call the shadows off.

None of that mattered now. She'd stuffed up so frigging badly. Goddess, why hadn't she just accepted from the start that the Templars should find the relic? Could all this have been avoided? She'd been so certain she could get it back, prove her innocence. But now, all she'd done was fuck it all up and make things so much worse.

"Eve. Eve!"

Someone was shaking her—Raph. She grabbed his arms. "Stop shaking me!"

"Let go of the crystal," he murmured. "They're gone now."

"It doesn't matter," she whispered. But she let the crystal slip go. "My relic's gone."

"Come on; we need to get out of here. Like now. I need to check on Arthur, and then we need to get back behind your wards."

"It doesn't matter!" Eve jerked Raph's hands off her arms. "Nothing matters! Not who the fuck you are and or why, by the goddess, you think I would ever go anywhere with you again, you lying, traitorous, mother-fucker—"

"Wow, impressive, but—"

"In fact, I'm going to do the world a real favor and take you out myself." Eve grabbed her athame from its sheath.

"You're going to stab me?" Raph said.

"I'm going to curse you, you son of a frogspawn."

"Uh, I'm already cursed, so no thanks. But really, we have to go. And I know I have a lot to explain, and I will; you have my word. But first, we have to get out of here. *This*"—

Raph tapped the bag hanging over his shoulder—"needs to get out of here."

"Like I'll ever trust your *word* again." Eve flipped the athame between her fingers, then drew the tip slowly across the fleshy pad at the base of her thumb. "This curse is for unending pain. Like how I'll go for the rest of my exista—"

"Eve! Just look, damn it." Raph opened the bag.

Her heart stopped. Sweet goddess! Eve yanked the bag away from Raph. "You're never touching this again." She swung the strap over her shoulder. "But how—and what did Creepy—oh goddess, what did Forneous take?"

"I took a jewelry box from Arthur's shop and hid it below the cardboard box with the relic. After Forneous saw the real deal, I swapped them around."

"You switched a jewelry box for the gift of gold?"

"Yes, then Forneous portaled off to who knows where, which is why we—"

"—have to get out of here. Got it. But I'm not going anywhere with you. In fact, I don't ever want to see you again."

"You have to." Raph grimaced; his eyes went dull.

Eve snorted and ran for the steps. "Not happening."

"Eve, Forneous will be back." Raph followed her up the stairs. "And maybe with more daemons. The only way to scare them off is the shadows—the shadows you can call. But you can't control them. For that, you need me. I'm the one who can send them away."

Damn the man to Hades, but he had a point. The relic was more important than anything—even her feelings.

Eve gritted her teeth but didn't stop running. "Fine. You can stay until I get the relic back to safety. But don't think this conversation is over."

27

Eve slid into Raph's car and slammed the door shut as soon as they'd dropped Arthur off with one of his family. The old man had been too shaky to leave at his shop alone.

She clutched the bag with the relic to her chest and swiveled to face Raph as he started the engine. "Time to talk. Now."

"I know," he said softly as he drove them through the city. "And straight up, I'm sorry I didn't tell you about—"

"You can shove the sorrys where the sun doesn't shine. Zero interest in your apologies. And where are you driving us?"

"My place. Your ward is still in action, so we can bunker down and figure out the next steps."

"You can take us there, but whether or not I go inside depends on how much explaining you do. Start with who you really are. And how you control the shadows."

Raph's lips tightened, but then he nodded. "You know my curse."

She stared at him. "So?"

"That curse comes from my mother's side of the family."

Raph's jaw ticked. "This isn't something I talk about, you know?"

"Yes, I do know." Eve folded her arms over the relic. "So spit it out. And is that why Creepy was talking about your grandfather?"

"Creepy? You said that before."

"Forneous. And don't change the subject."

"Right. Well, creepy is a good description to start with. He's my mother's sire's right-hand daemon."

"Your mother's ... you mean your grandfather, right? Just say so."

Raph's jaw clenched. "I don't use that term for the relationship. Ever. He sired my mother. That doesn't make him my *grandfather*. He means nothing to me. Or to Isa. We've spent our entire lives trying to disassociate from him and his world."

"Raph! Who is he?"

"I think you know," he whispered.

Her heart stopped. Oh goddess—she'd had sex with the grandson of the devil?

"Yeah, I can see you get it. And that's why I can control the shadows. But it's more than that. They're drawn to me. The shadows will come to me. Heed me."

"What exactly do the shadows do?"

"They live everywhere there is darkness, but always contained behind the first gate of Hell. For some reason, you can open the first gate, Eve, at least enough to call the shadows through. The task of the shadows is to take the souls of beings to Hell. Only ... only the Lord of Hell, or one of his blood, can control them. But more, they'll seek me out. Their job is to feed me the souls they've taken."

Eve's breath stopped. Goddess, that was awful. No wonder Raph didn't want her to do the spell—yet, he'd asked her to call it today, to save the relic. She squashed down the unwelcome feeling of … softness, pity even, that wanted to well inside her. This was about the relic. Nothing more. She hardened her resolve.

"Fine. You've got an interesting family tree. That's question one answered. Question two, what, by the goddess, were you doing with my relic? Three, why did you lie to me?"

"You've got a unique way of putting things, you know that?" Raph's lips turned up for a moment before they flattened again. "But yeah, I get this is the important part."

"Yes, Raph, this is the important part. The bit where you tell me why you stole my relic and risked it falling into the hands of a frigging daemon!"

"I know, I know. Okay." He blew out a steadying breath and then confessed everything. From Parsons and his binding contract to the threat to Isa.

"Hold on. You signed a magical *binding* contract?"

"It wasn't clear at the time, okay?"

"And the thing about Isa being hassled—and why she moved up to the farm—was that all a lie, too?" Eve's chest tightened. Damn it, she'd *liked* Isa. Had thought they'd kind of become … friends.

"No," Raph said, "that's the truth. But I did need to let her and Dad know about the threat."

The tightness in Eve's chest eased.

"Okay, so you were being pressured to hand over the relic. I get it. But then why take me on as a client too? What was …?" Oh goddess, now it all made sense. "You had to stay close to me, didn't you? You knew I would find the gift of gold no matter what, so you made me pay you to find the relic for me."

"You haven't actually paid me anything. In fact, I think I've paid you in craft items and ... okay, never mind."

"I made spells for you. I warded the farmhouse. I kissed you! I ... goddess, we had sex. All of that—everything was so that you could get to the relic. Raph, why by the Moon Goddess, would you do that?"

"I didn't have a choice! Yes, you were stubborn enough to find it no matter what. But I had to deliver the relic—you know I had no choice. Plus, at the start, I didn't even know if you were the original thief."

"But you had the choice to tell me or not. And that, you're wholly responsible for."

Raph went to speak, but they'd arrived at his apartment complex. He shot her a look—his jaw clenched so hard it ticked—as they drove into the parking garage.

"Keep an eye out," he said. "Forneous will know by now about the switch. Your magic is the best offensive weapon we have, so I'll watch your back, but you should go first. Do you want me to hold the relic? That is—if you're coming up?"

She gave him a withering look. "Yes, I'm coming up. But you're not ever touching my relic again." She tightened the bag over her shoulder but also readied a stun spell—just in case. The hum of power buzzed through her palms.

She only dropped the magic after they were safely back in Raph's apartment, and she registered that the power of her previous ward was still in place.

Eve stared at the kitchen ... her supplies were strewn over the counter. The counter where Raph had set her body on fire with his mouth. At the couch where they'd fallen asleep, and she'd woken up cradled in his arms.

Goddess, this wasn't such a good idea. She needed to get to Rome. Now.

"You can have a seat," Raph murmured into the silence. "If you want."

Eve made a beeline for the dining table. The only place she didn't have a memory of Raph and her together.

"Can I get you a coffee?" Raph asked.

She shook her head. "I don't want anything."

"Okay." He blew out a harsh breath and ran his fingers through his hair.

What did he have to be so upset over? He'd gotten what he needed—his contract was filled.

"I know I did the wrong thing," Raph said. "That I should've told you."

"Oh really? So why didn't you?"

"I tried to—but you've been so single bloody-minded about getting the relic back. I knew you'd never agree to my handing over the relic—even if I planned on taking it straight back."

"Well, you know what? We'll never know now because you didn't give me a chance."

"And for that, I'm sorry."

"And sorry's not good enough."

"Please, Eve. I delivered the relic, so the contract's over. But he's still out there. You need to be careful."

"Ooh, *he*? As in your grandaddy's sidekick?"

"Yes. Him."

"Well, no matter, I'm going to glamour the relic now. And my flight is booked to Rome at midnight. I'll get the relic to safety, and then it doesn't matter if Forneous or anyone else comes looking. I'll place a ward around it that no one will be able to get through."

"Don't underestimate Forneous. He's got sixth- and seventh-gate daemons working for him or with him. I'll come with you."

"I don't need your help. I'll call the coven, explain about Caterina and tell them I'm bringing the relic back. What I should've done from the start."

"Um, Eve, there's one more thing I need to tell you."

She slowly looked up. Raph was tugging at his earlobe."

"What more can you possibly tell me?" she said.

Raph blew out a short, fast breath. "The Templars know where you are."

"What do you mean?"

"When I realized the relic wasn't just a family trinket box, I called a contact of mine ... an old buddy I've worked with in the past. He's also a Templar. He was the one who confirmed the relic was the gift of gold. Although he failed to tell me exactly what the repercussions of it falling into the wrong hands are." Raph's lips tightened.

"And just who is this person?" Eve flopped back in her chair. "No, don't tell me. I know. It's Gray. And by the goddess, you were contracted by the Templars. You know that makes you one of them, right?" She shook her head. "I can't believe I had frigging sex with a Templar."

"Well—"

"Holy goddess, Raph, there was a Templar right here with me! But why didn't he just grab me and take me back? Or tell you to grab me and take me back since you're one of them."

"Contracted, technically. We knew you didn't have the relic. And to Gray, that was the more important outcome. Plus, he didn't know exactly how involved you were in the theft."

"Wait," Eve said. "Did you think I was involved in the theft?"

"At first, I wasn't sure if you were in on a deal that went bad or something, like maybe Frinecki cut you out, and you were trying to get it back after that. Remember, you said yourself, someone got past your ward."

A hysterical laugh escaped Eve. "Just great. You thought I'd stolen the relic."

"No—I just didn't know how involved you were in the disappearance. But I realized pretty quickly that you weren't part of it in that way. And I did try to get you to call the Templars, if you recall—"

"Oh, for the sake of the goddess, you were double-crossing me. And triple-crossing Forneous."

"Yeah," Raph said, "lucky he hadn't thought to put anything about that in the contract."

"Not funny. This is the most *not* funny situation I've ever been in. We had sex, Raph. And you used me to get to the relic. You lied to me. And you stole from me!"

"I know, but I promise you, I didn't make love—"

"Sex, Raph, we had sex. Like scratching an itch, although I normally don't scratch an itch with lying assholes."

"Eve. Well before you and I had sex, I knew you weren't involved."

"Fine," she managed to get out through gritted teeth. "But, Mr. Smith, the only reason I'm even considering letting you tag along to Rome is because you're a frigging daemon yourself—"

"Half."

"—and you might be useful if your *Forneous* returns. But as soon as the relic is safely in its vault, you and I are done. I never want to see you, hear you, smell you, ever. *Ever.* Again."

Ten hours into their thirteen-and-a-half-hour flight from Singapore to Rome and over eighteen hours after leaving Brisbane, Raph eyed the spare seat between Eve and the person fast asleep in the aisle seat. For the millionth time.

From where he sat across the walkway, it was clear Eve was awake, but she wasn't reading, or watching a movie, or doing anything other than staring out into the night sky. He could tell by the top and lower curves of her thick eyelashes.

She was pissed. And he got why; he'd lied to her. And the best of intentions didn't—couldn't—change that.

And Eve was right. He hadn't given her the chance to even prove him wrong.

Raph's gut curdled, and he looked away, focused on whatever the hell was on the screen ... but his gaze traveled back to Eve as if his eyes couldn't *not* look at her. Whenever she was in the room, she was the only person that existed. She was where his gaze went back to. Every. Damned. Time.

What was it about Eve?

Whatever it was, he was a goner for her. And what if she never forgave him? She was so stubborn and hot-headed that she might never let him get close enough to apologize. Hell, he'd grovel. Would gladly get down on his knees and beg her forgiveness if she gave him the chance.

Going back to the apartment in Brisbane without her ... his gut clenched. Left him hollow. His kitchen counter wouldn't be covered with her craft tools. Her smart mouth wouldn't keep him on his toes. Her perfume wouldn't fill his senses.

Raph mentally slapped himself in the head. He was a goner for her. Which was absurd—they'd known each other little more than a week.

Bloody hell, enough was enough. He squeezed past the person sitting on the aisle and maneuvered into the spare seat beside Eve.

Eve stiffened but didn't say anything. He met her gaze in the window's reflection and drank her in. She hadn't spoken to him since they'd boarded—and had said maybe ten words to him from the moment she'd finished glamouring the relic as a deck of tarot cards.

"I need to tell you one more thing," Raph whispered.

"Go back to your own seat."

"Just let me say one thing. Please."

Her lips pursed and her chin raised—she had a real talent for that—and then she turned to him. "No."

Raph's stomach dropped. He nodded once and held in the urge to tell her exactly how highly he thought of her and to try one last time to apologize. Clearly, she didn't care. He had totally and utterly fucked this up.

She turned back to the window, this time closing her eyes. Eve's angular profile was in shadow as she ducked her chin down. But her lips were still pursed and her jaw tight.

"Sorry," he whispered. Then he maneuvered back to his own seat.

But he didn't stop staring at her. She might not want anything more to do with him—and he'd have to bear that —but he'd still make sure nothing else happened to her until she got the relic to safety and her life back.

28

WAITING at the airport taxi rank, Eve pulled the edges of her coat tightly together as the icy dusk air snuck through her clothing. As soon as a cab pulled up, she hopped into the rear passenger seat and ignored Raph as he sat in the front.

She explained where they were heading, and the driver nodded and took off.

Within thirty minutes, they'd passed through one of the many openings of the circular wall that demarcated the ancient city. She'd made this drive less than two weeks earlier. On that morning, Eve's heart had been racing with excitement. Now, her muscles knotted, and nausea seesawed in her gut.

She glanced at Raph. He was chatting with the driver, discussing the regions like a real tourist and looking at the city passing by outside the car. But Eve saw through the chitchat. No doubt he was keeping an eye out for anything suspicious.

She was doing the same.

And then, the taxi pulled up at the drop-off in front of St. Peter's Square. In the early evening light, statues rose like giant sentinels above the surrounding colonnades. Lights illuminated every column and the buildings around the square.

Outside the taxi, Eve strapped the new leather bag she'd bought in Singapore across her body and drew her jacket close again. She blew out a steadying breath as she stared up at the obelisk in the middle of the square.

Almost there.

Raph joined her, his cheeks red in the icy evening air.

"This way," she said and took off at a fast clip toward the colonnades, dodging the people still coming and going around the square.

"Keep an eye out," Raph said by her ear. "Depending on who's still hunting the 'you know what,' they'll know you have to bring it back here."

Eve shivered—from the cold. Nothing to do with the heat of his body.

"I'm on guard," she snapped.

Goddess, but she wanted to put space between them. Except right now, someone would have to wedge between Raph and her to get to the relic.

The lights on every building and all around the square went out.

In the sudden dark, the colonnades loomed high into the early night sky. Some people held out their phones— their screens glowing.

"Eve. You holding that bag securely?"

"Tighter than a witch's grip on an athame for their first spell."

"Right. Sounds good. I take it the lights don't normally go out?"

"No clue. I'd only just arrived in Rome when this all started."

"Fuck."

A figure loomed out of the shadows, coming straight for them, and heart racing, Eve called up a stun spell—then stopped, hearing muttering in Italian. The approaching figure focused into a seventy-something-year-old woman, looking at the darkened lights with a frown.

"We need cover," Raph said.

"Through the colonnades. They're four rows deep, should give us plenty of cover." Instead of heading across the square to St. Anne's Gate, the entry into the city she'd used on her first visit, she veered hard right.

Around them, more mobile phones were being turned on for lighting, and people's voices rose as if the dark made it harder to hear.

Eve had just reached the first row of stone columns when running footsteps, a lot of them, echoed through the dark. The hairs on the back of her neck rose. That didn't sound good.

"Move!" Raph pushed Eve ahead of him deeper between the colonnades. Then two streams of silvery light shot between the columns.

"Witch!" Eve said. "Raph, this is magic."

"That's right. Mine," Caterina's familiar voice said from behind them. "I'll be taking that relic now."

Two more streams of magic shot straight at Eve, but she ducked and rolled. The spells shot overhead, singeing her jacket, and her chin stung from where it had hit the pavement.

"As if, bitch," Eve spat, tasting blood. "You should have crawled into some hidey-hole and hoped to the goddess we never found you. You're no match for me. That burns you, doesn't it?"

"You're nobody!" Caterina screamed.

In the pitch black, with the colonnades distorting sound, it was impossible to figure out where the loco Watcher was. Shit, she could be anywhere. But while the red-haired witch might be good, she wasn't as strong as Eve. Eve just had to outlast the other witch's energy until she could get her own opportunity.

Eve ran to the edge of the square and readied her magic.

Movement ahead caught her attention. Whoever it was, they'd darted to the outer edges of the colonnades too.

Eve followed them, skirting around the columns until she was right behind the person.

"Eve!" Raph's voice echoed from the square. "Where are you?"

The person in front of Eve called a spell and hurled a glowing orb of red energy ... a kill hex ... at Raph. For one moment, the glow of the spell revealed Caterina's face.

"Raph!" Eve screamed. "Duck!"

Raph cried out, then thudded to the ground. Eve's stomach dropped. Goddess, no! Please, please let him be okay. She went running for Raph, but then she spun.

Caterina was pulling another spell—the red of a hex coming together—but she was slow. Way too slow.

"Get the fuck gone, bitch." Eve threw her stun at Caterina.

As the silvery orb hit, it illuminated the redhead's face. Caterina froze in place; her eyes narrowed, lips pulled back in a snarl.

Eve didn't waste another second and ran toward where Raph had been, almost tripping over a lump on the ground. Her heart stopped. No. No, no, no, no.

She dropped to her knees—landed on a large body.

"Ugh," Raph groaned. "Ow."

Her breath whooshed out, and she ran her hands over

his chest and up to his neck. "Sweet goddess, you scared me. I thought she got you. Are you okay?"

"I ducked the spell, but my head bounced off the pavement when I hit the ground. Things are a bit fuzzy. Other than that, okay. How are you?"

"She had nothing on me." Eve stood and, in the dark, helped him to his feet. "She'll be stunned for a good thirty minutes—time enough to get inside the Vatican."

"Always so humble."

"False humility is a lie. And I don't lie to myself."

Her words hung out there. Crap. But she had to face this with Raph. He'd lied to her. And that had frigging hurt more than anything else he'd done.

An hour ago, Eve had never wanted to see him again. But when Caterina's spell had hurled toward him, and he'd gone silent, everything in her had stopped. She didn't want Raph to die. At least not by anyone else's hands but hers.

"Eve, I have to tell you—"

"Raph, I need to tell you—"

"Oh, how touching," an oily voice said at her back. "Fancy seeing you both here."

Eve stiffened. Who else was going to intrude on this party? She turned around as Forneous emerged from the dark, a phalanx of people in black suits—daemons no doubt—spread out in a V behind him.

Oh crap.

"Fuck," Raph muttered under his breath. "That's a lot of daemons."

"Yep." Eve glanced toward St. Anne's Gate. "Listen, my ward still stands inside the Vatican. He won't be able to pass through that spell. I get the relic there, and it's game over for Creepy and any chance to get his hands on the relic."

"The relic's the priority," Raph said. "You make a run. I'll stall them."

"You'll follow?"

"Yep. Couldn't stop me."

Eve took off. But just as she reached Caterina's frozen body, one of Forneous' squad yanked her arm. She spun away, called another stun spell, threw it at the daemon and ducked behind Caterina.

But another daemon with flowing black hair, punctuated with two rows of horns running over her head, grabbed Eve's satchel and whipped out a double-ended knife.

"Eve!" Raph yelled. "Watch out! That's a hellblade—"

Eve called a stun spell as the daemon slashed through the satchel strap, piercing Eve's chest at the same time, then spun, lifting the satchel into the air.

Eve grabbed for the satchel, but her arm wouldn't work. She tried to scream for Raph, but she couldn't catch her breath to make a sound.

With her hand that would work, she threw the stun spell. It froze the daemon holding her satchel in midstep. The hellblade clattered to the ground. Eve's satchel went flying.

And then Raph was there; his hand caught hers, and everything went dark.

Raph's heart stopped. Eve staggered and Raph dove, catching her head before it cracked on the pavement. "Eve. Answer me. Evangeline!"

Nothing.

Raph fumbled for her neck and felt for her pulse. Please, please, please ... nothing. No. Fuck, no, not this.

"Eve! Eve, baby, you've got to come back to me. Come on, princess. Come on."

He laid her down. Fuck. Her chest was wet. Sticky wet.

Oh fuck. That *had* been a hellblade. One slice to separate soul and body. He crushed Eve's lifeless body to his. Fuck no. No, no, no, no, no.

"The witch is dead, but don't hit Raphael," Forneous shouted. "He must not cross over. Get me the bag—yes! What? This is just a deck of tarot cards. Where is it? Search the square. Search everywhere. It must be here."

Cross over ... cross over ...

"*Embrace the dark.*" Isa's warning played back through his mind. The words were as loud and clear as if she stood at his side.

Fuck, he knew exactly what to do.

For the first time ever, Raph embraced his curse. He held a hand to the colonnade and opened his mind fully to the voices of the past—he raced back through time until he caught the ugly echo of darkness—a shadow.

Come to me, he mentally ordered.

The shadow surged through the past and then was there with Raph in the present and in the square.

"*Bring me the legion,*" Raph ordered.

The darkness flew at him. Into him. Through him. And suddenly, shadows streamed out of the dark, faceless, formless beings. Intense heat scorched him from the inside out; ash coated his mouth.

The pull of power unending made Raph's head spin. All of this—of them—they could all be mine.

No. No, he was not here for that.

Come to me, Raph demanded. *Protect us.*

"What will you sacrifice for this power?" whispered a deep voice through his mind. A chill shot to Raph's heart. He knew that voice. He'd run from it his entire life. But he wasn't running anymore.

"I'll give anything," he said.

A burning vise clamped around his bicep, and in his soul, Raph knew what had been given. But he didn't argue.

Come to me, he demanded again. *Protect us.*

And the shadows flew to him, surrounding him where he crouched over Eve. He stared at her face. The arch of her brows. The sweep of her lashes. The angle of her jaw. The curve of her lips. The imperial line of her nose. Eve. The woman he loved.

"Bring me her soul."

Please. *Please* let this work.

Eve sat up with a gasp. What, by the goddess, had happened? One moment she'd been flying through a welcome, endless night sky with a million stars shining back at her, and the next, something had caught her, sent her flying in the other direction ... and she'd seen something. No, *someone.*

Warm hands had reached out and clasped hers. But she'd slipped from the grip—almost fallen into an unending void of nothing, then the hands had reached again. This time they'd clamped around her in a vise-like grip and hadn't let go.

She strained to capture more of the image, but like a

dream teasing the edges of memory, it drifted away, and the more she woke, the less she recalled.

The remnant of something painful lodged in Eve's chest, and she scrubbed a hand over the skin there. Picked up her crystal. The warm weight of the amethyst hummed comfortably in her hand.

She reflexively ran a thumb over the fracture, but as she did, the seam rubbed against her thumb ... differently. Smoother. Harder. Still there but mended. And not just mended. Stronger than ever. She picked the crystal up and frowned at it. What, by the goddess, had happened there?

"Eve," Raph whispered her name.

She looked up to find him kneeling, facing her. His eyes roved over her, and he reached out, cupping her face.

"Why are you shaking?" she asked.

"Are you okay? How do you feel?"

She took stock. "I ... I feel fine. Different, but fine. Something aches here." Eve scrubbed a fist over her chest again. "But I'm okay. Hey, the lights are back on." She glanced around. Black-suited bodies were strewn across the square, as well as Caterina. The witch's face sunken, hollow, as if ... "Raph, did I call the Spell of Shadows?"

"No. I did."

She stilled, searching his eyes. Pain was there—deep in the glittering green of his gaze. "But we're okay. And the relic?"

He held up a hand—her satchel was right there. She scrambled to it and pulled out the relic.

"How?"

"Your glamour worked so well even Forneous thought it was a deck of tarot cards. He threw it away and ordered his daemons to search the square." Raph's jaw tightened. "That's when I called the shadows."

"Raph—" Eve bit her lip.

Something else had happened. To her. She knew it but, for some reason, shied away from interrogating that question any closer.

The relic. That was the important thing right now.

"Are there any other immediate risks to the relic?" Eve asked.

"Forneous ran as soon as the shadows came. Not sure where he went."

"In that case, let's get the gift of gold back to safety." Eve stood and found her legs wobbly. "And then you need to tell me the rest of what happened."

At St. Anne's Gate, the Vatican guards stopped them from entering; it was only after she called for the priest who'd escorted her on the last trip that she got anywhere.

"*Strega*," the priest said.

His eyes widened as he took in her singed jacket and scraped skin. Even her hair must look wild, given it had fallen out of its knot. But Eve held the priest's gaze, and then he nodded in acknowledgment.

"I have a ward to recast," she said. "Mr. Smith is with me. He's *my* guard." She glanced back at Raph. For the first time ever, she wanted to have someone else with her—supporting her. And even after all the crap he'd done, for some batshit reason, Raph was the person she wanted standing beside her. "Are you okay with that?" she asked him.

Raph nodded slowly. His eyes lit as he regarded her. "I'm okay with that."

The guards and priest once more led her to the vault.

Determination flowed through Eve as the guards swung the heavy gates open.

"This ward hasn't been made for you to cross, so stay here," she murmured, squeezing Raph's hand.

She didn't bother with a lantern this time, simply followed the trail of light cast from the corridor into the vault—the ward spell reacted correctly against her skin—so it still stood strong. No wonder Caterina hadn't wanted her in the vault after the theft. If Eve had recognized the spell as being correct and intact, she'd have known right there that only another witch who knew the spell could've passed through.

Well, Caterina was gone now. Although that meant Eve would have to take on the coven without Caterina to perform a truth spell. But that was a problem for later.

Eve withdrew the gift of gold from her bag, the hum of the glamour buzzing against her skin. She placed the relic in the middle of the table and removed the spell. Once the buzzing stopped, she stepped away.

Her breath whooshed out of her, but then she straightened her back. She'd done it. The relic was safe.

Now all she had to do was enhance the spell with her new addition.

29

____

IT WAS ALMOST midnight by the time Raph helped Eve out of a private car the Vatican had arranged to take them back to Eve's apartment. Carrying Eve's satchel, he supported Eve up to her floor. Her legs were trembling, and she leaned her full weight into him.

"Keys," she muttered. She ducked her head toward the satchel.

Raph eased the front door open and helped Eve sink into the nearest chair.

"Stay here while I check out the place." He waited for Eve to complain about being told what to do, but she said nothing. "Well, at least living in a shoebox is good for one thing. Nowhere for anyone to hide."

He came back into the kitchen and quickly set the thermostat to warm up the apartment. Given how small it was, that wouldn't take long.

But Eve didn't even blink. She looked ... done. And no wonder. She'd fought off a loco witch, died at the end of a hellblade, come back from the dead, returned the relic to safety, and then spent hours working on a new ward spell.

"Bed or shower?" Raph asked.

She lifted her head at that, but the fog in her eyes was clear, so he made the call for her. "You're covered in blood and scratches, so shower. Then bed. Here, lean on me."

The fact that Eve did without even a murmur of sass told him everything. His heart swelled with the need to protect her, somehow shield her from any more impact or shit or hurt. Fuck, anything bad at all.

Raph turned the shower on to let the steam warm up the bathroom, and Eve started to strip, but her movements were clunky and uncoordinated. Without a word, he helped her undress; as soon as the tips of her breasts were revealed, of course, his body went rock-hard, but he ignored that and concentrated on her. He dropped to his knees and removed her boots and jeans.

Bloody scratches covered one side of Eve's torso, and a long, shallow wound slashed from her shoulder to her chest. The hellblade slice. At least the wound was healing fast courtesy of the shadows—and him—bringing her back to life.

He clenched his jaw.

He shot a look up at Eve—did she know what had happened? But her eyes were closed, and she swayed on her feet. Hell, she was about to topple over.

"I've got you," he whispered. "Eve, do you want me to wash you?"

She muttered something, maybe fuck you, but he set about cleaning away the dried blood and grit, moving gently around the wounds, and then he turned the shower off. He wrapped Eve in a towel, her hair in another, then picked her up and walked over to the bed.

The room was warming up, but it was still too cold, so he found a pair of loose pants and a long-sleeved shirt. By the time he turned back, Eve was sound asleep. He got her into the shirt and pants and then pulled the blanket high under her chin.

Raph quickly dressed in the single change of clothes he'd brought with him and sat on the end of the bed. Heaviness dragged at his limbs, but he couldn't sleep while Eve was out. If anyone came for them—not that Forneous could remount an attack that fast after losing so many of his daemons—he needed to be awake and alert.

At least he had a weapon at his disposal. His gut churned. It might be a weapon he'd never wanted, but it was his now. And he'd be damned if he didn't use it—them—to make sure no one ever hurt Eve again.

He quickly sent texts to his dad and Isa. Although the farm was eight hours ahead of him—and who knew where Isa was—they'd want to know Eve and he were okay. Then Raph sent a text to Gray, letting the Templar know the relic was back and that he and Eve were holed up in her apartment while she recuperated. He got a thumbs-up text back from his dad but nothing from Isa or Gray.

He sighed and leaned his head back on the wall. Damn, but he hoped Isa was okay.

An hour later, his phone pinged with a message from an unknown number. *Clothes and coffee, from Grayson.*

That was it. A moment later, a soft knock rapped on Eve's front door.

In the corridor, Raph found two shopping bags filled with clothes for him and Eve, designer labels, of course —*bloody Gray*—and fresh food, and thank the stars, two large takeaway coffee cups in a cardboard holder.

How the hell had Gray arranged all this in the middle of the night? Whatever strings he'd pulled, Raph was going to kiss Gray the next time he saw him.

He sat back on the bed and took a giant sip of coffee. If Gray was sending coffee, his friend couldn't be in too bad of a situation—whatever it was the bastard had going on. And that meant Isa had to be okay too.

Four hours later, Eve sat up.

Her hair tumbled over her shoulders in thick waves. Color had returned to her cheeks, and the deep smudges beneath her eyes were lighter.

"Hey," Raph said, trying to hide how worried he'd been. Eve hadn't moved for four bloody hours.

"Hi," she whispered. She blinked and looked around the room. "What time is it?"

"Half past four."

"A.M.?"

"Yeah." Raph smiled. "Although my body clock is screaming it's the middle of the day. You must be thirsty. Do you want water or a coffee?"

"Water. No, coffee. Both. And I need to pee."

"Got it. Be right back."

As he returned with water and a cup of hot, rich brew, Eve was hopping back beneath the quilt. She took a sip of the coffee, and her eyes drifted shut.

"Thank you, goddess," she murmured as she leaned back on the headrest. Then her eyes snapped open. She stared at her mug. "Where did this come from? I didn't have anything like that here before I left."

"Gray arranged a midnight delivery, including coffee for your machine. He even sent two large takeaway coffees, but I, uh, drank both."

Eve's eyes narrowed, and she looked at him from his head to his toes.

"You haven't slept."

"Yeah, well, didn't think it was a good idea to have us

both snoring away."

"I don't snore."

"Princess, you definitely snore. But don't worry, it's gorgeous."

Eve smiled, but then it faded. "Raph, we need to talk."

"Yeah, I know."

"You lied to me. And don't say you're sorry—I get that you are. And you mean it. But you and I, we had something special. And I also know it's totally batshit that I could feel so frigging attached to someone so soon. It's like you're a growth that I can't get rid of."

Raph swallowed the lump that lodged in his throat.

"But I also realized that as hurt as I was," she continued, "I don't want to *not* have your big-ass growth attached to me. So I need to know. Are you going to ever lie to me again?"

Raph ran to the bed, stumbled over his feet and made the mattress shake.

Eve yelped and glared at him. "Watch the coffee!" She put the cup on the bedside table.

"I'm your growth?" he asked as he cupped her cheeks.

"Apparently." She snorted. "Although, by the goddess, I have zero clue why she chose you for me. But there you go."

Raph stared into her dark eyes. His chest tightened, and something locked inside him. "I might be your growth. But you're my heart. And yeah, I have no clue how that happened either. But something changed in me the day you busted into Arthur's antique store. And I have no idea what the future will hold, but I know two things—I want that future to include you in any way we can make it work. And I will never lie to you again. I know that's easy for me to say— but how about this?" He rolled up his sleeve to where the binding tattoo had been. "I want you to place a binding spell on me—give me another tattoo that I can wear for life. I swear I'll never lie to you again, no matter what."

"No, Raph, that's not need—"

"Yes. Yes, it is. And I want to wear a tattoo for you. Please, let me prove to you the only way I absolutely can, that you have my honesty—like my heart—forever."

Eve's heart stopped. Like literally stopped—and restarted. Raph's glittering gaze was so full of intent on her, *for* her, that she couldn't breathe. But crap, who needed air when you had a man like Raphael Smith.

"Thank you for the offer, but I think we can find another way to mark you up." She pulled him to her.

"Eve, Eve, Eve." He trailed kisses to her ear, and his teeth grazed her lobe. "My amazing, hot-headed, bloody-minded Eve."

His. Oh yeah. And he was hers.

Elation mixed with lust and a deeper emotion—a connection, a need for Raph that went beyond the physical —rippled through her. She couldn't contain a smile, and then he nipped at her throat, sucked the skin hard and an arrow of heat fired to her core.

She arced up against him, pressed her hips into his.

He nuzzled into her throat and growled again.

She pulled him closer. But damn it, he wasn't close enough. Eve rubbed her breasts against his chest. His lips trailed down her neck, and he nipped the skin above her collarbone. More arcs of fire rushed to her lady parts.

Eve ran her hands over his shoulders. But couldn't get to any skin. And goddess, but she needed skin.

"Raph," she gasped. "More."

"Why the hurry? We have all night—morning. Day. Whatever."

"No. I need to touch you. The shirt's got to go." Eve pulled his shirt up, and then he yanked it over his head.

Oh goddess, yes. Lean muscles, abs for days, his wide shoulders, miles of hot, delicious, tanned skin. Eve leaned forward and bit down on his stomach.

Raph hissed and his abs flexed. She grinned up at him.

"What, you can give it, but you can't take it?"

"Evangeline, are you challenging me to a hickey-off? Because I'm up for that challenge. But I believe we already have a competition to settle."

She took off her top. His gaze locked on her breasts. Another growl rumbled through Raph, and she hid a smile as she arched her back.

"Oh, and what competition might that be?" Eve asked.

"Think I recall someone saying she could make me yell louder than her." His gaze dipped to her lap beneath the quilt. "I think I'm going to spend a ... long ... time proving you wrong."

"Raphael Smith, you can try. But trust me, I have a way to blow your mind." She licked at the tight nub of his nipple.

"Two can play at that." Raph rained kisses down her chest to her breasts, drew her nipple into his mouth, rolled his tongue around and around the peak.

Fire shot to her core, and she gasped. Then he sucked hard, and her body flooded. She moaned, writhing as sensation sang through her veins.

"And that's just the start." Raph grinned against Eve's

breast and blew across her nipple. He kissed his way down her stomach to the hollow of her belly button, then pushed her pants down and wedged his shoulders between her thighs. "Eve," he murmured.

She levered up on one elbow. The need blazing from his eyes, the way his gaze locked on her core ... her body clenched.

His lips pulled back in a dangerous smile, and then he parted the curls at the top of her sex before his hot breath washed over her, and his tongue traced her folds. Delved. Found her clit. Sucked and licked and swirled.

Explosions of sensation crashed through Eve, and she cried out. Her hips rose, retreated, but the lashing of sensation didn't stop as he kept the pressure up. And then Raph dipped a finger inside her. She arched, tried to stop her scream ... failed. Went flying again.

When the world came back into focus, he was still between her thighs. His lips were red and wet. His hair mussed, his jaw tight.

"I want to be inside you so much right now. But no condom."

Heart racing, Eve waved over to the bathroom. "Check there. I would ... but my legs aren't working right now."

His low chuckle flowed over her core before he disappeared into the bathroom.

And then he was back. "Score."

"Score indeed." She managed to get to her knees. "Now get that body over here."

She plucked the condom from his fingers. As he lay back on the bed, a total smorgasbord of hot skin and ridged muscle, she knelt between his thighs.

"Raphael Smith, I'm one lucky witch."

She stroked his cock, the hot satiny skin making her body weep for more. Then she caressed his balls. Raph's back arched off the bed, and his hips surged into the air. Oh yes, this was going to be fun.

"I want you to see me this time," she purred.

Keeping her eyes on his, she leaned down and tasted him. His skin was salty with precum that she licked off, swirling her tongue over the tip. Then she took him deep in her mouth. Raph moaned and lifted his head, and Eve held his gaze as she lowered her lips all the way down—and back up.

"Oh fuck," he muttered.

She sat back on her haunches. "Sorry, I didn't catch that. Your voice was too low. Say again?"

Eve took him back into her mouth, moved up and down, over and over. Raph's words grew more and more hoarse. But with every sweep, her own body grew tighter—as amazing as the orgasm minutes ago had been, what she really wanted was his cock. Inside her. Now.

She let go and ripped open a foil packet, then rolled the condom over his length. His hips surged again into her hands. Eve wanted to tease him—let him know she was going to win this one, but suddenly the need to have him filling her was too demanding. Too hungry. And she straddled him, took him inside.

"Eve." Raph's back arched again, and he gritted his teeth.

She bared her teeth in response, but the demand was rushing through her, and she rose high—almost to his tip—and then slammed down. Sensation spiked; her nerves screamed. Eve did it again; this time, his hands grabbed her hips, and he thrust up as she came down. Stars shimmered behind her eyes. Her head fell back. Her body tensed.

Beneath her, Raph growled, and his hips thrust to piston

beneath her. The pressure in Eve gathered, crested, smashed through her again. Over and over, he hammered into her, and all she could do was hold on as the sensation surged through her.

Raph's neck muscles strained as he held her hips and ground into her, then his shout filled the room.

"Okay, you win. I definitely shouted louder," Raph said as dawn lightened the sky.

Eve smiled into his shoulder and pressed a kiss to the warm skin. Goddess, but he was fine. And this hunk of hotness was all hers. "It was my pleasure. And don't think I was far behind."

"Well, I'm only conceding the battle. The war is ongoing." His arm tightened around her, hugging her into his side.

Eve stared at the unfamiliar tattoo cuffing Raph's bicep. It was a series of lines and circles with a moon in the center. "This is new."

Raph lifted his head and looked at the tattoo. His lips flattened for all of a moment before he pressed a kiss to the top of her head and curled his arm around her again.

"I got it in the square," Raph said.

"How?"

"You were dying—your soul was already on its way."

"Raph, what did you do?" she whispered.

"I made a contract. A permanent one. I used the shadows to bring you back."

"And the cost?"

"I always knew if I ever used the shadows—if I ever made them work for me—that I'd have to give something up. The price was my mortality. Being part of the human world. Now I straddle both."

Eve turned in his embrace and met his gaze.

His eyes were serious but filled with a light blazing back at her. "And I would do it a million times over for you, Eve."

A shiver shook through her heart. He had sacrificed the ability—the choice—to disassociate with the supernatural world. For her.

"But Eve, I said I won't lie to you—and I mean that. So there's something else you need to know. Because I brought your soul back, and I'm now immortal, I think you are, too. I think we're tied together that way. If I die, so do you."

Eve stilled. "And me? What if I die before you?"

"My guess is I'll go too."

A sigh escaped her. "Watcher's live a long time, Raph. I've always known my power meant I'd be in this world longer than others—barring the odd hellblade altercation. Looks like that time's been extended. But I'm sorry you had to make that call."

"I'm not." His gaze grew fierce. "I would do it again in a heartbeat for you, Eve."

Eve wrapped her arm around his chest and held him tight. He'd been a shield for her against death? Well, she'd shield him right back against whatever pain or threat came at him.

"Hey, do you know what today is?" Raph said suddenly.

Eve burrowed into his side. "Apart from the day we spend eating, drinking mulled wine, sleeping and recovering?"

"Yeah, apart from that. It's Christmas Eve. Maybe ..." He cleared his throat. "Maybe we can start a tradition—you and

I spend Christmas Eve together. Wherever we each might be in the world, we spend Christmas together. If that means we're in Rome every year, that's where we are. Together. Mulled wine and all."

She raised her head and stared into his gorgeous face. "I'd like that." She kissed him softly before snuggling back into his side. "I won't know what my future holds until I get back to Cheshire and face the coven, but I can guarantee that no matter what they say, I'll be spending Christmases with you."

"So that's the next step? Back to the giant, old, craggy castle in Cheshire?"

"I have to explain about Caterina and the relic—hopefully, they're willing to hear me out."

"I'll be your witness. And Gray will too, without question. With the Templars on your side, the coven will have to listen. But then what for you? As a Watcher, I mean."

"I'm still willing to be a Watcher—I'm the best they've got after all. But the spells we have are old, used for hundreds, if not thousands of years. What if there are other Watchers disenfranchised like Caterina? The coven has pissed a lot of people off—*I've* pissed a lot of people off. While I'm there, I'll make it clear they need to change. Progress out of the past. And if they say no, then I'll find another way to look after the relics that need protecting."

"You could always do what I do—contract for the Templars. They'd jump at the chance to work with you. But you trained for a decade to become a Watcher. Is that still what you want?"

"For a long time, that was all I wanted. The prestige of becoming a Watcher. Of beating everyone else. To master the spells and my power. Of proving I could do it—kind of for both my mother and me. That's why I gave up so much over all those years to achieve that."

"Some things are worth sacrificing for." His arm tightened around her.

"And some things aren't."

THE END

THANK YOU & REVIEWS

Dear Reader, thank you so much for reading A relic of Magic And Gold, the first novel in The Relics & Legends series.

If you enjoyed Eve and Raph's story, I would be very grateful for a review on your favorite reading platform. Every review helps me pursue my dream of a career in writing.

ALSO BY HM HODGSON

Relics and Legends

A Wreath Of Thorns

A Relic Of Magic And Gold

A Relic of Magic And Myrrh *coming 2023

The Immortal Keepers

Book 1 The Last Keeper

Book 2 Keeper Of My Heart

Book 3 Keeper Of My Desire

Anthologies

Mermaid Kisses

Guarded Hearts *Featuring A Sword Of Stone And Magic, a Relics
& Legends novella

FREE EBOOK GIVEAWAY

Can a cursed Merprince blackmail his way out of a fairytale nightmare?

Read now to enjoy this Beauty and the Beast retelling!

Get your free ebook now by joining my reader group.

ACKNOWLEDGMENTS

This book (and the entire world of Relics & Legends with it) started with a question: What happened to the gold, myrrh and frankincense after the three gifts were given to Jesus?

So my first acknowledgement and thanks go to my father, Chris, who asked me that question. As a fantasy romance author, a world of characters and plots and possibilities instantly spun into being.

But ... a book eventuates from more than an idea. Planning, plotting, writing, rewriting, and editing, editing, editing. Throughout all this, my husband and children gave me the time and support to hit The End. I love you all so much. A special mention here to my wonderful hubby for listening to hours of book talk.

Then there's my writing wives, Jacqueline Hayley, Melanie Pickering and Jennifer Westgarth and our discussions over story, character, setting. To fellow author Renae Black, thank you for the feedback on my book baby. To another fellow author Louisa Duval, thanks your help with the greater Relics & Legends world and your support and friendship. I'm grateful to you all.

There's also my family: my mother, father, sister, and the entire crew who are always there for questions about covers and blurbs, details on investigative techniques, or an early pre-release read.

This book took readers to two wonderful locations, Southeast Queensland in Australia, and Rome in Italy. While I live in Queensland and happily write about my stunning home state, I visited the latter over ten years ago now. But the beauty and weight of history that presses down on you when you walk around Rome and the Vatican stayed with me, and I couldn't start or end this story anywhere else. I also can't wait for the day I get to visit again.

Another memory that influenced this book was the cow manure scene. I'm grew up on a farm, and one particularly cold, rainy morning, I was running around wearing a puffy rain parker with the hood pulled tight around my face. And … I fell face-first into a giant, stinking, steaming pile of cow poop. It was in my hair. My eyes. On my face. I cried out, of course, and Mum came running. But instead of helping me up; she darted inside, grabbed the camera and snapped a photo. Thanks a lot, Mum!

Once the story was down, I turned to Sarah Proulx Calfee from Three Little Words Editing for copy edits and manuscript assessment, and Jo Speirs from Nurturing Words for the final proofread. Together, these two brilliant editors made my story shine. Thank you!

Then there's the cover which I *adore*. I'm thrilled to work with Amanda Pillar from Smoking Hot Covers.

And now one more acknowledgement—you. Because what is a book without readers to read it? Thank you.

ABOUT THE AUTHOR

Brisbane author, HM Hodgson, has always loved stories. Creating her own is the natural evolution of a passion for reading, a love for what makes people tick, and the fantastic places that can be imagined.

Today, she writes about romance (steamy scenes a must!) and magic. Magic that moves worlds and takes her to another place. When not writing or reading or reluctantly cleaning up after her children, she loves looking after her veggie patch and a little flock of chickens.

Keep in touch with HM Hodgson at: www.hmhodgson.com

www.ingramcontent.com/pod-product-compliance
Lightning Source LLC
Chambersburg PA
CBHW020329120726
47904CB00002B/345